# catfishing
## in america

A
Camilla
Randall
Mystery

# ANNE R. ALLEN

THALIA

D1701662

# one

. . .

## Catfished

*O*wning a bookstore is like running a neighborhood bar. Everybody tells you their troubles — often at length. Unfortunately, the tips aren't nearly as good.

It was sometime around the middle of March — which tends to be blustery on California's Central Coast — and Ginny Gilhooly was telling me all about her catastrophic love life. Luckily, she didn't ask me about mine. I hadn't heard from my boyfriend Ronzo for three weeks, and I was afraid my Mr. Right was turning out to be one more Mr. Wrong.

The wind had blown Ginny's carefully constructed hairdo so two silver curls stuck up like devil's horns. I pretended to ignore them as I gift-wrapped a copy of Angela Duckworth's *Grit* with the new wrapping paper with the books-and-cats design. I'd splurged on it because the cats looked like my tuxedo cat, Buckingham.

Ginny planned to send the book to her oddly unlucky oilman boyfriend.

"He falls apart whenever there's a problem." Ginny's gold bracelets jangled as she spoke. "Last month his mother broke her ankle, so he had to rush off to her villa in Naples — and his pocket got picked on the shuttle from the airport. There he was in a foreign country with no passport and no money, and his mother has Alzheimer's so she was no help. I didn't mind wiring him the cash he needed, but the man has had his pocket picked three times this year and he never fights back or tells the police. I'm hoping he'll read this book and develop a little backbone."

She tapped the cover of the copy of *Grit* just as I was scotch-taping the wrapping paper over it, and I got a little tape on her long, green faux fingernail. Ginny loved to celebrate holidays, and I suppose with a name like Gilhooly, St. Patrick's Day was one of her favorites.

I gave her an apologetic smile as I carefully peeled the straying tape off her finger, hoping I wouldn't peel off the little gold shamrock.

"Naples is known for pickpockets, so I'm sure he's not to blame." I tried to sound sympathetic. Ginny seemed to have even worse taste in men than mine.

Buckingham jumped from his spot on the remainder table and sidled up to Ginny. He wound around her leg and gave her his "I'm so adorable" look.

She sniffed, obviously not charmed.

"It's not only Naples. Brownie gets robbed in a different place every time. He works on an oil rig in the Persian Gulf, and he's always bopping around the world. He's promised to take me next time he travels somewhere nice. I've bought one of those passport cases you can wear under your clothes for when we go. All these foreigners seem to be pickpockets."

Buckingham gave a small meow.

Ginny looked down at my kitty as if he were some species of vermin.

"Oh, ick. A black cat. I'm not superstitious, but black cats... They always bring me bad luck."

"He's not all black." I had to defend my little guy. "He's a tuxedo cat. White face and paws, see?"

"Well, he gave me a chill. Like somebody walked on my grave."

I worked to keep my smile in place.

"I hope you'll have a great trip, wherever you and your boyfriend go. After he reads this book, I'm sure he'll toughen up."

I wanted to be kind, in spite of her disparagement of my cat. It sounded highly unlikely this man was ever going to take poor Ginny anywhere, if he even existed. He sounded like a typical "catfish" romance scammer. But it wasn't up to me to burst her romantic-fantasy bubble.

"I used to think Brownie was a tough guy. He sure looks like it in his photo. Look at that six pack."

She pulled out her phone to show me a photo of a very fit forty-something White man wearing a hard hat, skimpy cut-offs, and not much else. I had to stifle a laugh. Ginny had to be at least sixty, with a less than girlish figure.

"He keeps putting off our trip. I was supposed to meet him in Athens last Christmas — that's in Greece — but that's when he got the infected toe, so he couldn't walk, and he had to stay in some Arab place for the whole holiday and they didn't even have a Christmas tree."

I managed to keep my smile bland. "It sounds as if your Brownie has had some seriously bad luck."

"His luck is the worst. Even worse than my luck around black cats." She peered down at Buckingham with another icy stare.

"Brownie. That's an unusual name." I rang up the book and her other purchase — one of the floaty pens we keep at the register for tourists. Hers had an otter in the barrel, floating past a picture of our landmark Morro Rock.

Buckingham turned a raised tail to Ginny and went to prowl back in the YA section, where two middle-school girls were giggling.

Ginny patted her hairdo, which only made the devil horns stick up further.

"His name is Brown David Jack, which is real unusual. He's from Texas and I guess they have all kinds of funny names. His father, Billy-Bob Jack, is a big oil man and Brown is a family name. I don't know why they didn't send him to better schools, though. The poor man's grammar is atrocious, and his spelling is worse. He spells Texas, 'Taxes' you know, like what you pay on April fifteenth."

Oh, I knew about April fifteenth income taxes all right. The date was looming. My bookstore had crawled out of debt, since I'd finally got the insurance payout after our disastrous fire last summer. But I still didn't have cash to spare. I needed a full staff, but so far, I'd only been able to hire one clerk — my best friend Plantagenet Smith — and I wasn't paying him enough to take the job seriously.

Yes, that Plantagenet Smith, Oscar-winning screenwriter and gay icon who had somehow got himself MeToo'd by a loathsome woman named Kensie Weiner. His Princeton education had filled him with esoteric knowledge, but he had no experience working retail. He'd get into long discussions with somebody who wanted to buy a $1.99 used paperback of *King Lear,* and ignore the customers who were lining up to plunk down $28 for the latest Danielle Steel.

I was carrying used books now. They had a better mark-up than new, and they sold fast. But as a writer, it made me sad. I don't make a penny from a second-hand sale of my etiquette books. It had been a long time since my alter-ego, "The Manners Doctor" had a bestseller. My publisher hadn't sent me royalties for at least six months.

I heard the girls giggle again as Ginny clutched her bag of purchases and walked out to the street with her devil horns twitching in the wind.

Plant appeared from the back room, where he had been unpacking our new shipment. He looked elegantly put-together as usual, in a bespoke sport coat and pressed khakis, not a graying hair out of place.

"Camilla darling, I couldn't help overhearing that poor woman's story," He watched Ginny making her way to her Cadillac Escalade while pretending she didn't see Hobo Joe, the homeless musician who played his guitar on the bench directly in front of her car. "I hope she can afford to keep paying that freakishly unlucky oilman of hers."

"It is sad. I'm afraid she's fallen for one of those catfish romance scams. And yes, she's well-off. She inherited buckets of money from her husband. You know — Gil Gilhooly."

A customer in the mystery section turned and gave me a sharp look, as if I'd said a dirty word. I realized we were being rude, gossiping about Ginny when we had customers in the store. Mentions of Gil did tend to upset people. Gil had owned half the low-income

4

apartment buildings from Morro Bay to Paso Robles. Some were so full of mold and vermin the tenants had sued. So Ginny and her son simply evicted everybody and sold the property to developers. The unhoused population in Morro Bay almost doubled. Ginny had not endeared herself to the chamber of commerce. Or, indeed, the unhoused.

"Oh, I know Gil Gilhooly." Plant lowered his voice. "At least I went to his funeral. Silas used to date a Gilhooly brother, so we had to make an appearance at the memorial last year. It was hilarious how everybody pretended to be devastated when they all despised him. So, our talkative customer is his grieving widow? I must have met her at the funeral, but she spent the whole time weeping into a large handkerchief, so I didn't recognize her."

"She conquered her grief quickly. Brownie seems to have been part of her life for almost a year. Maybe that's why she had to sell all Gil's properties — to send cash to the hapless Mr. Brown Jack."

Plant looked through the new titles I'd put on the shelving cart and picked up a handful of sci-fi and fantasy paperbacks. He gave me a sly smile.

"You know, Silas told me Ginny's giving the wedding of the year for her son at the Madonna Inn next June, and people are threatening to boycott the Inn. I wonder if Brownie is invited?" He raised a snarky eyebrow.

As the Escalade pulled away, a customer opened the front door and I could hear Joe out on his bench playing "Ding Dong the Witch is Dead." Plant laughed at the musical commentary.

"Even Joe? Ginny seems to have made a lot of enemies."

I felt a chill. "I fear some nasty karma is headed her way. Catfishing always ends in heartbreak."

# two

. . .

Catfishing 101

*O*ur two giggling middle school girls emerged from the young adult section with a stack of books after Ginny Gilhooly made her exit. The girls were regulars — Adriana and Britney. They were in the store almost every weekend. I loved their enthusiasm for reading, although they couldn't afford to buy more than an occasional used book or two.

Round, blonde Britney loved the Sweet Valley High romances, and dark, bespectacled Adriana was a mystery fan. They were inseparable, but they seemed to be disagreeing about something at the moment.

"That old lady is so being catfished," Adriana said. "Brown David Jack?" All the Nigerian scammers are clueless about American names. They call themselves stupid things like Steve Doug or Larry Bob. Then they steal a photo from some White businessman's website for their profile picture. They're hilarious."

Britney wasn't laughing. "Adriana, you're making that up. Just because somebody isn't named Diego or Manuel — or Ruben Moreno — doesn't mean they're a scammer."

Oh, dear. I didn't realize the girls had overheard Ginny's story of her hapless romance. Her voice did carry. But they seemed to know more about catfishing than I did.

Adriana gave Britney a dark look over her glasses, accompanied by a derisive laugh.

"These guys are so obvious, Britney. They hang out on Facebook because that's where the old ladies are. My grandma down in LA showed me some bananas stuff she got. These guys pretend to work on oil rigs and they're oh, so lonely and make tons of money, but then they have accidents or get arrested in a foreign country and need a quick loan and these old ladies fork it over."

Britney's pudgy little face had reddened and she looked close to tears.

"Adriana, you're so ageist. Those old ladies deserve some fun and romance, even if it isn't real."

Plant laughed along with Adriana. But I agreed with Britney that it was all rather tragic. I had those "friend" requests from wannabe-Romeos on social media all the time, and couldn't believe anybody would fall for them. But obviously some people did.

"Why do you suppose they call it 'catfishing'?" Plant said.

Adriana pushed up her glasses and gave him a professorial look. "The term catfish comes from fishermen putting catfish in with the codfish to nip at their tails and keep them swimming around. So, it's like they're pretending to be codfish, but they're catfish. On the Internet, the term means creating a false identity — usually to romance somebody."

"You're a catfishing professor now, Adriana? You sound like you memorized Wikipedia." Britney rolled her eyes.

Plant gave Britney one of his professional charmer smiles and took her well-worn books up to the register.

"Sweet Valley High. We keep selling out of these. I think it's great that kids are still reading them. Can I ring them up for you?"

Adriana followed them clutching a "Pretty Little Liars" mystery.

Plant had bonded with the girls over the past few weeks. They knew the ins and outs of the store and were probably better at training him than I was.

I'd hoped that Ronzo would be back from New Jersey by now to

7

help out with the store. He'd worked here before and was a persuasive salesman. I missed him terribly.

As Plant chatted with the girls, who were happily giggling again, his face went suddenly white. He stared out the window at the street.

"Dear God. That's her car pulling into the space in front of Joe's bench. The lime-green VW. I have to hide. I'm not here."

He ran down the hall and out the back door just before a bottle blonde sauntered in, wearing a Dolce and Gabbana ensemble two sizes too small: the one and only Kensie Wiener. She was Plantagenet's #MeToo persecutor as well as the daughter of Harold Wiener, the disgraced Hollywood producer.

Adriana grabbed Britney's wrist and made a sign to be quiet. They darted back into the YA section.

"Hello, Kensie." I managed to work my face into something I hoped looked like a smile. "It's been so long."

"Not long enough." Kensie gave me her usual Mean Girl sniff. "Where are you hiding Plantagenet? I know he's here."

"How is your writing going, Kensie?" I wanted to distract the dreadful woman long enough for Plantagenet to make his escape out the back, where his Ferrari was parked. "Did I hear that you had a contract with a publisher for your romance novel? Congratulations!"

"I'm not only getting the book published. *The Far Loveswept Shore* has been optioned for film by Zac Efron's people. We're friends, Zac and me. He grew up right near where I live down in Nipomo. So, I'm a star now and Plantagenet Smith is a nobody, so I don't really have time to bother with him, even though he did harass me."

"Is that why you're here, then, to tell him you don't have time to bother with him?" My teen years as a New York debutante had taught me to keep my face a mask of politeness no matter what sort of nonsense was going on.

Giggles came from the YA section. Adriana and Britney obviously did not have the benefit of debutante training.

I was relieved to hear the Ferrari take off down the gravel drive next to the store.

"Well, yes, actually." Kensie went into a 'Hollywood celebrity' pose.

"I'm going on the TV show #MenToo, to apologize to Plantagenet. It's part of a deal my dad got with the producers."

"#MenToo? Is that a thing?" I'd stopped getting cable, so I didn't watch any broadcast TV shows unless I was visiting Plant and Silas.

The girls came out, apparently too intrigued by a possible celebrity sighting to hide any longer. Adriana carried the bag of books and Britney cuddled Buckingham, who was purring away as she petted him.

"My mom totally loves that show," Britney scratched behind Buckingham's ears. "She thinks #MeToo is unfair because they only tell one side of the story."

Adriana gave a snort. "Your mom has a crush on that guy — the host. My mom likes him too. I don't see it. He's so old. Jonathan Kahn. That's his name."

I winced.

Jonathan. My ex.

All the debutante training in the world could not have kept my smile pasted on my face at that point. I looked down at the counter, took a deep breath and tried not to let it out as a scream.

# three

. . .

#CatfishToo

*O*kay, it seemed my ex-husband had started an anti-#MeToo show. I needed to take that in without making a drama in front of Kensie Wiener.

But the woman was relentless as she played celebrity for the benefit of Britney and Adriana.

"My dad thinks Jonathan Kahn is an opportunist, and he doesn't trust him any farther than he can throw him, but we have a contract with the network that says Kahn won't pull one of his numbers and make my dad look bad. Kahn is such a sleaze. He used to get BJ's from hookers right on Hollywood Boulevard, you know…oh, wait. You used to be involved with him or something weren't you?"

Her evil little smile showed she knew exactly what she was doing.

"Yes. I was once married to Jonathan Kahn. Many years ago, when he was a serious journalist."

I knew Jonathan was working at rehabilitating his image after his alcoholism and sex scandals ended our marriage. But I didn't know he had a new show. I wondered what he was being paid, and if there was a chance in Hades that I'd get any of my unpaid divorce settlement out of him.

Britney let out a little squee. "OMG, my mom is so totally going to freak! I know Jonathan Kahn's ex-wife! This is epic! Why didn't I know that? Adriana, why didn't we know she was Mrs. Jonathan Kahn?"

Adriana rolled her eyes. "Because we don't care what's on cable news, Britney. It's for old people."

Kensie sniffed. "Well, I'm not old, and I'm going to be on the show, next week, to show support for my dad, who did not rape all those women. It was consensual. But Jonathan Kahn wouldn't sign the contract unless I was willing to go on and say I overreacted to Plantagenet Smith's harassment. So, I wanted to tell Plant about it, okay? So he can stop being mad at me. Will you tell him? I honestly don't care if he watches or anything. I just wanted him to know."

Oh, my. Jonathan had been so awful to Plant over the years. Could he really be doing something kind for him? Help him get his career back after Kensie's ridiculous claims of sexual harassment got him blacklisted? Amazing. Maybe Jonathan was working his twelve steps and trying to be a good person. Finally owning up to what a creep he'd been when he was drinking.

Kensie flounced out of the store, a bit unsteady on what looked like brand-new Christian Louboutin heels. The red soles were barely scuffed.

As soon as she was out the door, Britney mocked Kensie's walk with giggly precision.

"Oh, so who's ageist now?" Adriana pretended to slap Britney, while letting out a big laugh.

Ageist. I suppose forty was ancient to these girls. I happened to be forty myself, but I tried to laugh it off.

Adriana was still laughing. "That lady with the shoes is such a moron. Doesn't she know that Jonathan Kahn completely shreds everybody who comes on his show?"

"I thought you didn't watch it because it's for old people." Britney made a face, then turned to me. "But yeah. You should watch it. It's hilarious. He's totally brutal. He always makes the women cry."

So much for Jonathan's rehabilitation. As much as I disliked Kensie, I felt sad for her if she was going to be the victim of Jonathan's snark. He could be pitiless. I'd been the victim of one of his hit pieces myself, back when I was New York's "debutante of the year."

"#MenToo? Is that really what he calls his show?"

"Yup." Adriana was a world-class eye-roller. "And people eat it up. A lot of old people think there's nothing wrong with sexual harassment, because everybody put up with it back in the olden days. Maybe they'll have one for romance scammers next. You know, #CatfishToo."

Britney shot eye-daggers at her. Catfishing was a mysterious bone of contention between the two. I wondered what that was about.

My cellphone rang. Probably Plant wanting to know if the coast was clear.

"Hello Babe. How's it goin'?"

Oh, my goodness, it was Ronzo. His tough-guy New Jersey accent always made my heart give a little flip.

"Sorry I've been out of touch, Camilla. I've been traveling."

"Traveling? You mean down to the Jersey Shore?" As far as I knew, Ronzo didn't leave Newark — or his ailing grandmother's side — except in emergencies.

"No. LA." He must have heard my wounded intake of breath. "I would have gone up to see you in a heartbeat, but I was only there for a day — for meetings with Jonathan Kahn about being on his new show."

"Jonathan. You flew all the way to California to talk to my ex-husband, but neglected to tell me you were here?" I couldn't keep the icicles out of my voice.

"Yeah. He's gonna get me on that show. You know, #MenToo? He's going to tell the truth about how Mack Rattlebag and Saffina slimed me with those fake videos. He says it was my story that gave him the idea for the show."

"That's wonderful news." It was. Ronzo was a music blogger who had been forced to go underground after his reputation was destroyed by a vindictive band who didn't like his review. They circulated a bogus video making him look like a kitten killer. His reputation was still a mess even though the man who orchestrated the video was behind bars now.

So why didn't I feel more joyous?

"I'm really happy for you," I managed to say.

"Yeah. Saffina's real happy too. We flew out together to get everything in writing with the network and Mr. Kahn."

The ice had gone from my voice to my face. It was frozen. For several moments, I could not make a sound. Then the words gushed out.

"Saffina? Jonathan's having your sociopath ex-girlfriend on the show too? You flew out to LA together? I'm surprised you didn't get Mack Rattlebag out of prison and have a little reunion. You didn't even bother to text me? Was something wrong with your phone?"

As if to mock me, the landline phone rang at my desk. Plant obviously wasn't there to answer it, so I'd have to deal with it myself. I felt like screaming.

But Adriana gave me a little smile and picked up the receiver.

"Morro Bay Bookshop. Adriana speaking. How can I help you?" She sounded like a professional salesperson.

Meanwhile, Ronzo was whining in my ear. "Babe, don't be like that. This isn't about Saffina and me. This is about being on national TV and getting that whole kitten-killer thing wiped off the slate…"

"Of course." I managed to get the words out calmly. "And I wish you and Saffina all the best. I have a call on the other line. I have to go."

But Adrianna was already hanging up the desk phone.

"That was the lady who was just here. Mrs. Gilhooly. She wants to return that book. I said she could. I hope that's all right. She was real upset."

"The one I gift-wrapped?"

"I guess. She said it was called *Grit*. And she decided her boyfriend didn't need it because he's got too much grit already. Plus, he's got another girlfriend. Mrs. Gilhooly is coming in first thing in the morning. Is that okay?"

Adriana sounded like a thirteen-year-old again. I nodded and gave her a big, if not entirely heartfelt smile.

"Thanks. You sounded very professional on the phone." I stifled my feelings about Ronzo and Saffina along with the tears that stung my nose. *Grit* wasn't a popular title in my beachy bookstore, so I'd be losing money on that as well as the wrapping paper, but I sympathized with poor Ginny. I knew exactly how she felt.

Britney sat in the easy chair with her new book, petting Buckingham. "Adriana talks like that all the time. She does a real good job of convincing people she's a grown-up, even though she's younger than me."

Adriana stood over her, hands on hips.

"By three months! And you have to drop the cat because we're going to miss the bus home and my mom will go ballistic."

It was past closing time anyway. I ushered them to the door.

"Thank you for answering the phone for me, Adriana."

Adriana stopped laughing. "I hope that lady is okay. She sounded like she was crying. I still say she's being catfished."

Britney stood and grabbed her bag of books. "Every time some old lady finds romance online it's not necessarily catfishing. I wish you'd give it a rest."

Buckingham gave a meow.

"He thinks you're mad at him now," Adriana said.

"Or that you're talking about his dinner. He loves fish." It was time for me to get to my cottage behind the store, and feed both of us.

Plus, I had to figure out how I was going to deal with my boyfriend and his ex-girlfriend cozying up to my ex-husband on national television.

# four

• • •

## The Fisherman Cometh

*P*lantagenet was over the moon when he heard from Jonathan's producer. He phoned me as soon as he got the call that evening. I was back in my cottage, relaxing in my sweats after the long day. So far, I'd resisted a meltdown over Ronzo and Saffina's little transcontinental jaunt, but I was afraid Plant's warm, sympathetic voice would start the waterworks.

Instead, he launched into a long monologue about how #MenToo was not about justifying sexual harassment or assault. He said Jonathan was simply trying to right some wrongs that happened when men were sexually harassed or falsely accused of it. Or their reputation got smeared by Twitter trolls. Jonathan had told him the show offered "a rebuttal of the unchallenged accusations that could destroy a man's life when he had no venue to defend himself."

I poured a glass of wine while he went on and on. I could see Plant was feeling some guilt about being on a network that wasn't famous for its LGBTQ tolerance. And of course, he had to be conflicted about being on a show with my caddish ex-husband.

Okay, he was not going to provide a shoulder to cry on tonight. For Plant's sake, I needed to be calm and polite about what was going on with Ronzo. I didn't know if they'd see each other in the course of filming, but it wouldn't be kind to insert conflict into the scenario.

Of course, maybe he already knew. The dumpee is often the last to know. I took a gulp of wine.

"It's fine, Plant," I said when I could get a word in. "I'm so glad you're going to be on Jonathan's show. It sounds like an amazing chance for you to clear your name and get your career back. I'm glad to hear Jonathan is doing something good for a change. I hear he's doing an interview with Ronzo too. Ronzo is ecstatic about it."

Plant stopped and took an audible breath.

"Oh, that's great news. #MenToo is helping Ronzo? So maybe his reputation as a kitten-killer can be erased?"

"Let's hope. Ronzo had to fly back and forth to LA." I stopped to take a calming breath to avoid bringing up Saffina. "I suppose you'll have to drive down to sign some contracts, too?" I hoped my voice sounded calm.

Keeping calm was increasingly difficult. Knowing Ronzo and Saffina were going to be thrown together for days while recording Jonathan's show had planted a cold seed of fear in my heart. I knew nothing good could come of it.

"Going to LA. Yes. That's what I was calling about, darling. Well, partly what I was calling about. I need to drive down tomorrow. Will you be all right in the store without me?"

I wouldn't really. Tomorrow was Friday. One of my busiest days. Being alone in the store would be exhausting, and I might lose sales for lack of a clerk. But it wouldn't be polite to tell him that.

"The store will be fine. Of course you must go."

I hung up and took another gulp of wine. Somehow it had to be "fine" that all my menfolk were leaving me at the same moment.

The phone rang again. Plant was probably going to tell me he wouldn't be able to work on Saturday either, but I'd already figured that out.

But it wasn't Plant. It was Ginny Gilhooly. She was in tears.

"Can I bring that book back right now? I do not want it in my house." She paused to take a dramatic sniff. "Did that girl tell you? I

16

found out Brownie has plenty of grit already. I got a crazy email that got sent to me by mistake. From some other woman. It was all lovey-dovey sweet talk like he always sends to me, but it was signed 'Tiffani' with an 'i.' She must have meant the email for Brownie but somehow it got sent to me. A couple of my friends kept telling me he's too good to be true, and now I know they're right. They think he's playing both of us — me and Tiffani. I'm so hopping mad, I can't stand to look at this thing. I've given him thousands of dollars. And I'm sure he's taking more from this bimbo." She blew her nose with vigor.

I tried to make sympathetic sounds. "There's no reason to think Tiffani is a bimbo, even if she spells her name with an 'i.' She's probably another victim like you."

That was obviously the wrong thing to say. Ginny let loose a rant about the morals of women called Tiffani, Crystal, Ruby and other jewelry-related appellations, as she sniffled and honked through her rage.

"I'm so sorry you're going through this, Ginny." I chose bland words I hoped wouldn't set off another rant.

"So, can I come over and get a refund on this damned book? Otherwise, I might go out and kill this Tiffani woman."

I didn't know what to say. Of course, it was unlikely Ginny seriously contemplated killing her rival. Her friends who said Brownie must have hundreds of women on the hook were probably right. Tiffani could be anybody, anywhere in the world. Her real name might not even be jewelry-related.

"Of course you may bring the book back for a full refund. But it will have to be tomorrow. I'm at home now, dressed for bed. I share my landline with the store. But I'll have your money for you first thing when we open at 10 AM. So don't go out and get involved in any homicides, okay?" I tried for a light laugh.

"But..."

"Tomorrow at ten, Ginny. So sorry your Brownie turned out to be a cad."

I hung up. I couldn't have listened for one more minute. I had my own pain to process. I felt so horribly alone. The thought of Plant,

Ronzo, and Jonathan getting together without me made me inexplicably sad. It would have helped if I hadn't got a card from my old boyfriend Rick Zukowski last week saying he and his wife Dolores had reconciled and renewed their vows in Las Vegas on Valentine's Day.

Even my publisher seemed to have abandoned me. Where on earth was my royalty check? It was more than a month overdue.

I reached for the bottle and then realized I was being stupid. I didn't need a pity party. I needed a cup of hot cocoa, a good book, and my cat.

"Buckingham!" I called him as I heated up some milk. I got out his bag of treats and rattled it. That usually got him to come out of hiding.

But it didn't work. There was no cat.

Then I heard the screen door bang. I didn't remember letting Buckingham out after I fed him dinner. He did know how to bang that door by hooking his claws into the screen. How had he got out?

"What are you doing out there?" I opened the door.

But it wasn't Buckingham on my doorstep.

It was a strange fisherman, wearing a windbreaker and a three-day beard, carrying a beautiful salmon, wrapped in plastic.

"Don't say I never brought you anything, lass," The man spoke in a Northern English accent. "Fresh off the boat. Along with yours truly. I don't suppose you could make me a spot of tea?"

# five

· · ·

## A Lovely Fish

"*P*eter!" His name exploded from my mouth as I realized the man who was standing at my door holding a dead salmon was my publisher, former boyfriend, and international smuggler, Peter Sherwood.

When I opened the door, he handed me the fish.

"It's a lovely salmon," I said, because I had no idea what else to say. So many questions swirled in my brain, I couldn't focus on one. So I put the fish on the kitchen counter, got out a platter, and tried to extricate the thing from all its clingy plastic wrap.

Buckingham emerged from his napping place in my bedroom, padded into the kitchen and gave a polite meow, indicating that he too, thought it was a lovely fish.

"You'll want to gut it first." Peter washed his hands in the warm water from my kitchen faucet. "Let me do it for you. You put the kettle on. It's bloody freezing out there. That wind is brutal."

Buckingham meowed again, this time a little louder, as he snaked around Peter's leg. Maybe he remembered Peter from his last visit three years ago, or more likely, he was lured by the salmon.

I filled the kettle as Peter dried his hands. I needed to put first things first. I tried not to use an accusatory tone of voice.

"Have my books not been selling at all? Sherwood hasn't sent me my royalties since last November." It wasn't the politest way to open a conversation with a former boyfriend I hadn't seen in three years, but it needed to be said.

"I apologize for that. Unfortunately, Sherwood Ltd. has fallen on some difficult times, so I've had to buy the company back from Pradeep. He seems to have lost Fanna Badjie." Peter took a small knife from the drawer and proceeded to open the belly of the fish. It gave surprisingly little resistance. He cut off several bits and put them in Buckingham's bowl.

"Fanna Badjie? The woman who writes those African mysteries? We've been selling them like mad. Has she left for greener pastures?" I got out the tea pot and looked for my decaf Darjeeling. "I guess Sherwood doesn't have a lot of big-name writers anymore, since your Hinckley Lutterworth hasn't come out with a new historical mystery recently."

"The Hinckley Lutterworth backlist was the only thing keeping us afloat until Fanna came along. And I'm afraid your etiquette books aren't exactly jumping off the shelves. This isn't an era when anybody much cares about good manners."

Peter opened the belly of the fish and pulled out a thick cylinder wrapped in plastic. Unusual fish guts to say the least.

He washed and dried his hands again, then pulled the cylinder from the plastic, unrolled it and flattened something on the cleaner part of the counter. It appeared to be a little booklet, dark blue, with a gold insignia on it. And the word Canada. A Canadian passport.

I sighed. People don't change.

"You're Canadian this time? What's your name?"

"Peter. It's Peter again. Peter Pelletier, eh? How aboot a cup of Tim Horton's?"

He managed to sound not at all Canadian. His Midlands accent always came through. He reached into his pocket and pulled out an Australian passport. Inside was some Australian currency. He handed me three one-hundred-dollar bills.

"What's this?"

"Your royalties for the past six months, more or less. As I said, sales haven't been brisk."

"That's why you're here, to pay me my royalties?"

"And drink a cup of tea. I could really use that tea. Milk and sugar, please."

Before I fixed his tea, I re-wrapped the salmon in clean Saran wrap and put it in the fridge. I had no idea how to cook a whole salmon, but I could probably find some instructions on YouTube. I could make some nice salmon salad with the leftovers. And I could freeze a bunch and have cat food for a month.

Peter didn't seem to have any further interest in it beyond its passport-hiding properties.

He removed his damp jacket and hung it on the back of one of my Chippendale dining chairs. I stifled my urge to cringe. I still had a few antiques left from my former life as the heiress to the Randall newspaper fortune, which became the Randall pile of debt after my mother married her Eurotrash fake Count.

"Would you rather I put me windcheater somewhere else?" Peter looked a bit chagrinned.

"No. Of course not. Please sit. Would you like something to eat with your tea? I have some chocolate chip cookies from Kat's Kitchen across the street."

"A cookie sounds delightful. Even though it's really a biscuit."

As soon as Peter sat down, Buckingham jumped up to avail himself of his lap. Buckingham always preferred men to women, but Peter had probably made it to the top of his list with that gift of salmon belly.

Peter ran his fingers through his dark blond hair. It was shorter than usual, cut in the current style — very short on the sides and long and tousled on top. The look suited him, and he'd probably look almost respectable if he shaved his grungy stubble. His chiseled face was a deep tan, showing a few more wrinkles than it had three years ago, but he still had a smile and twinkly blue eyes that could make me melt.

I watched him drinking tea and munching on the cookie for a few moments, wondering what questions to ask him first. Like what was he running from this time, and was he going to keep the publishing company going and, um, how long did he intend to stay — minutes, days, weeks?

I finally settled on the subject of the publishing company.

"So, tell me about Fanna Badjie. What did you mean that Sherwood Ltd. has lost her?"

"I mean we've literally lost her. Our Vera had been sending Fanna's royalties to her business partner in Leeds, but about three months ago, Fanna wrote to say she no longer trusted the business partner and we were to send the money directly to Banjul. But the wire transfer never went through because the Banjul account had been closed. Her new book is overdue and she's not responding to texts or email."

"That's all pretty terrifying. Banjul? Where's that? Kenya?"

Peter laughed. "It's amazing how little you Yanks know about Africa. Banjul is in The Gambia in West Africa. About 4000 miles from Kenya."

I tried to ignore his condescension.

"So, are you going to try to sign some new authors? What is Pradeep going to do? Pradeep is still managing the business, isn't he?"

"Yes. Pradeep is still managing, and with all of Fanna's success, he hasn't had time to put on his Hinkley Lutterworth hat and write some more of those Tudor blockbusters. He's sick that all the advertising and energy they put into Fanna may be lost. And of course he's worried about her. She's a charming lady."

"Should I be shopping for another publisher?" That came out before I thought it through. Peter looked wounded.

"You'd abandon ship because of a bit of bad luck? That seems harsh."

Now I felt terrible. I was being rude to my guest.

"Oh, no. I didn't mean...Peter, what are you doing here? The last I heard, you were happily living in Australia as Piotr Stygar."

"Piotr got himself in a spot of bother with the customs people in Queensland, and soon after, he unfortunately met his maker in a boating accident. That's why I needed to switch nationalities." He gestured at the Canadian passport. "And since Peter Sherwood isn't entirely welcome in the UK these days, I figured I could come to North America via a friend's fishing vessel and establish myself as a Canadian tourist in the US before I fly to Banjul."

"Banjul? So, you're going hunting for Fanna?"

"I am. But I'll need to stay here for a few days. I hope that won't be too much of a bother?"

There. He finally came out with it. He had come into this country illegally and now was hoping to be reborn as Mr. Pelletier, right here on my living room couch. I hoped it wouldn't be a long visit.

"Will I have to break any laws?"

"Not a great number." He gave me a puckish grin. "I don't suppose you have a drop of cognac I might put in this tea? I don't seem to be able to warm up. That wind is merciless out there."

I got out the Paul Masson. Imported cognac wasn't in the budget these days.

"Just some California brandy."

"When in California…" He poured a dollop of brandy into his tea. Then another. "Can I pour you a glass?"

I sighed and got out one of my brandy snifters.

"Please. It's been sort of a roller-coaster day."

"The dramatic life of a bookstore owner?" Peter gave me a silly smile as he filled my glass. It was a sexy, adorable look, but I wasn't going to let him work his wiles on me tonight.

Buckingham jumped down from Peter's lap and went to the door. I didn't usually let him out this late, but he probably had business to do. Besides, it gave me an excuse to avoid Peter's seductive looks.

"Peter, if you're going to make fun of me, you can leave." I closed the door behind Buckingham. "Excuse me if I don't live the exciting life of an international criminal."

"So sorry, lass. I didn't mean to offend you. Please, have some brandy." He lifted the glass he'd poured for me.

I sat across from him at my little table and his eyes met mine. He reached for my hand. I felt a familiar tingle at his touch as he brought my fingers to his lips.

I pulled away. "That's not going to happen this time, Peter. I have a boyfriend."

"You're still involved with the handsome musician from New Jersey?"

"Yes. He's taking care of his grandmother now, but he plans to visit me soon."

I certainly hoped I was telling the truth about that. But it was necessary to say it in order to establish boundaries with Peter. The last thing I needed at the moment was to get involved with one more bad boyfriend.

# six

. . .

## Fish and Visitors

*P*eter woke me by shaking my shoulder with a heavy, clammy hand. I wasn't hung over — I'd only had the one brandy — but I could hardly get my eyes open and my head hurt.

"What time is it?" I smelled coffee, turned over and saw he was holding one of my mugs, full of steaming liquid. But the sky was still dark outside my window.

"It's around four AM."

No wonder I was still sleepy.

"Give me three more hours. I don't open the store until ten. I need to sleep." I pulled the quilt over my head.

I felt Peter sit down on my bed and heard him slurp the coffee. He didn't show any signs of leaving. I peeked out from under the quilt. His frown and slumped body language said he was not happy.

"Is the couch that uncomfortable?" I tried to sound sympathetic. "I have an inflatable mattress if that's better. It's in the store in the office closet. The keys are…"

Peter jangled my keys in front of my face.

"You told me about the inflatable last night. And yes, the couch is uncomfortable, so I went to get the mattress."

"And…?" What kind of stupid game was he playing?

"And it's a bit difficult to get in the back door. There's what appears to be a corpse on the doorstep."

"A corpse." If this was a joke, it was decidedly unfunny. "Like a human one?"

"Human, yes. A woman. In her sixties probably. A bit portly."

Good Lord. This couldn't be happening. A dead person on the back steps of my store? It was dark out there. Maybe Peter was confused about what he saw.

"Are you sure it isn't a homeless person having a nap? They sometimes come into the courtyard, thinking the place is empty. Not too many people know there's a house back here."

"No. The person is definitely deceased. No breath. No pulse. And I can't imagine this woman was homeless. She's wearing Italian shoes. Prada, I believe."

Peter did know his designer leather goods. He'd done time in Tasmania for smuggling designer knock-offs.

I took a breath, trying to calm myself. If he was right about the Prada-wearing corpse, I needed to call the police. Right now.

He'd left the bedroom door open, so I wasn't surprised to see Buckingham come padding in. The kitty looked distressed, and meowed at me loudly. I could see something green and sparkly stuck on the back of his head. He kept batting at it with his paw, but it stayed put.

I sat up, covering my chest with bedding. I did not want Peter to see me in my threadbare silk nightgown. It was practically transparent. Now that I had a little money again, I needed to do some clothes shopping.

"Did Buckingham go over to the store with you?"

"Yes. He'd been sleeping with me on the couch. Well, he slept and I tossed myself about."

The cat came over to the bed and meowed.

I had to let go of the bedding to pick him up. Fine. Let Peter get an eyeful. It wasn't as if he hadn't seen it all before. I pulled the sparkly thing off the cat's head and saw it was an acrylic fingernail. Painted green. With a little gold shamrock on it.

"Ginny Gilhooly! Dear God. Is that Ginny Gilhooly out there? She's dead on my back steps?" I sprang out of bed and grabbed my robe.

Peter sat on the bed, drinking coffee and petting Buckingham, as if stumbling across dead bodies were an everyday occurrence. Who knows? Maybe it was for him. He certainly wasn't in a hurry. He was fully dressed, so he must have taken the time to put clothes on since finding Ginny's body. If that's who it was. He'd also made coffee.

I gave him a stern look. I was not going to let him watch me.

"Do you mind? I need to get dressed. You could make yourself useful and report this to the police. The number is 911 in this country, not 999, like in the UK."

Peter gave me a funny look.

"Not the best plan. I'm technically an illegal alien. I didn't arrive at a designated port of entry. I need to avoid the coppers."

"But you're Canadian now. I'll say you're my cousin. It will be fine." I gave an exasperated sigh and shooed him out of the room. If I was going to have to talk to policemen, I didn't want to do it in see-through designer silk.

"Would you mind fixing me a cup of coffee, too?" I called to him as I scrambled into my underwear. "I like cream but no sugar."

The door immediately opened a crack and a mug appeared.

"Yes. I remembered." Peter gave me a grin and shut the door as soon as I took the mug.

Caffeine helped a little. I knew I had to get a grip and call 911, no matter what Peter's legal status was at the moment. I couldn't very well ignore a corpse in my courtyard. Unfortunately, I didn't have a good history with the Morro Bay Police Department, who usually treated me like an intellectually disabled nuisance.

I should probably phone from my landline. It was also the line for the store, so they'd know I was a respectable local merchant. But I had to get dressed before I called. Sometimes they could be very speedy. The police station was only a few blocks away. No way did I want to be caught dressed improperly.

I put on dark slacks with a buttoned-up blouse and tweed blazer, with a little light make-up. I didn't have time to work on my hair, which was a shocking mess, so I pulled it back in a bun. I looked like the head of a girl's boarding school. Or maybe one of those librarians who's always shushing people. Which was fine. I only cared about not looking like a dingbat. Peter would probably laugh, but it was more important for me to impress the police with my credibility.

But before I talked to the police, I needed go out there and look at the body and make sure it was Ginny. I still thought it might be a homeless woman. The local homeless camps had been overflowing since the Gilhoolys evicted all the low-income renters.

When I got out to the kitchen, Buckingham was happily eating a salmon breakfast. Peter had obviously fed him.

But Peter wasn't there. Which was weird. Was he so afraid of the police he was hiding somewhere? That was unlike him. He'd at least wait until I made the call. He was probably outside with the body.

The body. I really did need to go look and see if it was Ginny's before I called 911. I took another sip of coffee, grabbed the flashlight and went out to the courtyard. The night was foggy and moonless. The wind had died down but there was a chilly drizzle. Why would Ginny Gilhooly have come out here on a night like this?

I walked the gravel path to the back door of my store and aimed the flashlight beam at the step.

But I saw nothing there.

No corpses.

Not a one.

I called to Peter, but got no answer.

I called again. Where was he? Was I out here in the dark, freezing off my derriere...for nothing? Had Peter been pranking me all this time?

I called his name again, then walked to the driveway, where my ancient Honda was parked. Nothing was parked behind it. How had Peter got here? I'd forgotten to ask.

No doubt about it. Peter — and his vehicle, if he had one — had disappeared.

Had I somehow hallucinated the whole thing? Peter, the salmon, his tale of a corpse on the doorstep — they would seem pretty prepos-terous to the police. Well, to anybody. Thank goodness I hadn't called them. They'd think I was certifiable.

I tried the backdoor to the store. It was still locked. I shone the flashlight all around the concrete steps and surrounding shrubbery.

Finally, I saw something in the bush on the right side of the step.

It was a shred of paper about two inches long. Gift wrapping paper. I pulled it out. It had little books and cats on it — the new store gift-wrap. Like the paper I'd used to wrap Ginny Gilhooly's book.

I hadn't done any other gift wrapping in days. And this scrap wasn't soaked from the drizzle. So it had to be pretty fresh — and from Ginny's book. A very strange clue.

Speaking of clues, there was also that fingernail Buckingham had found. They both seemed to be evidence that Ginny had been here.

But I had no idea if that meant she was dead or alive. Or why Peter thought she was dead.

And where was he? Was he really ghosting me in the middle of the night? At least I hadn't let him talk me into anything romantic.

Maybe it was just as well. Peter said he wanted to stay awhile to establish his identity. But my cottage was tiny, and as Benjamin Franklin said, visitors, like fish, stink after three days.

# seven

. . .

## Something Catfishy

*F*riday felt eerie — foggy, cold, and still. In spite of the
coffee, I'd managed to get back to sleep for a couple of
hours after the bizarre incident with the corpse that wasn't there, and
the chronically evaporating Peter Sherwood.

Except for the large fish in my fridge, I could believe I'd imagined
the whole thing.

Usually Friday was one of my busiest days, but this one was dead.
Maybe because of the uninviting weather. Morro Bay fog could get so
thick it felt like rain.

All morning I only had one customer — a solitary tourist looking
for a paperback to read while his wife explored the Embarcadero
shops.

"She's shopping for clutter," he said. "Like what we need is more
tchotchkes."

Even Hobo Joe was missing from his usual spot on the bench in
front of the store where he busked for spare change. I always enjoyed
his virtuoso playing on his beat-up old guitar. His absence made the
silence even creepier.

Besides, I'd been thinking I might need his help if I got busy tomorrow. He sometimes helped me out at the register when I was alone in the store. Even though he was unhoused, he managed to bathe regularly, so he passed muster with most of my customers.

Without Plantagenet, Saturday afternoon could be exhausting. I'd love it if Joe were around to take over for a half hour so I could take a short break for lunch.

Plus, Joe could help me with that salmon and take some to his camp outside of town. I hoped he'd be back tomorrow.

Around two o'clock, the sun broke through the marine layer and I had a sudden rush in the store. Customers came in by twos and threes and fours. Keeping up was exhausting. One patient woman wanted a copy of a Louise Hay book I knew I had, but she couldn't find it and I couldn't leave the register to help her.

An authoritative female voice behind me interrupted. "I can show you where the New Age books are, ma'am."

It was Adriana. She and Britney had materialized in the crowd, and Adriana was putting on her grown-up act again. I have to admit I was awfully grateful. She led the customer to the display in the back where we'd put the most popular self-help and New Age books.

I was doing pretty well keeping up with the people at the register until a woman asked for her book to be gift wrapped.

"I love that wrapping paper with the books and kitties on it. It's a birthday gift."

Britney shot around the counter and gave me a big smile. "I can wrap that for you, ma'am. I love that paper too. So, who is this for...?"

I was too busy to marvel at how beautifully Britney wrapped the big hardcover copy of the *Vegan Instant Pot Cookbook*, but the customer was all smiles as she walked out.

"It's so sad about Mrs. Gilhooly," Britney said when there was a small lull in the traffic.

Ginny. I'd almost let myself forget about Peter and his corpse-on-the-doorstep story. It must have been some kind of a crazy prank Peter had pulled on me. Nothing else made sense.

"Yes. Poor Ginny. She called me at home last night. She's having boyfriend problems and wanted to get rid of the book she bought yesterday. But you know, she hasn't come in to return it yet. Maybe she'll be in later today."

Britney looked at me as if I'd developed dementia.

"Well, duh. It's hard to return a book when you're dead."

I think I gasped. This was too creepy. Could that corpse on the doorstep have been real after all?

"What do you mean she's dead? You think Ginny Gilhooly is dead? Why? Did you see something?"

What if the girl had seen the body on the back step? What was she doing here in the middle of the night?

Britney laughed. "Well, I didn't personally see her die or anything, but it's all over the news. They found her dead in the homeless camp out on Highway 41. My mom says it serves her right. She said Mrs. Gilhooly made a whole lot of people homeless by tearing down those apartments instead of fixing them."

Okay, it seemed there really had been a corpse. But not on my doorstep. Somewhere miles away. This was even less believable than Peter's story. I looked over at Adriana, who had been dusting off the History section with a paper towel she must have found in the bathroom. An enterprising young woman.

"Adriana, have you heard this news about Mrs. Gilhooly?"

"That they found her body in a homeless camp this morning?" Adriana dropped her improvised dust cloth in the trash basket near my desk. "Yeah. That's like the biggest news story all day. I guess she won't return that book now, will she?" Adriana gave a little laugh.

The *schadenfreude* of the young. I could only shake my head.

"What happened?" I hated to sound clueless, when everybody else seemed to know all about it. "Did Ginny have a heart attack or something?"

Let it not be murder. Somehow it would make me feel better if it hadn't been murder. Of course, murder or not, it made no sense that her body had left my property and ended up in a homeless camp on Highway 41, five miles away. Poor Ginny. She owned so many houses, but ended up in a camp for the unhoused.

"The people on TV didn't say what killed her." Britney spoke with way too much cheer. "But they did say the death was 'suspicious.' So that doesn't sound like a heart attack. They must have found something fishy."

"I'll bet that catfishing boyfriend bumped her off," Adriana said. "She finds out he's a catfish, and a few hours later she's dead? Britney, that's not just 'something fishy' that's more like 'something catfishy.' The boyfriend killed her. I'll bet you five dollars."

"What, he flew all the way over from Africa in record time to knock off one of the fake girlfriends he was scamming? That makes no sense, Adriana. Unless he's maybe *not* one of those Nigerian catfish scammers and an actual real-life boyfriend who was cheating on her. I guess maybe her boyfriend killed her, but not because he was some African catfish."

I tried to smile. I hadn't raised children, so I didn't know how to deal with squabbling teenagers. I didn't want them to disturb the customers, but I also wanted to find out what they knew about Ginny's corpse.

"Girls, 'suspicious' doesn't mean it was murder." I tried for a calming, reasonable tone. "It could have been a heart attack or a stroke with unusual circumstances. I agree with Britney that even if it's murder, an African romance scammer doesn't seem a likely killer."

Adriana gave a shrug. "I didn't say he came from Africa, did I? He could be somebody right here in Morro Bay and still be a catfish. I know girls at my school who catfish people all the time. Like Willow O'Malley pretends to be an 18-year-old model on Snapchat. But anyway, I don't believe the homeless people killed Mrs. Gilhooly like they say on TV. Especially not Joe. Joe is awesome. He was teaching me guitar. And he takes showers at the shelter. He hardly even smells."

Why was she talking about Joe? I knew Adriana sometimes hung out with him and he'd let her play some chords on his guitar. It would be stupid for the police to suspect him only because he was homeless and Ginny died in a homeless camp.

"Joe? You're talking about our guitar player who calls himself

Hobo Joe? They suspect him of having something to do with Ginny's death?"

"They've got one of those BOLOs on him," Britney said. "They've got witnesses that say he threatened Mrs. Gilhooly yesterday. Right here in front of this store."

This news was going from bad to worse. Way worse.

# eight

. . .

## Ding Dong the Fish is Dead

*I* looked at Britney, and then Adriana, hoping they were joking, or at least they were mistaken about Joe being a suspect in Ginny's mysterious death. But their faces were full of sincerity and confidence.

I glanced around the store. We had about four customers browsing. I wondered if they all knew the sweet old man who usually played guitar in front of the store was a suspected murderer.

"The police totally think Hobo Joe killed Mrs. Gilhooly." Britney stepped closer to the counter. "I guess when Ginny left the store yesterday, he played that *Wizard of Oz* song on his guitar — 'Ding Dong, the Witch is Dead'."

Adriana came closer too. "Like that was a threat. It's just a stupid nursery rhyme. He didn't even sing the words. Who knows, it could have been ding dong the wish is dead or the fish is dead, or whatever. They're so wrong to say he made threats. Anybody could tell them Joe wouldn't hurt a fly. In fact, I saw him take a giant spider off the bench once and set it down into the planter out there instead of squishing it. He's like Mr. Rogers or something."

A woman in the Romance section looked over and gave Adriana a sympathetic nod. Joe had friends in this town. I was glad of that.

Still, it was rotten news. If Joe was in trouble, he was going to need help. And God knew he had no money to get it. My first instinct was to phone Ronzo. Joe had been a good friend to Ronzo after his music reviewer career at *Rolling Stone* had been cancelled by Mack Rattlebag and Saffina. Joe had even let Ronzo live at his campsite.

But what could Ronzo do? Did I even want to talk to him? If he lied to me about Saffina, I would be done with him. Nothing is ruder than gaslighting — flat out denial of somebody's reality. Jonathan used to do that and I still hadn't forgiven him.

"Do you want us to shelve these?" Britney wheeled out the book cart with the new order.

"I'll help and make sure she does them right." Adriana gave me a big smile.

I had to nod gratefully. Right now, all I could think of was Joe. I knew he hadn't killed anybody, but he did have dark secrets that would be exposed if the police arrested him. Secrets only Ronzo knew for sure, but I strongly suspected. "Hobo Joe" was an alias that had been protecting Joe while he stayed off the grid, but it would not hold up under scrutiny from the police. Or prying journalists.

I took out my phone to call Ronzo, but couldn't do it. There had to be a way to help Joe without acting like a clingy girlfriend.

Britney and Adriana were arguing over whether to put a book in Romance or Mainstream Fiction. Shelving was one thing Plant did very well when he wasn't chatting up customers. He might have to redo some of the girls' decisions, but I was going to let them try to work on their own.

Plant. That was it. I'd call him about Joe. He and Silas might be able to help.

But then Plant was in LA and probably wildly busy with Jonathan's show and seeing old friends. And his husband Silas probably never had any interaction with Joe. Silas came from a wealthy local family and it was unlikely he knew any unhoused people.

Of course, the person I really wanted to talk to was Peter. He could clear Joe's name in a heartbeat. He had to know what happened to Ginny's corpse. If there had actually been a corpse on my back steps in the first place. And if the corpse had been there, he might have had something to do with moving it. Or at least know who did.

If only Peter would un-evaporate.

Two women came in who looked familiar — Ginny's friends from her book club. They often came in together. I strained to hear to their conversation, hoping they might have clues about Ginny's mysterious demise. They were talking about how her son Larry's big June wedding should be cancelled, and the couple should wait at least a year. There were some harsh words about 'that Crystal' and her 'bridesmaids from hell.' There had to be a story there, but it was unlikely to help me find Ginny's killer.

The phone rang. I picked it up eagerly, hoping it might be Peter. But it was one more scam robocall telling me my computer was about to expire. I slammed down the phone, getting angrier at Peter by the minute. How could he have disappeared like that? Did he expect me to believe he'd never been here?

Of course, I had been incredibly sleepy last night. Maybe I'd had one of those lucid dreams or something.

After a weird fisherman brought me a salmon.

Maybe the weird fisherman wasn't Peter? Maybe he was some kind of serial killer who brought fish to people and then killed them?

But then I'd be dead and not Ginny.

My cellphone rang in my purse. Did Peter have my cell number? I reached in to grab it — the first time I'd opened my purse all day — and there, stuffed in the main compartment was a wad of money. Australian dollars. Okay, so that part had been real.

I looked at the number on my phone. Dear Lord, it was Marva.

Marva was so much not who I needed right now. She was a drag queen dominatrix who called herself "Mistress Nightshade" and occasionally impersonated my alter ego, the Manners Doctor, for her kinky performances. Unfortunately, her faulty moral compass did not always steer her in the direction of friendly behavior.

But I took the call anyway. A customer came up to the counter with a question, but sweet Adriana rushed over to help. I turned my attention to the call.

"Camilla dear, I know you're worried about Hobo Joe Torres." Marva spoke in a conspiratorial whisper. "Don't worry. He's safe. But don't pry. Peter says you mustn't get mixed up in any of it."

"Peter says...?" I'd forgotten that Marva and Peter had formed a friendship the last time he was here. So that's where he'd disappeared. "You mean Peter is there? At your house? Does he intend to come back here? Does he want his fish?"

"I said you mustn't pry, Doctor Manners." Marva's voice got sharp and her pitch lowered. "I can't tell you where Peter is. Or Joe. All I can say is that you need to stay out of this."

"Out of what? All I know is he told me there was a corpse on my back steps. A dead..." I stopped myself as I realized the two girls and several customers were paying close attention to my phone call. "Um. I didn't see it. But I did see a fingernail. And a scrap of wrapping paper."

"Unsee them, dear. It never happened."

The phone clicked off. I felt a little dizzy. This was getting weirder and weirder.

"You look like you had some bad news," Britney said. "Are you okay, Ms. Randall?"

"I can get you some coffee. I know where your coffee maker is in the back room." Adriana gave me one of her smiles.

I shook my head. "I'm fine. I had a houseguest last night and thought he'd be staying longer, but I guess he's staying with...another friend."

Dear Lord. I did not want to have to explain Marva to a couple of thirteen-year-olds.

"But you said a corpse," Britney said. "You said there was a dead something. A corpse."

"Um, a dead — mouse. Yes. He said he saw the corpse of a mouse." I hoped I was managing to sound sort of believable. "A poor little dead mouse. Buckingham isn't much of a hunter, but my friend said the kitty killed a mouse and the corpse was on the back steps to the store. But when I went out to look for it, the corpse was gone." Oh, dear. Here I was lying to a child.

"Eeew," Britney said. "Is that why your friend went to your other friend's house? It would freak me out too. Where is Buckingham?"

My poor kitty. I hadn't brought him into the store today. I was so rattled by everything that happened last night that I'd left Buckingham in the house. I'd have to run back and get him. He was an indoor/outdoor cat and didn't use a box. I had to pray he had the bladder control of a camel.

But I heard the bell on the door jingle and in came one of my most talkative customers. She might keep me forty-five minutes or more.

"Girls, I've got to run back to my cottage. Can you hold the fort for me for a couple of minutes?"

They both beamed at me. They actually seemed to be enjoying all this work.

Buckingham was fine, sound asleep in a sunbeam on the living room floor. But he was grateful to see me. As soon as I opened the door for him, he bounded out and disappeared into the bushes which hid his commode.

When I got back to the store, my talkative customer turned and smiled at me.

"I'm so glad you've hired some professional help," she said. "These young ladies are so much more helpful than your man friend. He'll talk your ear off."

Of course, I knew she'd done most of the talking. Like Ginny Gilhooly. Plant had been good with both of them. He was generally a good listener, and gave good advice. I needed to talk to him myself about all this mysterious stuff as soon as he got back.

The girls glowed from the customer's compliment.

"She's right. You have done a great job," I told them after she left. "I don't suppose you'd like to come in tomorrow? Plant won't be back from LA and it's our busiest day..."

They both grinned and gave emphatic nods.

"We'll be here at ten," Adriana said. "That's when you open, right?"

As they ran off to do more dusting, I realized they really were working for me. Which meant I must find a way to pay them.

But I wondered how many child labor laws I'd be breaking when I did.

Probably fewer laws than I was breaking by not telling the police about Marva's phone call. Plus my illegal alien friend Peter "Pelletier."

And, of course, the disappearing corpse of Ginny Gilhooly.

# nine

. . .

## Catfishing in America

*I* expected Plant to be back at work at ten on Tuesday morning. I was desperate to talk to him about Peter. And the missing corpse. And how the police were calling Hobo Joe "a person of interest." And that Marva seemed to be hiding him.

I wasn't happy with Marva. I hadn't heard a thing from her since that one ominous phone call on Friday, and she wasn't returning my texts.

Buckingham didn't seem happy either. He sat out on Hobo Joe's bench, looking forlorn. I missed Joe too. I hoped he was somewhere safe.

Unfortunately, Plant didn't show up until well past eleven. He looked much the worse for wear. And he was sipping coffee from a Starbucks cup, which was odd. He usually brought some of Silas's special brew from home.

"I heard about the demise of our chatterbox, Ginny Gilhooly. It's sad she died in that homeless camp, but suitably ironic. After all, she took homes from a lot of people."

I already had several customers in the store, so it wasn't the time to talk about all the drama concerning Ginny's traveling corpse.

"What have you done to the store?" Plant surveyed the place with bleary eyes. I wondered if he'd driven all night from Los Angeles. "Either you've been cleaning like a madwoman, or you've hired a service."

"That was our little YA book duo. Britney and Adriana jumped in and helped out on Friday afternoon and most of Saturday. I paid them minimum wage. I hope that wasn't illegal."

"It might have been." Plant gave a thoughtful smile. "I think you have to get a special permit to hire children under sixteen. It's something studios do for child actors. I think you can get permits from the school system." He looked around the store again. "It might be a good idea to look into those permits. They did a fabulous job."

I laughed, glad his feelings weren't hurt. "It's not as if I'm going to need to hire them now that you're back."

Plant gave a strained smile. "Well — you might. That is, I'm not exactly back. Not for long. A few weeks maybe. But I've had an offer of a job in LA."

"A writing job? You're going to work on a film?"

Plant's face broke into a grin. "Yes, darling! I've got a job writing on a series for Netflix. It's about a support group for people who've been catfished. TBS has that reality show about catfishing and this will be a kind of fictional version of it. Ten stand-alone stories. An anthology series. It's called *Catfishing in America*."

"Will you have to live down there? How does Silas feel about it?"

"I don't have to live in LA permanently. But Silas is..." Plant sighed. "He's not ecstatic. Unfortunately, I told him about the job when I got home last night around eleven and we argued until two. We didn't resolve anything. But we did kill half a bottle of Grey Goose. That's why I overslept."

"I'm so sorry about Silas. But congratulations!" I gave Plant a hug. "So your appearance on Jonathan's #MenToo show is putting you back in the game?"

"I think Kensie's appearance is what's going to clinch it." Plant laughed. "She's so comically transparent. In the course of denying everything, she made it pretty clear she knew I was gay and married, but she stalked me for months thinking she could 'convert' me."

"Well, I'm sure Silas will be happy for you once he thinks it over. He has to realize that writing a Netflix series is a fantastic opportunity for you to get your career back." I laughed. "But you'd better go comb your hair. It looks a little bed-heady."

"Oh, damn. Do I look awful?" Plant tried to smooth his hair and only managed to make it look more tangled. He slurped the dregs in his Starbucks cup. "I think I'd better get some more coffee. Silas usually makes it for us with the French press, but when he's not speaking to me, he's also not cooking."

I was genuinely thrilled for Plant about the job, but, like Silas, I'd miss him terribly.

The door banged open and a man I'd never seen before stomped into the store as if he were storming Iwo Jima. He clutched one of our signature green paper bags.

"This was supposed to be returned!" His face turned a frightening shade of pink.

I hoped he wasn't going to give himself a stroke right there in front of me. One corpse was enough for any four-day period.

"We accept returns, as long as you have the receipt and the book is in a condition to be sold as new." I gave him my Manners Doctor smile.

"The receipt is in there." He tossed the bag onto the counter. "The thing is gift wrapped. That's not supposed to make any difference. That's what your employee told my mother."

"Then there's no problem." Maybe the friend of the woman who'd bought the *Vegan Instant Pot Cookbook* Britney giftwrapped on Friday had decided to go back to a carnivorous lifestyle.

I pulled the book out of the bag. The wrapping paper had been torn off one corner. I felt a chill as I looked at the receipt.

Mrs. Gilbert Gilhooly. This had to be her son. Keep calm, I told myself, the poor man has just lost his mother. A year after losing his father. He had a reason for acting a little unhinged.

"So, you're Ginny's son? I'm sorry for your loss." I gave him a warm smile. "She was such a good customer. And she always had interesting stories to tell. We'll miss her a lot."

The man scowled in furious silence.

So I got down to business.

"This was bought with a MasterCard, so I'll simply credit that. The credit will appear on your — that is her — statement next month. I'll only be half a minute." It was probably going to take three minutes, but I thought talking to him in a calm tone might keep him from exploding his brain right there in front of me.

"I don't know what you did to her, lady, but she was real upset about this book. She wanted it the hell out of her house. She was threatening to come over here in the middle of the night. Thank goodness my fiancée got her to take a sleeping pill and go to bed."

Oh, my. Ginny had planned to come here in the middle of the night. Well, that was a juicy bit of information. Maybe she actually had been here.

But her son thought his fiancée had stopped Ginny from coming.

He was a large man, tall and burly, wearing a well-cut bespoke suit. He didn't seem much over thirty. This had to be the son who was having the controversially lavish wedding at San Luis Obispo's famously pink Madonna Inn. Poor little rich boy.

I kept my voice calm. "I don't think it was anything we did, Mr. Gilhooly. Ginny was upset when she found out that oilman boyfriend of hers wasn't what he seemed."

"Boyfriend? My mother just lost her husband. She did not have a boyfriend!" He gave a large sniff and I could see his eyes were glistening with tears. "And I'm not Mr. Gilhooly. That was my father — rest in peace. I'm Larry. Plain old Larry. The orphan."

The poor man. He was hopeless. I couldn't imagine what sort of woman would be able to put up with him.

But the bell on the door jingled and there that woman was: a scrawny, horse-faced redhead wearing so many bejeweled rings and gold bracelets, I wondered how she lifted those emaciated arms. The gold bracelets looked remarkably like the ones Ginny had been wearing last Friday. I supposed the fiancée might have inherited Ginny's jewelry, but it seemed a bit too soon.

"Larry, what's takin' so long? This place always gives me the creepy-crawlies. That's where the murderer always sits. That bench outside. Right outside this store. Smelly old homeless guy. I don't like bookstores anyways. Why not go to the freakin' library? It's free." Her accent was from the San Joaquin Valley. Probably Bakersfield. She said "binch" for "bench' and "innyways" for "anyway."

"I'm ringing up the return now, Miss." I tried to keep my voice soothing. "I'll be done in a flash and you can be on your way."

"Why the heck was Ginny buying more books, anyways?" The scrawny woman was in even higher dudgeon than her fiancé. "It's not like she didn't have a buttload of them. Those huge book shelves are going to be a bear to move out of the front room. We're going to have to get movers in before we paint the place. I want to do the room in sunset orange and pink. Our wedding colors." She pulled herself back from her home decorating reverie and shook her head. "If only your mom hadn't come in here last Friday, she'd be alive right now. That criminal probably scoped her out while he picked at that garbage guitar. I'm sure he figured she was a rich target."

The woman took out a tissue and dabbed at some less-than-genuine tears.

"Crystal, it will be all right." Larry's voice softened as he patted the woman's shoulder. "The police have a BOLO out on the homeless guitar guy, and they'll find him. I know they will. These homeless have their little hidey-holes, like rats. But the cops will smoke him out. The guy took her phone. They have ways of tracing a phone."

I handed Larry the new receipt and gave him a quick smile. I had to feel a bit of compassion for the poor man. His mother had been a little difficult, but it looked as if he was taking on a total disaster in marrying this Crystal woman. I couldn't help thinking about what Ginny had said about jewelry-related women's names. She must have had her future daughter-in-law in mind.

There was a knock on the display window, and a gaggle of four or five women who looked like Crystal clones waved and giggled outside. A tiny one, dressed in various shades of purple, with almost-matching violet fingernails, knocked on the window and mouthed the words "hurry up." Maybe they were afraid if they came inside a bookstore, they'd lose their bimbo cred.

Crystal waved back and grabbed Larry's arm. "We're outta here, Larry. We need to go for fittings of the bridesmaid dresses and you know how picky the girls can be."

Bridesmaids. So, they really were going through with the elaborate wedding in spite of Ginny's death. That was not only dreadful manners but presented a real dilemma for guests. Attending would disrespect the dead and staying home would infuriate the bride. Whatever they did would seem rude. No wonder Ginny's friends were so agitated about it the other day.

Plantagenet had materialized with a steaming cup of coffee sometime during my encounter with Larry and Crystal. As they rushed out to meet their fan club, he grabbed me in a sideways hug and handed me the coffee.

"That's why you can work retail and I can't, darling. You kept a straight face all the way through that little scene." He let out a big laugh. "And his name is Larry. I wonder if he left Moe and Curly in the car. And that bimbo battalion outside — what was that all about?"

I started to explain, but another couple of customers came in. Plant greeted them with a hearty smile. He was better at working retail than he thought, in spite of his tendency to be overly loquacious. I was going to miss having him here.

I tore the rest of the wrapping off the copy of *Grit* and started to toss the paper, then wondered if I should save it for DNA or something. Plus, I should see if it fit with that scrap I'd found the other night. It might have been torn right there on my back step. Maybe the killer had tried to take the book away from Ginny and she hung on.

I folded the paper carefully and planned to put it in a plastic bag with the other "clues" in case anybody asked.

But a big question loomed in my mind: how had Larry got hold of the book if Ginny had it on my back step last night? If the scrap of paper I found fit with the big sheet of paper, it had probably been Larry on my step last night. With Ginny.

That meant Larry was her killer.

But somehow, I couldn't picture it. He'd been so devoted to his mother. And he seemed like someone who was genuinely grieving.

Should I tell Plant about it? I could use his advice, but I was wary of telling him about the mysterious disappearing body. He'd think I was losing my marbles.

And maybe I was.

# ten

. . .

## Catfishland

*a*s I re-shelved the late Ginny Gilhooly's copy of *Grit* in the Self-Help section, I tried to make sense of all the bizarre details her son Larry's visit had revealed.

First, Larry obviously didn't know about his mom's two-timing boyfriend "Brownie." That was weird. She'd talked my ear off about her sweetheart "oilman" over the past six months. Could she really never have mentioned him to her son?

Ginny had been highly strung, and I could understand why she was upset that night, and why the anger might focus on the book — probably the only solid thing that existed in her "love affair" with Brownie.

Except for that hole he must have left in her bank account. I wondered how she'd explained all those PayPal transfers to Larry if she hadn't told him about her relationship.

Maybe she'd kept a tight rein on the purse strings and didn't let Larry nose around her personal finances. That would have annoyed him, I should think, since they were partners in their rental business. Maybe that's what kept him dependent and babyish. He couldn't think of himself as a grown-up "Mr. Gilhooly" although he wore the costume of a successful businessman.

But the details didn't add up. I had to get Plant to sit down and listen to the full story so he could help me make sense of it all. Even if he thought I was bonkers.

But right now, Plant was happily chatting with a retired school teacher about what a shame it was that high school students didn't read George Eliot anymore.

I sat down at my desk behind the counter and numbed my brain with a bunch of paperwork, until a familiar face peered at me over her dark-rimmed glasses. Adriana.

"I hope you're not mad at me too? Are you mad at me?"

I stood. "Oh my, no. Why would I be mad? I thought you and Britney did a fantastic job on Saturday. In fact, I need to talk to you two…"

She sniffed. "It's not us two anymore. Britney says she's never going to speak to me again." Adriana's face scrunched up with incipient tears. She looked very much the thirteen-year-old schoolgirl, and not the efficient worker she'd been last weekend.

"I'm sorry to hear that. What's the problem?"

I looked around to see if maybe I could take the conversation to the office. Only two customers, which Plant could handle if he let go of George Eliot.

"Let's go back to my office. I can make you some hot chocolate."

Adriana gave me a tearful smile. I signaled to Plant that I'd be in the back.

I turned on the tea kettle and poured the contents of a packet of hot chocolate in a mug, then poured myself some java from the ancient Mr. Coffee I'd inherited when I bought the store. I motioned for Adriana to sit in the chair facing my desk.

"So, tell me what happened. Was it something major?"

"About as major as it gets." Adriana sniffed and sat up straight, putting on her grown-up smile. "I know Britney's mom is being catfished, and nobody will believe me. Shannon — that's Britney's mom — keeps sending money to this so-called boyfriend in Africa. But he stopped writing to her about six weeks ago." Adriana gave a big sigh.

"They usually do." I gave a sympathetic smile. "Con men move on to greener pastures once they think the money might run out or somebody's on to them."

Adriana's brow furrowed.

"That's the weird thing. She says she sent him money last month but it came back. I guess he'd sent her another one of his bogus sob stories. He told her he was in all this trouble because his business partner hijacked his bank account and stole all his money. So Shannon got super worried and sent him a boatload of money through PayPal. But his account was closed. And he didn't answer her emails. She's sure he got thrown in jail because he couldn't pay his bills."

Adriana pushed her glasses farther up her nose.

"So, Saturday night I told Shannon, well, duh, of course he's in jail. He's a criminal, and that's where they put criminals — in jail. That's when Britney decided to go bananas on me. Then Shannon cried and called me disrespectful."

I made sympathetic noises although I could imagine Shannon didn't appreciate getting snark about her boyfriend from a thirteen-year-old.

"I found a bunch of articles on catfishing and romance scams and sent Britney the links and begged her to read them and give them to her mom." Adriana sniffed back tears. "But she blocked me on Instagram and pretends I'm not even in the room."

I'd met Britney's mom, Shannon Fiorentino — a massage therapist or something. Very New Age, usually draped in hand-painted scarves and jingly jewelry. She once told me she wanted to write a novel, so I sold her Stephen King's *On Writing*.

"I'm so sorry, Adriana. It sounds as if you're the only sensible one and you're getting hurt because of it. But people do get angry when you pop their fantasy bubbles, so it's better manners to say things like that gently. Sometimes pose it as a question. Say something like 'Do you know why the police might think he's a criminal?' Something like that."

Adriana gave me an expression that was very nearly an eye-roll.

I realized it was not time for etiquette advice.

"It sounds to me as if Britney is trying so hard not to face the facts about her mom that she's shooting the messenger. Having a mother who's gullible is very difficult. My mother was gullible too."

I wondered if I should tell the story about how my mother married a fake Portuguese Count who stole every penny we had.

But Adriana looked unreceptive. She finished her hot chocolate and put her mug on the desk with an emphatic thump.

"Yeah, well it's going to be even tougher to have a mom who's dead. You should read the stuff about this catfishing mafia."

"There's a catfishing mafia?"

"Yes. I saw it on TV. They have their headquarters in Lagos, Nigeria. That's Catfishland. They're scary guys. I'm so afraid Shannon's going to get hurt — or worse. I don't want to tell Britney 'I told you so.' I just want Shannon to stay alive."

The bell I keep on the checkout counter started ringing. Where was Plant?

I ran into the store. Plant was still in deep discussion about the merits of *The Mill on the Floss* vs. *Middlemarch.*

And there was Britney, holding Buckingham in the crook of her arm while frantically ringing the little bell. Buckingham watched it warily, as if he expected the bell to attack at any moment.

Britney was breathless, her face pink.

"A bunch of awful people threw Buckingham off the bench outside. They were sitting on the bench and Bucky jumped up, like he does with Joe, and a horrible lady picked him up and threw him in the street. I can't *even*. Do you think he needs to go to the vet?"

I took Buckingham in my arms and peeked out the window. Crystal and the "bimbo battalion" were eating frozen yogurt from the place next door. Larry Gilhooly hovered over them, looking somehow dorky and menacing at the same time.

Buckingham seemed to be all right. He was used to being removed from furniture in the store. But all I could think of was poor Ginny Gilhooly. Even being catfished couldn't have been as awful as having to deal with those people.

# eleven

· · ·

## A Very Real Salmon

*I*t wasn't until Thursday evening that I was finally able to tell Plant about Peter and Joe and Marva and the mysterious disappearing corpse. I figured it was worth the risk of his initial mockery in order to get his advice, which was usually sound.

Also, I couldn't decide what to do with my "clues." I'd folded up the sheet of wrapping paper — the first piece fit with it like a jigsaw puzzle — and stashed it in a Ziplock baggie, along with the acrylic nail, the way they do in TV police dramas. What would Plant think of them?

I was also full of curiosity about his meeting with Jonathan.

I hadn't heard from Ronzo, but I almost didn't expect to. Things between us seemed to be deteriorating fast. No point in postponing the inevitable. Saffina was younger, richer, and a whole lot more geographically appropriate than me.

No word from Marva, either, and she wasn't returning my calls. That was probably because she was hiding Joe. Peter wouldn't have stayed there long. He was probably halfway around the globe by now.

I'd persuaded Plant to come over to my cottage after work for a glass of wine. I tried to talk him into joining me in a nice salmon salad that needed eating, but he said it wasn't a good idea for him to miss dinner with Silas when things were still rocky.

Buckingham would have to take care of the rest of Peter's salmon.

Right now, the cat was occupying Plant's lap while Plant sat on my living room couch, sipping a local Pinot Noir.

"You are absolutely, positively sure Peter saw a corpse on your back step on Friday night? What made you think it was the body of Ginny Gilhooly? Peter Sherwood didn't know Ginny, did he?" Plant leaned over carefully so as not to disturb Buckingham as he refilled his glass from the bottle on the coffee table.

"No. I'm not absolutely, positively sure of anything. Even that Peter was really here. But there was the salmon. The remains are in the fridge if you want to check. It's a very real salmon. Also, I have the Australian dollars, which I must take to the bank, hoping they can convert them to US currency. But otherwise, it doesn't seem likely, does it? At one point, I almost managed to talk myself into believing I'd dreamed the whole thing. But then I had to rethink when I heard the news that Ginny was actually dead. And I still have the shred of wrapping paper from my back step that fits exactly with the wrapping paper on the book Larry brought in for the refund. Oh, and I've got Ginny's acrylic fingernail. It was stuck on Buckingham's head."

Buckingham gave me a heavy-lidded look, as if he were warning me not to repeat the story of the embarrassing incident.

"The acrylic nail? Do you still have it? You should give it to the police. They need all the evidence they can get to prove Joe is innocent." Plant looked a little rattled.

"But how would I explain it? My cat — who never leaves my property — wandered in wearing Ginny's fingernail as a hat? Wouldn't that make Joe look guiltier? I don't know what evidence they have, but apparently, they know Joe hung out here. And people heard Joe play "Ding Dong the Witch is Dead" when Ginny walked by his bench. The police think that was meant as a threat."

Plant set down his wine glass.

"What? That's what he played? Did you hear it?"

I nodded. "The incident happened a few hours before she died. It's one of their reasons for naming Joe a 'person of interest.' I guess a bunch of tourists coming out of the yogurt shop next door heard Joe play it. They've been playing the song clip on the local TV news as if that's evidence of guilt."

"How do you know he didn't do it?"

Buckingham made a sudden jump from Plant's lap.

I agreed with my cat. "How can you even ask me that? Of course I know he didn't do it. I know Joe. He wouldn't kill a fly. Literally. He doesn't even squish bugs, according to Adriana. I trust him completely."

"Then why not give the police the fingernail? It probably doesn't mean anything. She was in the store that afternoon, and it could have popped off then. Buckingham could have rolled on it later."

"He'd have to have rolled on it in the courtyard. He didn't go back into the store after dinner and he didn't have the nail on him then. My worry is that if the police see evidence that both Ginny and Joe were here in my courtyard on Friday night, that could look bad for Joe."

Plant took a thoughtful sip of wine.

"But Camilla, you're withholding evidence."

"Evidence of what? A body that wasn't there? Do you think I should give them the wrapping paper too?"

I showed him how the pieces of paper fit together.

Plant jumped up as soon as I showed him the jigsaw-puzzle fit.

"Wait a minute. How did Larry get the book with the torn paper if Ginny had it when she was dead on your doorstep?"

"I don't know. Maybe he was the one who took the book from her?"

"On your doorstep? Was that before or after he killed her?"

"I don't know!" Now I was confused. "Maybe Larry did kill her. But if she was murdered, I think it had something to do with the catfish scam. She found out Brownie was two-timing her, and she was dead within hours. How can that be a coincidence?"

Plant gave me a hug. "This is a matter for the police. I'm only thinking of you, darling. You don't like jail. Remember last time?"

"Yes, I do, thank you very much." How rude for Plant to remind me of my past patches of bad luck. "Anyway, Marva told me Peter said I should keep out of it."

"Marva and Peter. A drag queen dominatrix and an international smuggler. They always give you good advice, do they? How do you know they didn't kill Ginny themselves?"

I wanted to slap him. "I told you Peter didn't know Ginny. And Marva may have met her a few times in the store. But Marva had no motive to kill her. Why would she kill Ginny?"

"Well, there were those tacky green fingernails…" Plant gestured at the green nail, which Buckingham had been eyeing as if he thought it might morph into a tasty lizard.

I had to laugh. Time for a Manners Doctor change-of-subject.

"You haven't told me anything about your meeting with Jonathan. Did he tell you that Ronzo and Saffina are going to be on his show too?"

Plant gave me a quick kiss on the cheek.

"I've got to go home or things will get even more stressful with Silas." He took a last gulp from his wine glass. "Yes. Jonathan told me Ronzo and the former Lady Ruffina are going to be a big hit. She's terribly contrite, apparently. And it turns out she's very telegenic without all the Goth make-up."

Telegenic. In other words, stick-thin and drop-dead gorgeous. I didn't need to hear that.

Plant picked up his coat. "We'll talk tomorrow, but I think Larry is your killer. The wrapping paper proves it. Call the police."

My landline phone rang.

"That's probably your hot Jersey boy now." Plant blew me a kiss as he rushed out the door.

I admit my heart raced a bit as I reached for the phone.

But it wasn't Ronzo. It was Adriana. She sounded a bit weepy.

"Can you talk to my mom and tell her you paid me this money? She thinks I stole it."

I heard a woman's voice come on the phone.

"Hello? This is Morro Bay Bookstore lady? I am Luisa Garza, Adriana's mom."

Her voice was heavily accented. I told her yes, I was indeed Camilla Randall, and explained I paid Adriana and Britney for their excellent work helping me in the store over the weekend when my employee hadn't been able to come in.

"She is not a bother for you?"

I assured her the girls were very welcome. This seemed to satisfy her.

"Better your store and not the library. Too many homeless men there. They say bad words for children."

She was right there. The library and its computers were a fantastic resource for all residents of Morro Bay, but it had become a haven for some of the less savory members of the unhoused population. Joe said a bunch of men had been asked to leave after using the computers to look for porn.

"I have question," Luisa said. "You sell books from Fanna Badjie? This is famous writer, Fanna Badjie?"

This was an odd question in light of all the news from Sherwood Ltd.

"Yes. We carry all five of her books. Do you want to buy one?"

"No. Thank you for money for my Adriana." The phone clicked off.

That was all very strange. Fanna Badjie was internationally known, and I was sure some of her work had been translated into Spanish, but it was weird that a woman without strong English skills would want one of our English copies.

Fanna Badjie seemed to be at the center of some mysteries that were even more complex than the mystery novels she wrote.

# twelve

. . .

## A Telegenic Fish

*a*fter the call from Adriana's mom, I felt a bit off-kilter. Plant hadn't been as soothing as I'd hoped. Maybe he was right and Larry had killed his mother and I should tell the police about my clues.

Buckingham was still keeping an eye on that green fingernail.

"What am I supposed to say, Bucky? Should I call the police and say, 'I'm calling to report a dead body I never saw that apparently got up and walked away from my courtyard last Friday night? And also, I have two pieces of my store's wrapping paper and a fake fingernail that was stuck to my cat's head. I think they have something to do with the body you found in the homeless camp, which an evaporating faux Canadian said was at my house first. And my friend Plant says I have to call you to keep Joe out of jail. And me.'"

Buckingham sauntered off into the kitchen for a drink from his water bowl.

"The police would probably to lock me up, wouldn't they?"

Buckingham wasn't going to dignify that with a response.

They probably would. The Morro Bay P.D. never believed me about anything. Like those horrible death threats I got because I responded to an Amazon review. And that Lexus I totally didn't steal. They always think I'm the one who's guilty of something.

Anything I did would probably bring attention to Joe and put him in more jeopardy.

What I needed to do first was find out what on earth happened to Peter and get him to tell me what he knew. I couldn't believe he would have lied about the corpse being there in the first place. Stupid pranks were not his style. He must have some clues about what happened. If I could only find out how to contact him.

Marva was still incommunicado.

I booted up my laptop and checked my email, but all I had was catfish spam from all those phony oil rig workers and servicemen with two first names. David Henry, Jack John, and my favorite, Denise Tom Dick. They often got the gender wrong. I used to think these wannabe lover-boys were hilarious with their identical, semi-literate love letters to perfect strangers. But after what happened to Ginny, I wasn't laughing any more.

And right now, it was time for business. I dumped all the lover-boys in the spam folder and sent an email to Vera. She was the office manager at the headquarters of Sherwood Ltd. in England. I asked her to forward Peter's latest phone number or email address or whatever means she used to communicate with him. Then I let her know Peter had paid me my back royalties. That should put her mind at ease. She'd been evasive about my money, and that usually meant Sherwood had spent it.

Of course there was nothing from Ronzo in my inbox. I wasn't even sure if he had access to the Internet these days. He used to email at least once a week, but the messages had been getting shorter and less frequent. And I'd had no real phone calls in forever. He sent the occasional text, but it was usually when he was waiting in some doctor's office with his grandmother. She seemed to be sicker recently.

Maybe he was torn between his promises to me and his duties to his "Nana." Both his parents were dead and she had raised him. That meant he'd be pretty much orphaned when she died. I certainly didn't want to pressure him by saying how much I missed him.

But I did. I couldn't help it. The fact that Saffina was getting so much more of his time than I was made me furious.

I poured myself the last of the wine and found a nice period drama on Netflix. But after a few moments, I turned it off again and grabbed a book. I did not want to spend the rest of the evening looking at people who were "telegenic."

Buckingham didn't either. He wandered off to the bedroom.

After a bit of reading, I decided to join him and make it an early night. I checked my email once more before going to bed, hoping against hope that I'd have a message from one of my evaporating men.

Instead, I saw a note from Vera, which brought me huge relief at first, but unfortunately, she didn't offer anything very helpful.

> I've come to the office early to tidy up the bits and bobs before the men come in and make a muck of it all again. As you may have surmised, things have gone even more catawampus at dear old Sherwood than usual. Pradeep is in a tizzy about Fanna, whose bank keeps sending back her royalties, so he's sure she's been mauled by tigers or eaten by some venomous crocodile. And of course, we've not heard a thing about her overdue manuscript. She was supposed to come to England to promote it and we've lined up television interviews on all the chat shows. But now there is no book.
>
> To add to the merriment, Fanna's former business manager is suing us. This daft cow seems to think we are responsible for Fanna's disappearance and she insists that Fanna owes her money. Dreadful piece of work.
>
> And, alas, we haven't heard a peep from Peter. Not since he left Australia. He promised Pradeep he'd find a way to sort the Fanna mess, but I have no idea how he intends to do that. I'll send you along his latest email

address, but I doubt it will work anymore. You know how he moves about."

I wrote a quick note thanking Vera and sent off an email to Peter's new address. I asked him what was going on and why he'd disappeared. I didn't mention Ginny's name. Apparently the police can read your old emails even if you delete them, and I didn't want to send anything incriminating out into the cyberverse. Not that I'd done anything wrong. But I didn't know that Peter hadn't.

You could never be sure, with Peter.

Who knew, maybe the murderer was the shady character who gave him the passport-stuffed salmon. All I knew was it wasn't Joe.

I don't suppose I expected a reply, but I could always hope.

Then I Googled Fanna Badjie. I hadn't paid much attention to what Peter had said about her, but now I was curious. However, I didn't find much. Apparently, Sherwood was keeping her disappearance under wraps. There were plenty of photos of her — a stunningly beautiful West African woman, always dressed in traditional garb — usually wearing a towering head wrap that accented her high cheekbones and luminous eyes.

She was beautiful in still photos and I imagined she'd be even more impressive on a television talk show. Another telegenic beauty.

I went to bed and had a disturbing dream where I was devoid of make-up and about to go on a television show carrying a large aspic-glazed salmon decorated with mayonnaise florets and "scales" made of roasted peppers. Apparently, I feared I'd become less telegenic than an over-decorated fish.

Sometimes our fears are quite reasonable.

I also feared that something terrible was going to happen to Joe, and that was probably reasonable too.

# thirteen

. . .

## A School of Catfished Ladies

Over the next few days, I kept digging through the local papers and news blogs for more information about Ginny Gilhooly's death, but there wasn't much. Finally on Sunday the local paper published an overview of the case.

The situation wasn't exactly what we'd been led to believe by the early hysterical news coverage.

The article said police were still looking for Joe Torres for "questioning," but it seemed they hadn't definitely ruled Ginny's death a homicide. They said Mrs. Gilhooly was believed to have sedatives in her system and they were waiting for the results of more tests. Interesting. Maybe Ginny had been trying to return that book in some sort of drugged state. Her son Larry did say she'd been talking about returning the book "in the middle of the night." Maybe his lovely bride Crystal hadn't talked Ginny into going to bed after all?

Unfortunately, after that Sunday story, Ginny's name disappeared into the back pages of the local newspapers and I didn't hear a peep about her on TV.

Later that week, I asked Plant if he'd heard anything.

"From what I've read, it looks as if it was an unfortunate accident."

His tone was dismissive. "I hope that means Joe will come back soon. I think he brought in customers."

"But how do you explain the book? How could Larry have it the day after she died? He must have killed her — out there in my courtyard. There's no other way to explain how the piece of wrapping paper got on my back step."

"Maybe the police gave Larry the book?" Plant had that glazed look he got when he didn't want to talk about something. He turned to shelve a wayward psychology book that I'd found in science fiction.

"You think the police are clueless enough to give a suspect a major piece of evidence? He has to be a person of interest, even though they're looking for Joe."

"A suspect? Now you agree Larry is the most likely suspect if it was murder? I thought your money was on the catfish." Plant made it sound so stupid.

"I don't know who I suspect, or who the police suspect. Maybe Brownie's other girlfriend wanted Ginny out of the way."

"Unlikely." Plant moved back to the counter and straightened the free tide charts we kept near the register. "If the killer moved the body from your courtyard to the homeless camp, they had to be awfully strong. Ginny was seriously plus-sized."

"Well, who knows, maybe Brownie's girlfriend has a lot of catfished friends."

"So, you suspect more than one of them?" Plant laughed. Now he was mocking me. "A whole school of catfished ladies?" Plant gave a rough laugh, leaned on the counter, and gave me the dark look he reserved for serious matters.

"Camilla, I know I first told you to talk to the police, but after reading that article last Sunday, I'm glad you didn't. There's no logical way that disappearing corpse thing could have happened. Your friend Peter Sherwood pulled something on you. I don't know how he did it, but I do know Peter Sherwood. There have to be perfectly mundane reasons for finding the fingernail and the scrap of paper. It looks as if Ginny took too many sleeping pills, went for a drive, got out of her car on her way up Highway 41 — maybe to have an emergency rest stop — and fell down on a rock or something. End of story. Forget about it."

He sounded like Marva. Whom I still hadn't heard from. But unfortunately, Plant made sense. Peter was unreliable at best.

I tried to put the whole Ginny incident on a back burner. But it would have helped if I had some idea of where Joe had gone and if he was okay.

I tried to talk with Plant about the situation over the next few weeks, but he wasn't interested. As the date of his move approached, I could tell his mind was elsewhere. He was probably writing his new Netflix series in his head. I was dreading May first, when he planned to leave for LA. I'd be alone again. And I'd have nobody but Buckingham to listen to my complaints about Ronzo's non-communicative texts.

Adriana and Britney occasionally came into the store, but they weren't using it as their own personal playhouse anymore. Sometimes Adriana came in alone. She and Britney were speaking again, but things sounded prickly. They didn't seem to have patched things up very well.

I didn't know if their absence had anything to do with my mysterious phone call from Adriana's mother Luisa. But something seemed to have soured the girls on the store.

So, I didn't ask them about working for me and decided to put an ad in the local paper for a part-time bookstore clerk starting in May. I didn't look forward to interviewing prospective employees. It was so hard to find somebody knowledgeable who was willing to work for the tiny amount I could pay. Plant's husband Silas, who sold me the store, once said looking for good bookstore employees was like fishing for trout in a goldfish bowl.

I needed to go fishing.

# fourteen

· · ·

## The Thing about Catfish

*A* week or so before Easter, Adriana came in looking weepy and red-faced. When I asked what was wrong, she whispered a plea to go into my office again. Luckily Plant was on duty. I sat Adriana at my desk and handed her a tissue while I set about making hot chocolate.

After blowing her nose and composing herself, she started her story. She spoke stiffly, as if she were on TV, reporting the news.

"Britney's mom, Shannon, flew to Lagos, Nigeria on Tuesday morning to go look for her so-called boyfriend."

"By herself?"

Adriana nodded.

No wonder the girl was weepy. Shannon had always seemed a little flakey, but not the sort of woman who would fly off to Africa to follow a phony lover-boy who had been hitting her up for money — not when it meant leaving her child alone.

Adriana gave a sniff. "I told my mom how those catfishing rings are run by a Nigerian mafia. I showed her the news stories and told her how bananas Britney is for not believing me. My mom said she believes me, and I could see she was scared. But then she shrugged and said '*lo que paso, paso.*' It's what she always says. 'What's over is over'."

"But it's not over, is it? Shannon's all right?" I handed Adriana her hot chocolate. I shared Adriana's fears. Shannon wasn't exactly worldly.

Adriana gave me a look of exasperation. "We don't know how Shannon is. My mom thinks because Shannon's already taken off, we have to hope for the best. But it's kind of hard to keep hoping when you know bad things are going to happen. Or maybe they did already."

Buckingham woke from the nap he'd been taking under the desk and jumped onto Adriana's lap. She gave him a few strokes and looked a bit more relaxed.

"Who's watching Britney?"

I tried to keep my disapproval of Shannon out of my voice. Adriana needed me to be soothing. Her mother was right that working herself up wasn't going to help.

"My mom is taking care of Britney, like always."

"They're close friends — your mom and Shannon?"

"Yes. They've been friends forever but now my mom is Shannon's maid. That's because she was Mr. Fiorentino's maid, and then Mr. Fiorentino married Shannon, who was his massage therapist. But then Mr. Fiorentino died last spring and so Shannon is the boss and our landlord, since and we live in the guest cottage."

Oh, my. That would make for odd employee / employer boundaries. Poor Adriana. I needed to say something to quell her fears. It wasn't as if she could do anything. I sipped my coffee.

"I can imagine it feels terrible to know how bad things could be in Africa. But you know —" I tried to put on a bright smile. "I think everything will be okay. And it will be less awkward for you and Britney if you don't talk about catfish. Do you think you could do that?"

Adriana gave me a sulky look and kept petting Buckingham.

But I kept talking in what I hoped was a reasonable, soothing tone.

"You see, that's the thing about catfish. They are fictional personas dreamed up by some con man — or a café full of con men. You can't find somebody who never was. All Shannon probably has is this man's name, address and phone number. And those are all bound to be phony. So she won't find anything. Maybe she'll have an interesting African adventure and come home a little sadder and wiser — but no harm done. And we can hope she'll be more careful about her choice of boyfriends next time."

As if I had made any careful choices of boyfriends recently. Ronzo had become more and more distant. I knew I needed to let go of my fantasies about him coming back to me.

Adriana gave me a look that showed she did not feel soothed.

"But Shannon might be dead already! She was supposed to text my mom when she got to her hotel in Lagos, but she didn't. If she ever got there. Britney hasn't heard one thing since her mom left LAX. That's almost three days without even a text. And Britney somehow makes it all my fault because I knew it was going to happen."

Buckingham jumped down, having failed at his mission of calming her down.

I have to admit the situation did sound pretty frightening. It had to be even worse for poor Britney. I hoped Luisa would be able to cope with both girls and their drama. I didn't envy her that.

Plant knocked on the door and signaled we needed to close up. I'd forgotten that was the night Plant's interview with Jonathan was going to air. He and Silas had invited me over to watch it on their big TV, since they still had cable.

I watched Adriana run off to her bus stop. I hoped her little family would be all right. It was tragic how much damage a catfish romance scammer could do.

One had caused Ginny Gilhooly's death and another might already have killed Shannon.

# fifteen

. . .

## Fishing for Trout in a Goldfish Bowl

*S*ilas seemed to be resigned to Plant's temporary move to LA. He was gracious and funny as he fed us a sumptuous meal to accompany Jonathan's show on Friday night. He'd fixed duck breasts with Cumberland sauce, Chantilly potatoes, and asparagus from their garden, *en croute*.

Silas seemed to be making sure that Plant remembered what he'd be missing down in LA.

He even poured his sixty-year-old Armagnac when we adjourned to the living room to watch Plant's interview on their big TV. Silas was certainly making this a special occasion.

It felt oddly normal seeing Jonathan on television again. His new set looked a bit like his old one for *The Real Story*, so it seemed as if he was getting a do-over in his new-found sobriety. I was happy for him, but felt a bitter knot in my stomach from all the anguish he'd put me through. Being the wife of a celebrity who has famously visited sleazy prostitutes reduces you to a pitiable punch line. I'd had to run home to hide myself in my mother's Connecticut mansion while her friends pretended I didn't exist.

But there was Jonathan again, the impossibly handsome "silver fox" displaying his famous interviewing skills.

In Plant's segment, he asked questions about Plant's Academy Award-winning film about Oscar Wilde, and how it felt to be a "gay icon."

With each question I could see that Jonathan was subtly building the case that Plant was a happily "out" gay man who was not interested in women.

As Plant and Silas cuddled on the couch, they looked more relaxed than they had in ages. Plant's time in #MeToo jail was finally over.

Now I understood why they had made this such a celebration.

Kensie, in a separate interview, did not fare as well. She came across as needy and more than a little disturbed. I'm sure the poor woman didn't realize how completely she was being savaged.

"Did you know about this?" I asked Plant. "He's being pretty rough."

"Wait. It gets better." Plant laughed, displaying a *schadenfreude* I didn't often see in him.

"So, Jonathan showed you previews of all this?" It felt odd to think that Plant and Jonathan had got so cozy after disliking each other for so many years.

"Oh, no. We haven't seen it before, but he told me what he'd planned."

He and Silas both giggled as Jonathan pretended to be sympathetic to the difficulties a woman faced in the "Hollywood jungle" and asked Kensie if she'd been harassed before. Jonathan segued into questions about her former boyfriends, including Conor McDara, the Irish poet.

Plant gave a hoot when, in a typical Jonathan move, he introduced Conor himself via Zoom. At Jonathan's prompting, Conor, with a wealth of Irish charm and humor, told the story of Kensie's relentless pursuit of him.

Even before the second commercial break, Kensie Wiener was toast. I doubted anybody would believe she'd had so much as a hug from Plantagenet in her life. And even she admitted he'd never been her mentor as she claimed, and she said he'd mocked her romance novel, *The Far Loveswept Shore.*

But Jonathan allowed her to explain that Plant had told her she had a great future with the Hallmark card company with her poetry, which she took to be "strong support" for her writing ambitions.

Jonathan didn't ask her a thing about her Hollywood project with Zac Efron. It had probably fallen through as most options do. In any case, if Kensie still had that film deal by the end of Jonathan's hatchet job, it would have been astonishing.

Of course I joined in Plant and Silas's joy at the restoration of Plant's career. But I couldn't help feeling a little sorry for Kensie as I drove home. After all, she had Harold Wiener for a father. She'd obviously been raised with too much money and not enough love.

I wondered if Jonathan would do the same kind of scorched earth job on Saffina. I was half-dreading and half-anticipating her appearance on Jonathan's show. The woman deserved roasting for what she did to Ronzo — destroying his career with a faked video that made the world think he'd killed a kitten.

But I was afraid if Jonathan was that fierce in attacking her, Ronzo might spring to her defense. He was, after all, a deeply moral person and a gentleman — which is why I loved him. Why I ached for him.

I needed Ronzo now with all the weird stuff about Ginny's death still unresolved. Plus Joe's disappearance and poor little Britney and Adriana's woes. Ronzo normally would offer sensible advice and comfort.

But not now. His texts were increasingly perfunctory and decidedly unromantic. Everything was about his Nana's health. I was sympathetic, but I would have liked some news besides updates on her blood pressure and oxygen levels.

He was obviously a good caretaker for his grandmother, but I wanted my boyfriend back. Unfortunately, it looked as if that wasn't going to happen any time soon.

I wasn't sure I was going to get help in the bookstore soon, either.

Over the next few weeks, the responses I got from my ad were discouraging, to say the least. I feared I'd end up running the shop by myself again.

Silas was so right when he said it was like fishing for trout in a goldfish bowl. Nobody was remotely right for the job.

One woman showed up to her interview wearing a skimpy tank top over a very visible and rather grimy pink bra, and another had alcohol on her breath at ten in the morning. Two seemed barely literate. A few retirees looked promising, but most of them said they wouldn't be able to lift cartons of books.

When I had only two days to go before Plant's departure, I finally got a call from a job applicant with potential. He was a well-spoken older man who said he'd once worked in a bookstore in the Bay Area. He said he was retired, but looking for part-time work. He talked about books like a college professor, and said he could still lift a carton of books with no trouble.

At last. Morris Fishman, his name was. I asked him to come in the next morning at ten for an interview.

But the man who arrived at ten on the dot the next morning was more than a little disappointing. His look was what my mother used to call "unprepossessing." He wore old jeans and some sort of Mexican shirt, much faded. His unruly gray hair was tied in a ponytail with what looked like a leather shoelace. The effect was decidedly "old hippie."

But instead of introducing himself, the man went to the Literature section and searched for something.

I hoped maybe he wasn't Mr. Fishman after all. Just an eccentric customer. I breathed a sigh of relief and glanced outside for signs of the distinguished older gentleman I'd spoken to on the phone.

But the sidewalk was empty.

A few minutes later, the old hippie came stomping over to the counter.

"*Trout Fishing in America!*" His tone was belligerent. "You don't have one copy of Richard Brautigan's *Trout Fishing in America*. Or *Confederate General from Big Sur*. Not one Brautigan book. And here you are right on the way to Big Sur. You call this a bookstore?"

He leaned over the counter and pushed his face so close to mine I could smell the coffee on his breath.

I was alone in the store. Plant wasn't due for an hour. I wondered if I should be looking for a weapon. I hovered near the phone, so I could call 911 if need be.

"Are you Mr. Morris Fishman?" I desperately hoped he wasn't.

"Fish. Just call me Fish. Everybody else does." He extended his hand.

I shook it. The handshake was firm but not aggressive. He did look a bit like a fish, with a big mouth that turned down, and large, buggy eyes. Steve Buscemi might be able to play him in a movie.

I tried to smile. "You're the gentleman I spoke with on the phone? About the job?"

"I am. This isn't a bad little store. You got used books too. I like that. Keep things in circulation. Nothing I hate more than seeing a book thrown in the trash."

"So, you're interested in the job?"

God help me, was I going to hire this man?

"Only if you'll stock some Brautigan titles. At least *Trout Fishing in America*. That's one of the great classics of twentieth century literature."

I had never heard of the author, or either of the titles Mr. Fishman mentioned, but maybe he knew something about local authors that I didn't. We did get a lot of tourists on their way up Route One to Big Sur.

"I can do that," I said. "I'll need you four days a week, including Saturdays. We're closed on Sundays. I can only pay minimum wage right now, but…"

"Deal." The man held out his hand again and gave me a big grin. "When do I start?"

Oh, dear. What had I done?

# sixteen

· · ·

## Catfish Scary

*F*ish showed up right on time for work on the first of May, his long gray hair neatly confined in a braid that hung down his back. He even looked freshly shaved and showered, although his fashion choices were again heavily influenced by the Age of Aquarius.

Buckingham became his constant companion. My cat followed Fish wherever he went in the store. It always made me a little sad that my cat preferred men to women. But Ronzo had been his first owner, so I guess preference for male company had been imprinted into his little psyche from an early age.

Fish turned out to be good with customers, too. Especially those old men who came in looking for strange books about cars or out-of-print Westerns. And he was remarkably helpful with the college students. He seemed to know every book they studied in their literature courses.

He even bonded with Adriana. She came in one Thursday — without Britney — in quite a good mood, looking for a mystery to read. She said she'd finished the *Pretty Little Liars* series and wanted something more adult. She and Fish had an enthusiastic discussion about mystery novels and he declared her to be grown-up enough to read Arthur Conan Doyle. He found her a paperback copy of *The Sign of Four* and ushered her to the register. I'd swear he under-charged her for it, but I didn't care. She left happily reading the book as she walked out to the street.

Of course I was pleased Fish was so helpful with her, but I wished I'd had a moment to talk alone with the girl. I wanted to ask if Britney had heard from her mom and why the two of them weren't coming around anymore. I hoped the fact I'd paid them for their work hadn't offended Adriana's mother.

And I still didn't know if Shannon had died in some Nigerian city looking for her catfish. Those poor girls.

Ronzo's interview with Jonathan aired the next night, but I wasn't going to be able to see it. I was furious with myself for dropping cable TV. I could probably afford it now. I wondered if I should get one of those satellite dishes.

I had dropped hints to Plant in my emails that it would be nice if Silas invited me over to watch it while he was gone, but he said Silas was sulking and that would be a bad idea. Silas had never really warmed to me. I guess because I'd been Plant's best friend for eons before they met. And Plant and I had once been engaged, back in my debutante days. Even though it had mostly been a sham on Plant's part, Silas still treated me like the competition.

Plant and Silas adored each other, but their relationship seemed to thrive on strife. Maybe it was good Plant was taking a vacation from married life in the wilds of Hollywood.

But that meant I had to settle for searching for clips of Jonathan's show on YouTube over the weekend.

I was ruminating over all this on Saturday morning when Adriana came into the store. She was obviously disappointed that Fish wasn't in yet. I explained his hours didn't start until eleven, when the customers start coming in.

I sat at the desk behind the counter, trying to get some paperwork finished before the rush. I hoped she had some good news about Britney's wandering mother.

Adriana leaned on the counter.

"I like Fish. He reminds me of Mr. Fiorentino. He was a professor at Cal Poly."

"Shannon's husband? Have you heard from Shannon? Did she ever make it to Nigeria?"

Adriana nodded yes, but she didn't look overjoyed.

"She got there. I guess when she first landed, she didn't stay in Lagos, and had to take another plane and then some rattletrap bus full of chickens and goats that took like, two days to get to where her boyfriend supposedly lives. And she couldn't charge her phone until she got to an Internet cafe. That's why we didn't hear from her for all that time after she landed."

"But that's wonderful news! Shannon is all right? She found her romantic pen pal? He's a real person?" Oh, good. One worry I could cross off my list. "I hope you and Britney can be friends again."

Adriana looked at me over her glasses, expressing a skepticism beyond her years.

"A real person? I doubt it. At first Shannon was all happy he was okay and not in jail. He had some lame excuse for why he hadn't picked up the money she sent and couldn't text her or email. Like his bank account got closed by mistake, so he had no cash and couldn't pay his phone bill. And no, Britney is still not talking to me."

"But this man is simply a romantic pen pal and there's no catfishing going on, right?"

"I did not say that." Adriana gave her head a frustrated shake.

I had never parented a teenager, but I supposed this was part of the teen hyper-hormonal personality — an exaggerated need for drama.

"But it sounds as if everything's fine, doesn't it? He's not a very good catfish scammer if he asked for money and didn't take it. Why are you still worried?"

"Oh, he's a catfish all right. He doesn't look anything like his photo on Facebook. Not even a little bit. The photo he put on social media was of a hot guy who looks like Idris Elba who's got great abs and a six pack. She says this Derrick is a little white guy from England. But it's all fine because he's cute and she's totally in love with his accent. Like that means he's not going to rob her blind."

"But he's refusing to take any money? I'd say he's a pretty bad catfish."

Adriana drummed her fingers on the counter. "The last time Shannon texted my mom, she said she hadn't seen any of the stuff she was supposedly paying for when she sent all the money before. There was supposed to be a school and a village, but this guy lives in a fancy guest house at the beach and there's no school. So, I still think there's something scary going on. Catfish scary."

"Scary? Because he used the picture of an African man on his profile? Because he's well-off? Maybe he didn't want to look like a catfish, so he used the picture of a Nigerian. Sort of reverse psychology. Those guys always pretend to be white, don't they?"

"You sound like Shannon. With her, everything is always rainbows and unicorns." Adriana gave a dramatic shrug. "But it's not. Believe me."

"But what's the problem?" I realized there was no chance I was going to get these accounts done. I'd have to work on them in the office when Fish arrived. I turned and gave Adriana my full attention.

"The problem is—" Adriana leaned in to whisper. "The problem is that she checked out of her hotel five days ago and we have not had one word from her since. Not one text. She didn't even tell anybody what her plans were."

Oh, dear, now I was on a roller-coaster ride along with Adriana's hormones. I took a sip of my cold coffee.

"Shannon checked out of her hotel and hasn't been in touch since?" Talk about burying the lede. I wished the girl had started with that part of her story.

Adriana gave me a fierce look. "Britney and my mom say I'm being negative and paranoid and she's probably spending a fun time being shown around the country, and I shouldn't deny Shannon her happiness."

"Even though there's been no word for five days?"

Adriana nodded, but her attention concentrated on the front door as Fish walked in. She was full of smiles as she ran to greet him.

But I had seen real fear in the girl's eyes when she talked about Shannon. I wondered if the poor woman was still alive.

# seventeen

· · ·

## Not about Singing Lobsters

*I* took my paperwork back into my office, where Buckingham had been enjoying a nice nap. But when he heard Fish's voice, the cat darted out the door to greet him. A few customers had come in behind Fish, and I thought he could handle them. He had been in an intense discussion with Adriana about Sherlock Holmes.

I wished he had the same patience with paying customers. After about ten minutes, he called me into the store to talk to a customer who wanted a bestselling book. She didn't know the title or the author — only that it was a bestseller and the cover was a kind of orangey-pink, and it might be about singing lobsters. Questions like this weren't an unusual occurrence, but they infuriated Fish.

He was an odd man. He seemed to be easy-going most of the time, but he had a short fuse on some subjects. I'd seen his eyes flash in a way that scared me. There was darkness in him that he didn't want any of us to see.

But nothing scared me as much as Adriana's story about Shannon. If nobody had heard from that woman for days, it changed things. Shannon was a mother. She wouldn't leave her child with no word after checking out of her hotel.

It sounded to me as if Shannon at been conned by a charming crook who played into her fantasies. There was no rule that all the Nigerian catfishers had to be African. Maybe this was a guy who'd come as a tourist and decided to extend his stay by writing catfish letters for West Africa's thriving romance scam industry. Who knew what he and his cohorts might have done to a gullible American widow?

Once I'd fixed up the forgetful customer with Delia Owen's *Where the Crawdads Sing,* I asked Adriana to come back to my office to tell me more about her disturbing news about Shannon.

"Are you sure Britney's mom hasn't been in contact with anybody in five days? That doesn't sound good."

Adriana perched on an unopened carton of books.

"I sure don't think it sounds good, but nobody listens to me. My mom's pretending she's not worried, but she can't even sleep. She gets up about ten times in the night and makes her sleep tea concoction. And Britney just keeps playing Candy Crush on her phone and doesn't talk. She's like a zombie."

The whole adventure did sound very bizarre. And more than a little scary. Catfish romances didn't tend to end well. But I didn't want to share my fears with Adriana. She had enough of her own. I had to think of something hopeful to say.

"You know what?" I gave her a reassuring smile. "Internet and phone connections are probably really iffy over there. Shannon is probably fine — maybe enjoying a sight-seeing trip with her cute Englishman. Once she contacts your mom, I'm sure you'll get an explanation for everything. Then everybody will know if this man is a scammer or not. So there won't be any reason to quarrel."

Adriana gave a noncommittal shrug.

"Do let me know when you hear something. But remember to give the catfish talk a little rest."

Adriana turned and gave me her fierce look.

"You want me to stop talking about it? How? I know something terrible happened to Shannon. Just like Mrs. Gilhooly."

I cringed. I did not want to picture Shannon meeting the same fate.

"I don't think it's anything like Mrs. Gilhooly. Ginny didn't go to Africa." I opened the office door and held it for Adriana, then walked her down the hall to the store.

She gave me a reproachful look.

I smiled and tidied things up on the counter. Then I focused on the accounts, hoping to convey to the girl that I needed to get back to work.

But she obviously had more to say.

"Mrs. Gilhooly didn't go to Africa, and she didn't need to, because this romance scam mafia is everywhere." Adriana put both elbows on the counter and looked down at me as if I were a very slow child. "Last year they busted a bunch of Nigerian catfishers who were living right here in California. East LA or someplace. They run it like a regular office except the employees are all writing bogus love letters to old ladies. They have the love letters all written into an app and just change the names. Like Ginny or Shannon. I'll bet they'd pay an English guy a lot because he could write letters with good grammar."

Poor Ginny. I tried to keep her from my daytime thoughts, but she'd been a regular visitor to my nightmares this past two months.

Joe too. I still didn't know what had become of him. Or Peter. But right now, it was probably Shannon I needed to worry about. Adriana did make some sense.

"Do you really think Shannon's English boyfriend is involved in organized crime?"

"Well, we know he's a liar because of that photo. Plus, this guy claims to be a famous English author. And he said he had a boatload of money from all these bestselling books but his business partner stole most of it. But he's not in Wikipedia. In fact, I couldn't find him anywhere in Google. Only on that stupid Facebook page. And it's been taken down now."

"This famous author's Facebook page is down? What's his name?" That stopped me. It did sound like a red flag.

"Derrick Alan George." Adriana laughed and tossed her hair.

"Sounds like he got it at Fake Names 'R' Us. Two first names are always a red flag. Three is a total give-away. He's not a real author, is he?"

I shook my head. "No. I have never heard of a British author named Derrick Alan George. And I do know something about books. I agree that he sounds suspicious. And the name does sound a little as if it were invented by somebody who doesn't know much about English names. Like whoever named Brown David Jack."

Adriana gave another snort. "It gets crazier. I guess he had to explain why he lives in Africa instead of London, England, so in his emails he told her some story about how he lived in a remote village where he started a school. Totally Oprah stuff, right?"

That part sounded almost believable, but Adriana's tone dripped sarcasm.

"And of course, he wrote her how the schoolkids don't have medicine or enough to eat and, bam! He hits her up for a donation. A couple weeks later, he said his business manager stole his advance and all his royalty payments from his books. So he needed a loan..."

Adriana gave a big laugh. "...and then the roof blew off the school in a freaky storm right before it was going to open. So of course, Shannon had to send him more money. Then to top it off, some burglar stole the new roof fund, so he needed the money all over again. Or maybe the goat ate it. And on and on and on. Oh, none of that is fishy at all, right?"

I had to stop and help a customer find a local guidebook. When I got back to the counter, I had more questions for Adriana. I wished she'd told me all these tidbits before.

"Do you think Shannon maybe went Africa partly to check up on her investment? To see if Mr. Derrick Alan George was actually spending money on a school?"

"No. She freaked because he ghosted her. As soon as she wired him that last payment, he disappeared without taking the last payment she sent. He was just gone. No 'so long and thanks for all the Benjamins.' Nothing." She ran off to join Fish in the Mystery section.

I have to admit the girl was convincing me. Shannon sounded like a good soul, but a remarkably gullible one.

Fish lit up with a warm smile as Adriana ran back to talk to him, full of questions about Sherlock Holmes.

I was glad the two had bonded. I hoped he could help cheer the girl a little. Losing the trust of her best friend must have been so painful, especially since they lived together.

Adriana appeared to be the most responsible person in that blended family. Or maybe she was simply the most imaginative.

Maybe everything was fine and someday she'd write an orangey-pink bestseller about singing catfish.

# eighteen

. . .

## Fishing for Clues

*O*n a Saturday evening in mid-May, after opening a bottle of chardonnay, I went searching You Tube for clips of Jonathan's Friday night show, featuring his interview with Ronzo and Saffina. It didn't take long to find one. Jonathan was becoming wildly popular.

I started the video. It was a short clip, but it told me everything I needed to know.

Jonathan had interviewed Ronzo and Saffina together, not separately like Plant and Kensie. And he did not say one unkind thing to Saffina. In fact, he seemed rather smitten with her himself. Saffina told him she was oh-so-sorry about circulating the fake kitten murder video that had destroyed Ronzo's reputation. But it wasn't her fault. She'd been under the control of her evil ex-boyfriend, steampunk rocker Mack Rattlebag, who was now safely behind bars for his numerous crimes.

Jonathan kept nodding, as if he believed every word.

He was equally understanding with Ronzo, who came across as articulate and sympathetic in spite of his New Jersey street accent. I think anybody watching would understand he was simply a victim of a sadistic prank and not a kitten killer.

Saffina's hair was a honey blonde now, and she wore an elegant professional-woman pantsuit — with pearls, no less — and Ronzo wore the Armani jacket my friend Mickie had bought for him, along with a pale shirt and a handsome tie. Very corporate-class.

When Buckingham heard Ronzo's voice, he jumped up on my lap and stared at the screen, but when Saffina spoke, he let out a low growl. I agreed completely.

But Jonathan treated both his guests with warmth and helped them create a sympathetic, good-citizen image by asking about Ronzo's ailing grandmother and letting Saffina talk about how she was back at Sarah Lawrence finishing her degree in music, and singing in the church choir.

They could have been a couple of Sunday school teachers in love, not a down-and-out music blogger and his sadistic Goth persecutor.

In love. That's what I was looking at. Two people in love. It felt like a punch in the stomach.

Buckingham jumped off my lap, flicking his tail back and forth, low to the ground. He did not feel any better about Saffina than I did.

So much for Jonathan's snark attack. He'd given them hearts and flowers. I wondered if his network approved.

I could feel my nose sting with tears. No wonder Ronzo hadn't been able to tell me anything except the state of his Nana's blood sugar.

I poured myself another glass of chardonnay and let the waterworks flow.

The ring of my landline phone startled me. It was nearly 8 p.m., and nobody much called the landline except people doing business with the store.

It couldn't be Ronzo, could it? Maybe it was. He must have figured I'd watch the show. Maybe he was finally going to tell me the truth. On my business landline phone so he could dump me in a businesslike way. That would go along with the professional image Jonathan had so kindly created for him.

I picked up the receiver, not sure how I was going to react to

Ronzo's voice. I did not want to make a fool of myself with a torrent of tears.

But it wasn't Ronzo. It was Adriana. Her voice sounded small and childlike, but agitated.

"Are you all right, dear? Is something wrong?" I hoped it wasn't anything to do with Fish. He was such an odd duck, but I didn't think he'd be weird with children. At least I hoped he wouldn't. Oh, ick. I didn't want my brain to go there.

"No. Nothing's wrong. Something might be right. I've been sleuthing."

"Sleuthing?"

"Detecting. You know, fishing around for clues like Sherlock Holmes. Well, not on purpose, but I didn't want to go home today with Britney not talking to me and my mom all in anxiety mode about Shannon. So I went to visit some friends from school who live up in that homeless camp where they found Mrs. Gilhooly."

"I'm not sure the police would want you sleuthing up there, dear. Isn't it a crime scene?" Now I was sounding like Plant. But oh, my goodness — she went to school with homeless kids. Housing prices in our county were so obscenely high. Families were losing their homes like mad. Those messy tent encampments were the only place they could go.

Adriana gave a powerful sigh that told me I was being a moronic adult.

"Of course not. Not anymore. The police took the tape down a couple of days after they found the body. It was sort of out near the road, anyway, not really in the camp." Her voice lowered to a near-whisper. "Besides, you're going to change your mind when you hear what I got. My friend's little brother found a phone out along that road. They're always scavenging for stuff people throw out of their cars. They couldn't unlock the phone, so they asked me to try to get into it — cause I'm kind of the class geek. And guess what? It's Mrs. Gilhooly's. I'm sure of it. I mean, the case is green with shamrocks on it, so duh. Exactly like her manicure. Then I had a hunch, so I used the password BrownDavidJack and it worked."

"Oh, my! That was brilliant!" The girl did have a remarkable mind. "Do you have the phone now? Or did you give it to the police?"

The police. I guess now I understood how Plant had been feeling about the fingernail and wrapping paper before he read the newspaper article about how it could have been an accident. But what if it wasn't?

If it had been murder, this was real evidence — not a dubious scrap of wrapping paper or an artificial fingernail.

Adriana snorted.

"Of course not. I'm not going to the police until we can prove this catfish guy killed Mrs. Gilhooly. I'm sure he totally did it. Did you see the TV news last night? The police are still calling it a suspicious death."

"I don't see the TV news that often. What did they say?"

"They say she got bashed on the head twice. Most people don't fall on their head two times. That's why we have to start sleuthing. ASAP."

"We? Are you sleuthing with Britney?"

"No. I told you. She's totally freezing me out. But I figure I'm sleuthing with you. You can be my Dr. Watson!" She gave a girlish squeal. "Can I bring the phone over Monday after school? We can fish around for clues. You know — messages from this guy Brown David Jack and find some incriminating evidence. I know there has to be some. You should see his Facebook page. It's screams 'I'm a scammer'."

Incriminating evidence. This was not good. If she brought that phone over, the person who was going to be holding — or withholding — incriminating evidence was me.

Of course, nobody knew it was Ginny's phone but Adriana.

Still, I didn't feel very good about her bringing me something that obviously belonged with the police. I hoped we (well, she) would be able to do some very quick sleuthing and find out what transpired between Brownie and Ginny on that fateful Friday. We needed to be able to shed doubt on Joe having anything to do with Ginny's death. It seemed so obvious it must have had something to do with finding out Brownie was two-timing her.

"I wonder if you can find out anything about the other girlfriend.

Like, does she live around here? Maybe this woman got an email meant for Ginny too, and went off the deep end and killed her."

Adriana laughed and hummed "dum-de-dum-dum."

Oh, dear. She saw this as some kind of game. Should I be encouraging her? But this was our first real chance to find a suspect other than poor Joe.

"So it's okay if I bring the phone by the store on Monday? I won't start sleuthing unless you're there. So we can do this together. Also because I don't want Britney to walk in on me. She'll know the phone isn't mine."

"Monday. Fine. But we can't keep it too long. Or we'll be withholding evidence. We can fish for clues in the phone on Monday, then give it to the police on Tuesday."

Oh, dear. I was about to break a rather large number of laws playing Holmes and Watson with a thirteen-year-old. I hoped I wasn't utterly insane.

But I felt oddly exhilarated and suddenly not the least bit weepy about Jonathan's interview or the Ronzo and Saffina situation. Situation. I should call it what it was: a love affair. But I figured if Saffina wanted a boyfriend who cheated, fine. Let her have him.

I had a life to live. And a mystery to solve.

# nineteen

. . .

## Fishy Stuff

$\mathcal{O}$n Monday after school, Adrianna bounced into the store wearing her school backpack. Purple and sparkly. A good reminder I was dealing with a child.

I parked her in my office where she pulled the green phone out of her backpack while I made her hot chocolate. There were indeed glittery shamrocks sprinkled on the phone case. It certainly looked like Ginny Gilhooly's phone.

Adriana seemed to think she was going to find emails like the ones Shannon had been getting, with preposterous stories about roofs blowing off schools and burglars stealing the school building fund.

"I told you they sit in these offices and turn this stuff out," she said as she sipped chocolate. "They have a script they all use. I know I'm going to find some of the same fishy stuff as Shannon's catfish told her. Like 'oh, the goat ate my travel visa and I have to bribe the police to get a new one,' or 'a local kid got bitten by a poisonous snake and I had to use all my money to get him to the hospital.' I'm going to find one and then Britney will have to believe me."

I had a store to run, and Fish didn't work on Mondays, but I ran back and forth to the office whenever I could, hoping she'd find some kind of clue. Unfortunately, Brownie's emails seemed to be mostly romantic nothings with no red flags to suggest he was planning anything untoward. He always claimed to be somewhere far away, mostly Europe and the Middle East, but not Africa. And no goats were involved.

He said he'd been born and bred in Texas — sometimes spelled "Taxes", and loved country music. His favorite way to be romantic seemed to be to quote Garth Brooks lyrics.

Later in the afternoon, Adriana found some other emails in Ginny's "sent" folder that were anything but hearts and flowers. They were emails from Ginny to her son, complaining bitterly about his bride-to-be and her friends. "Trixie Trailer Trash," "Betty Boobs," and "Princess Gold digger" were a few of her choice epithets.

Adriana said it seemed as if the upcoming lavish wedding had not been Ginny's idea at all. It's true Ginny had hardly mentioned the wedding to me. The subject of Brownie dominated all our conversations. The over-the-top wedding ideas seemed to have all come directly from Crystal — with Ginny resisting every one.

"This Crystal lady sounds like a total bridezilla." Adriana gave one of her epic eye-rolls.

I hoped I wasn't making a mistake letting her do her illegal hacking of Ginny's phone in my store's office. But it didn't seem wise for her to be playing with a phone that had belonged to a murder victim right there in the house with her undocumented mom. And poor Britney.

"You know who I really don't like?" Adriana swiveled in my desk chair. "This Larry guy. Ginny's son. He's being very disrespectful to his mom here — telling her she has to pay for all this crazy stuff. He talks like Crystal is the princess of the world. Who ever heard of a bunch of flowers costing twenty thousand dollars? And why should his mom pay?"

I had to agree. The plans were entirely wrong in terms of established etiquette.

"Larry is showing complete ignorance of good manners. The wedding expenses are the responsibility of the parents of the bride, not the groom. The groom's family pays for the rehearsal dinner, and the bride's parents pay for the wedding and the reception. That's how it's done."

I poured myself the dregs of the morning coffee and offered Adriana more hot chocolate, but she declined, holding up her water bottle and a granola bar. Kids these days never went anywhere without water. I wish we'd had the sense to do that when I was her age.

"It looks like Crystal is fresh out of parents." Adriana laughed. She was obviously having a fun time with all this. I wished I could find something that excited her brain that much that didn't involve lawbreaking.

I had to go back and tend to the store, so I didn't hear all of the choice tidbits.

Ginny's phone belonged with the police. But I hadn't quite figured out the right way to tell them how I got my hands on it.

I did know the one place such a valuable piece of evidence shouldn't be was a child's backpack, so when Adriana got ready to go home for dinner on Monday, I told her I was going to lock the phone in the office safe. I didn't mention law enforcement.

But she was a child, and this was a decision for an adult to make.

# twenty

. . .

## Fish or Cut Bait

*I* had to admit I was burning with curiosity about Ginny's phone. Before I put it in the safe, I had to take another look. So after I closed up the store, I sat down at my desk to read a bit more of Ginny's correspondence.

I approached it with equal parts eagerness and guilt.

The messages from Brownie were mind-numbingly similar. They seemed to be written from a template. He endlessly repeated Garth Brooks' lyrics to "Take the Keys to my Heart" and "Two Pina Coladas."

I tried to find something in his messages that suggested a stalker mentality or any kind of threat, but they were too generic to be emotionally charged. Occasionally he'd talk about her shiny hair or nice fingernails or pretty smile. Again, he must have been following a script. Ginny must have been in a pretty bad way to fall for a man with so little originality.

But the emails between Ginny and her son Larry held the fascination of a train wreck. Larry seemed to think Crystal needed to have everything she ever wanted or he'd lose her.

And Adriana was right that Crystal was apparently parent-free. From what I could cobble together from Ginny's emailed rants, Crystal's birth mother seemed to have met her demise early in Crystal's life, via overdose, and her father was incarcerated. She'd been raised by an aunt who went AWOL when Crystal turned eighteen. Her only "family" was the bunch of friends from high school who made up the "bimbo brigade" we'd seen out the window when Crystal and Larry came in the store. Ginny didn't call them the bimbo brigade, but she had some other choice epithets, like the "Bakersfield Bit—s."

I suppose a background like that would have given Crystal a reason for feeling life owed her something, but it looked as if Ginny had been doing most of the paying.

No wonder Ginny had turned to a long-distance romance. Even if it wasn't real, her relationship with "Brownie" was better than her home life. First, she lost her husband, then her son got himself enslaved to Cruella de Vil and her posse from Hell.

So far, I hadn't seen anything that suggested Ginny had been likely to be murdered by anybody she knew. Certainly not by Crystal, who was depending on her for money for the big wedding. I sat in my office, mesmerized by the emails until Buckingham came in and announced it was dinner time.

I locked the phone in the safe and figured I could make a decision about the police later.

Buckingham seemed to agree.

After I fed him and myself and got into comfier clothes, I decided to phone Ronzo to ask him about the legal repercussions of being caught with Ginny's phone. A simple question. Nothing guilt-trippy. After all, Ronzo had worked as a detective for a law firm, so he might be able to tell me how much trouble I was in. And I suppose I wanted to hear his voice, no matter what might be going on with him and Saffina.

Okay, to be honest, I was hoping he'd say something to get me out of this limbo. Even if it was only "get lost." The TV interview certainly made it look as if he was romantically involved with Saffina, but I needed to hear it from his own vocal cords. Sooner, rather than later.

It was time for Ronzo to "fish or cut bait" as my dad used to say.

I needed to be polite about it, of course. I wasn't going to pepper him with accusations. I took a deep breath and got into Manners Doctor mode before I punched his number.

But I needn't have bothered. From the time Ronzo picked up the phone, he barely let me get in a word. First, he had good news about his Nana, which was of course lovely to hear. His grandmother was apparently doing better. She'd had hip surgery that seemed to have helped her pain level a good deal.

Mostly Ronzo was full of the fantastic news that he'd got a job as a music reviewer again. Not for *Rolling Stone*, but some Newark entertainment paper. Baby steps to restoring his reputation. He kept telling me he owed it all to Jonathan, and gushed copious thanks to me for introducing them.

I hadn't heard Ronzo so happy in months, so I made lots of enthusiastic noises, trying not to think about him going to all those clubs full of attractive young things. I wondered if he was attending with Saffina. She was probably as interested as he was in the local music scene. After all, she'd been the singer for Mack Rattlebag's band.

No. that was silly. She was in college. At Sarah Lawrence, way up in Yonkers, which would be a good two hours away, with all the New York traffic.

I also realized I'd probably be pretty miserable going to sleazy nightclubs listening to loud rock and roll these days.

Another deep breath. I needed to get to the matter at hand. I worked at making my tone friendly and light.

"So, I have a question for you. You know how I told you that the Morro Bay police suspect Hobo Joe in a murder investigation...?

"Hi Saffina!" Ronzo said. "I'll just be a minute. Camilla, I have to go. We're visiting a new club with a killer band. Tell Joe I said hi."

Thunk.

I couldn't even cry. I sat and stared at my stupid phone until Buckingham walked over and meowed, obviously sensing that all was not as it should be.

"I'm fine, kitty," I lied. "I'm fine. Ronzo's fine. Saffina is fine. Everybody's perfectly fine."

I tried to clear my mind and remember that a polite, mature person would simply put my question in writing in an email or text and not let the emotional nonsense get in the way of a request for information.

And I was a mature person. I'd turned forty last November, for goodness's sake. I'd write Ronzo a polite email. After all, Joe was his friend. Ronzo would want to help when he wasn't hyper-excited about going out clubbing with Saffina.

I booted up my laptop, working at staying in my Manners Doctor mindset.

Buckingham kept staring at me, swishing his tail as if he suspected trouble.

"I have to write a note to your friend Ronzo," I told him. "I have an important question for him. Unfortunately, he's going out to a night-club — on a Monday night — with the woman who tried to kill him. But hey, it's fine. He's got his groove back. His Nana's got her groove back. Everybody's got their groove back."

Buckingham turned and walked away. He was not buying a word of it.

I realized I had quite a lot of email I needed to deal with first. So, I had a short reprieve.

One was a message from Plant. He said he'd been wildly busy, but he was having great fun with the team working on his series. He said he was researching romance scams and catfishing to come up with new storylines. He wanted to know more about Ginny's catfish so he'd call later in the week.

Then I found a surprise email from Jonathan. He apparently expected me to gush with gratitude for his softball interview with Saffina.

 She's an amazingly nice girl," he wrote. "She reminds me of you when you were in college."

Great. Just what I wanted to hear. I'd been replaced by a younger version of myself.

Who didn't have evidence in a murder case in her office safe.

I closed up my laptop and decided to skip asking for legal advice from the new Ronzo or any of my other friends.

I had to make this decision myself. I was the one who had to fish or cut bait.

# twenty-one

. . .

## Like a Fish Needs a Bicycle

*A*driana didn't come into the store on Tuesday. I worried about her all day. If I decided to give Ginny's phone to the police, I didn't want the girl to be involved. I'd say somebody left it in the store or something. I hadn't quite worked out my story yet. Which is why the phone was still in my safe, sitting there like a time bomb.

I thought of calling Adriana to talk things out with her, but then I realized not only didn't I have her number, I didn't know her last name. I knew Britney's mother was named Fiorentino, but she was off chasing a catfish. And I didn't want to disturb Adriana's mother Luisa any more than necessary. She already seemed suspicious of me.

I was much relieved on Wednesday afternoon, when Adriana bounced in with her own laptop in her backpack, saying she'd had an idea and needed to explore Ginny's phone and do some more sleuthing. She obviously never believed I was going to turn the phone over to law enforcement.

I hesitated a moment, but decided to get the phone out of the safe and set her up at my desk in the office. I wanted to hear more about her idea, but the store was busy.

Out on the floor, Fish was in intense discussion with a tall older woman who looked vaguely like Gloria Steinem. She had the long blond hair of Steinem's youth, and under her tailored pants suit, she wore a tee shirt that said "A Woman Needs a Man like a Fish Needs a Bicycle."

When there was finally a lull around five, Fish sidled up to me behind the counter — very odd for him. He usually had impeccable manners. He slipped me a folded piece of paper as if we were a couple of cartoon spies.

"Keep that under your hat. You don't know anything and I don't either, okay?"

Unfortunately, a customer came in at that moment and I was afraid to unfold the paper — a lovely piece of Eaton's stationery. I had to wait until she had chosen a book and I'd rung it up before I could read the mysterious note.

As the customer left, I unfolded the elegant paper.

"I came by to see Fish and make sure he's keeping an eye on you." It began. "Yeah, that was me in the wig and falsies. I guess you didn't guess because you never seen me clean-shaved before. Marva has a giant wardrobe and a collection of the most humongous lady shoes you've ever seen. She keeps saying the best way to hide is in plain sight. So, I'm wearing her crazy drag stuff and staying in her spare room in exchange for cooking. She's hooked on my homemade granola and potato-leek soup. I stopped by because I want you and Ronzo to know I'm okay. Just laying low here at Marva's until they figure out who really did bump off that Gilhooly witch."

Of course. The person dressed as Gloria Steinem had been Joe Torres. I hadn't suspected a thing. Marva was good. And there was more…

"I also gotta tell you Peter made it to darkest Africa on some cargo ship. He's in Lagos now, but he's setting out for a country called Gambia to look for that missing writer, Fanna Something.

"He said his phone and laptop got ripped off from his hotel, so he emailed Marva from some café. He thinks he has an address where he can find this Fanna woman. As soon as he knows something, he's gonna contact us. Or so he says. You know Peter. Take care and be nice to Fish. Down on his luck but he's good people."

Well, it appeared Joe and Fish were friends. Which seemed extraordinary. And then it didn't.

Joe had never admitted it, but Ronzo was absolutely certain that "Hobo Joe" Torres was the rock god guitarist, J. J. Tower of Towering Inferno. Yes, the one who supposedly died in a Texas roadhouse fire all those years ago. I tended to believe Ronzo's instincts — at least I did back then — but I'd never breathed a word of it to anybody. I knew Joe wanted anonymity and whatever his past was, he'd sacrificed a lot to stay off everybody's radar.

So now Joe/J. J. Tower was going around in drag and living with Marva/Marvin, the drag queen dominatrix. Still sacrificing.

I wondered if Fish had a similar secret past. Who knows, maybe he'd been a rock star too.

Adriana came out of the office and asked if I'd found any new clues. She looked pointedly at Joe's note. I had to tell her it was nothing. I would have loved to be able to tell her that Joe was safe and in good hands. But Fish had been stern in his warning and I understood the need for secrecy.

Adriana looked as if she was about to jump out of her skin, so I asked if she'd found some new clue herself.

She leaned in and spoke in a conspiratorial whisper.

"Oh, maybe the guy who killed Mrs. Gilhooly."

"Adriana! You've found the killer? On Ginny's phone? Who do you think he is?"

"Brownie. I found the IP address where he'd been sending the emails from."

"In Nigeria?" My mind had been on Africa ever since I read Joe's note.

"Nuh-uh." She shook her head, but her eyes sparkled. "It's here in Morro Bay. The Morro Bay library, in fact. You know all those homeless guys that hang out in the library, using the computers? That's why my mom doesn't want me to go there anymore. But that's where Brownie was sending his catfishy emails from."

This was startling news. If the man lived here, Ginny's "catfish" zoomed to the top of the list of suspects for her murder. If it was murder. The library was only a few blocks away from my store. Maybe "Brownie" was one of the evicted former tenants with a grudge against Ginny and her real estate empire. Maybe he'd started by conning her for money, and when he was exposed by that other girlfriend, he got rid of Ginny.

Why he had to do it on my back step, I didn't know. Maybe he was stalking her and followed her here. I was pretty sure something happened on my back step, in spite of Plant's dismissal. It was ridiculous to think Peter would have made up the story to be nasty. He might not always be honest, but he was kind, and he never did anything without a financial motive.

"We have to go to the police with this." I gave Adriana a firm look. "It's time. We've been withholding evidence."

"Evidence of what?" That was Fish. He could move with the stealth of a cat. And there was his friend Buckingham, padding right behind him.

"Nothing." Adriana was quick to jump in. "It's just a game. A thing I'm doing for school."

She scurried off. Fish raised a single eyebrow, then shrugged. He might be willing to sit on this, but I wasn't happy that he knew we were hiding something. Adriana wasn't a convincing liar.

After I rang up purchases for a couple of customers, I realized the time had come to visit the police station and disclose what we'd found. Adriana might be precocious and intellectually gifted, but she was a child and shouldn't be involved in a real-life murder investigation.

I went back to my office, expecting to find Adriana there. But the office was empty. I suppose I looked bewildered when I went back to the counter.

"Looking for little miss Mensa?" Fish gave me a funny look. "She took off like a bat out of hell. You must have scared her with all that police talk. You care to elaborate?"

I avoided his eyes and shook my head. There were a couple of customers in the store, and even though they didn't seem to be paying attention, I didn't want to talk about Adriana's sleuthing in front of them.

"Not now. She might still be at the bus stop. Can you take over for me?"

Even though Fish had only been with me a few weeks, I had no trouble trusting him. He'd obviously been through some hard times, but he had the same sense of honor as his friend Joe.

I ran to the bus stop on the corner, but Adriana — and Ginny's phone — were gone.

I couldn't go to the police without the evidence on the phone. They'd think I was a lunatic.

Maybe I was a lunatic. I'd been trusting the ideas of a thirteen-year-old.

But her theories were convincing. Now I was worried for Adriana. "Brownie" was out there, in this town, and that little girl had the only evidence that he might be Ginny's murderer.

I'd been an idiot not to take the phone and put it back in the safe. Now Adriana could be in serious danger. And even Marva couldn't hide her from a murderous catfish with a giant grudge.

# twenty-two

. . .

## Trout Fishing in Used Graveyards

*M*y anxiety escalated when Adriana didn't reappear in the bookstore for nearly a week. Even Fish was worried about her absence, and he didn't know about the phone.

"That little girl is too smart for her own good. She's going to get herself in trouble. I think her mother is undocumented. If the kid gets on the wrong side of the law, her mom's going back to El Salvador, and the girl is an orphan. That's the way the government works these days."

I felt a wave of guilt. Here I'd been encouraging Adriana in her illegal sleuthing instead of protecting her. Shannon had left the children in a precarious situation. If Luisa were deported, both Britney and Adriana would have no official guardians.

I was glad Fish was looking out for Adriana. In fact, he was acting more like a responsible adult than I was.

Fish was such a strange man. Joe had mentioned him being "down on his luck" and Fish was very cagey about where he lived. I was careful not to pry, but it was pretty obvious he was homeless. He drove a beat-up Toyota truck he never parked near the bookstore. He usually left it in a secluded alleyway behind my property. I had a feeling it contained most of his earthly possessions.

On the day the new book shipment came in, I was happy to show Fish that I'd bought two copies of *Trout Fishing in America*.

"How much?" He promptly grabbed one and started to reach into a pocket for his wallet. Then he stopped himself. Poor man. Even with an employee discount, he probably couldn't afford a new book.

"Sorry," he said. "I spent the last of my cash on breakfast. Just take it out of my paycheck, okay?" He took a pen from the desk, wrote on the flyleaf and handed the book to me. "Here. A gift."

The inscription said, "thanks for letting me park in your used graveyard."

I hoped that would mean more to me when I read the book.

It was a trade paperback — too large to fit well into a purse. The Houghton Mifflin reprint had a childlike line drawing on the cover. It looked highly experimental. Not my favorite kind of read. But I knew Fish meant well. I smiled politely and thanked him. And of course I wouldn't take the money out of his check.

That evening I knew I needed to read it. No vegging out on mindless Netflix. I was going to read what was apparently an iconic book of the 1960s.

But it wasn't easy. Even after I'd poured myself a nice glass of wine, and got Buckingham to snuggle up next to me, it was a slog. A man kept mistaking a woman for a trout stream. I personally have never mistaken a human being for a body of water of any kind, and the man simply came across as rude. Plus, nothing in the "story" led up to anything else. It was all random musings, mostly about books and fishing. I found the line Fish quoted about six times, and read it out loud, but I still couldn't figure out what it meant.

"The bookstore was a parking lot for used graveyards."

Buckingham stretched and yawned. I agreed.

"Does he mean that books are graveyards? And used books are used graveyards?" I asked the cat. "Or are all books used, even when they're new?"

Buckingham jumped down and sauntered off to his water dish in the kitchen.

I agreed that Brautigan's assessment seemed harsh. I didn't think of books as dead. I found them very much alive, full of people and places that became real when I read them. Well, except maybe this one.

Okay, I had professors in my classes at NYU who made us plow through this kind of quirky literary writing. That dreadful Mr. Kerouac who thought all women were either homebody moms or dumb blondes. But I could see why Fish might like the trout fishing book. Fish and bookstores were fine things to write about.

But the book didn't have that one aspect of storytelling I most enjoy: a plot. It was more like a collection of weird poems by a guy who liked to go fishing.

I decided I needed a break. I figured I'd check my email and see if Ronzo had finally decided to tell me he and Saffina were an item and it was time for us to be realistic. I did hope he wasn't going to ask for his cat back. I went to the cupboard for a cat treat. Buckingham deserved a treat after all the activity in the store. I knew he'd prefer that I keep the clientele down to one or two at a time.

I had a new email. But it wasn't from Ronzo. It was from someone with the address: "Pelletier95@ gmail.com."

Peter Sherwood, a.k.a. Peter Pelletier.

 Hello Duchess," he wrote. "I'm in the city of Banjul. That's in The Gambia in West Africa. I hope Marva told you about my catastrophe in Lagos. I made the mistake of booking a room in a cheap guest house where my sailor friends stay. Pretty much everything I had was burgled when I went out for a bite to eat. So I'm writing to you on a used phone I managed to buy for about $50.

I'm working at tracking down Fanna Badjie. With no luck. I did find her one-time assistant, an ex-pat Brit whose mobile number Vera managed to get out of Fanna's toxic former business partner. But the assistant wasn't terribly communicative about Fanna's where-abouts. The man had an American ladylove with him who obviously didn't want him to talk to strangers.

Especially fellow Brits. But I heard the lady say she's going shopping tomorrow in one of the posher Senegambia beach towns. So, I'm going to attempt some communication again tomorrow."

That didn't sound very promising. If the author's own assistant didn't know where she was, Peter was going to have a hard time tracking her down. I hoped he'd finally tell me what happened the night he evaporated, so I was hopeful as I read on.

Marva has sent news that Joe is going to send a friend over to help you out. He's worried about you being in the store without him to watch over you. The bloke has the odd name of 'Fish.' I hope all is going according to Marva's plan and your mate Joe is still safe. Marva has some wild scheme to keep Joe out of the public eye until the mystery of the missing body is solved.

Ta for now."

So that was all I was going to get? I wanted to scream. Peter admitted there was a mysterious missing body, but he didn't tell me how he became mysteriously missing as well. And how he got to Marva's on the night the body disappeared. But he apparently didn't intend to answer any of the obvious questions.

Still, it was good to know he was safe, even though his mission to find the elusive Fanna seemed to be in vain.

All of his news percolated in my mind while I tried to decipher another chapter of *Trout Fishing in America*. It had been rather sweet to hear that Joe believed he'd been watching out for me while he busked in front of my store.

Buckingham came back to my chair, jumped up and purred, obviously grateful for the treat. I picked up the book and read a few incomprehensible lines out loud to the cat. He looked as baffled as I was.

I'd started to drift off when there was a knock on my front door.

"Open up, Sweetie. This is important."

# twenty-three

. . .

## The Floaty Otter

*J* opened the door and there was Marva. My friend the drag queen dominatrix. She and Ronzo had both served in Iraq, so Ronzo always gave her grudging respect. So did Peter, who had worked with her to smooth over a patch of bad publicity we had to deal with last year. Marva had been kind and helpful, so I suppose I considered her a friend now. But I still felt wary around her.

She was dressed as Elizabeth Warren this evening: short honey-blonde wig, wire-rimmed glasses, red jacket and sensible shoes. Marva always dressed as powerful women. That seemed to be what her clients liked. I'd met her when she was impersonating me, in my Manners Doctor persona.

But she didn't look powerful tonight. She looked worried.

"Is he here? Joe? Have you seen him?" Marva sat on my couch, carefully crossing her ankles. "I came home from visiting a client and Joe was gone."

I shook my head. "I haven't seen anything of him except a visit by, um, Gloria Steinem last Wednesday."

This was scary news. I thought he and Marva had worked out a comfortable arrangement.

"Josephine. That's her drag name. She's sorta cool, isn't she?"

Marva petted Buckingham, who had defected to the couch to snuggle up to her. "I didn't know she'd visited you. Joe doesn't much like drag, but I didn't think he'd take off like this without his wig. Not without telling me. He was supposed to cook potato-leek soup tonight. He puts kale in it. I didn't think I liked kale, but with his magic touch, it's delish."

"Do you think he could have been arrested?" My mind always went to worst-case scenarios.

"I don't know. I don't know anything except that he's done a runner from my house. Took everything. Not that he owned a great many things, but he's obviously gone. He left the dresses, pantsuits, and shoes I gave him, and that worries me even more. If he's not in disguise, he's likely to be spotted and scuttled off to jail. It will help that he's been shaving and I gave him a good haircut, so he doesn't look like that awful picture they've been showing of him in the media. But still, he's pretty recognizable."

"Did he give any kind of clue? Like where he'd go?"

"I do have one number. A man with an odd name..." Marva reached into her handbag and brought out a notebook. "Fish. His name is Fish. But I've called several times and it always goes to voicemail. I can give you the number. Maybe you can try, too." She took a pen from her bag.

I sighed. "Not necessary. Fish is working for me now. Joe may have told him I was looking to hire somebody. I do have a cell phone number for him, but he doesn't always keep it charged. I think he lives in that homeless camp where they found Ginny's body."

"No shit?" Marva gave me an intense look as she dropped character. "You better watch your ass. Joe thinks someone up there in the camp killed her. They all hated her guts."

"You don't suspect Fish killed Ginny, do you?" What a terrible thought. "Then why would Joe vouch for him?"

Marva carefully replaced her smile and her softened tone returned. "Oh, dear me. All I know is Joe is completely innocent."

That's when I noticed the pen. Marva held a floaty pen that

showed Morro Rock in the background. With an otter floating by it. Exactly like the pens we sell in the store.

And the one Ginny Gilhooly bought the day she died.

"That pen. Did you buy it in my store?"

"This silly thing? Oh, no. It's just an overpriced tourist-trap item, isn't it? No offense. It must have been Joe's. He left it by my landline phone."

"Do you know how, um, where Joe got it?" My stomach was taking an elevator ride to the basement without me. How did Joe get Ginny's pen — or what looked like her pen? Could he actually be the one who killed Ginny after all? Maybe with the help of Fish? Maybe the police were right to suspect him—and I'd been covering up for a murderer. Or murderers.

"Do you want it?" Marva handed me the otter pen. "I have no idea where Joe gets anything. But I think he does most of his shopping in garbage dumpsters, so it could probably use a wash." She pulled a tiny bottle of hand sanitizer out of her purse and cleansed her hands.

All I wanted to know was whether the pen had Ginny Gilhooly's fingerprints on it. I held it between two fingers and placed it on the coffee table. I'd have to put it in the bag of clues I still didn't know what to do with.

I offered Marva wine, but she stood, saying she was in a hurry.

"I have a few more places to look for Joe, Sweetie, but they involve turning myself back into Marvin. I'll do a quick change in the car. Joe mentioned a couple of fishermen's dives he used to frequent. Maybe he's off having a beer. I've been doing a cleanse, so I haven't had any alcohol in the house and he does like his 805 beer. Maybe that's why he left."

It was hard to believe Joe would be so thirsty for a beer he'd risk his life. He was never much of a drinker — at least as far as I knew. It was all very mysterious.

As mysterious as the otter pen resting on my coffee table.

# twenty-four

. . .

## Truth is Stranger than Fishin'

wo days later, we still hadn't heard anything from Adriana. Fish was fretting about her, and he didn't even know the girl was walking around with important evidence in a murder investigation.

I tried not to worry. I still didn't have Adriana's cellphone number — and I couldn't find a number for Luisa or the Fiorentino house. Frustrating, but it probably would have been rude to call and complain that her child hadn't been shopping in my store.

I felt some trepidation about the police investigation into Ginny's death. It might take a bad turn now that Joe was out and about without his disguise.

Meanwhile, the real murderer was probably hanging out right here in the neighborhood. Very likely in the public library.

Unless, of course, Joe Torres was the real murderer. Or Fish. But I wasn't going to let myself think about that.

Unfortunately, the otter pen wasn't sufficient evidence. I was pretty sure nobody would be convinced it proved Joe's guilt.

Still, I'd put the pen in my "evidence" baggie with the fingernail and the wrapping paper. I wondered if I should put them in the safe. At the moment they were still in my sock drawer.

I felt an urgent need to do something, but I was pretty sure that walking into the police station with a floaty pen, a scrap of gift paper and a fake green fingernail with a shamrock on it wasn't the something I should do.

I kept up with the local papers and watched clips of Morro Bay news online, but the last mention of Joe Torres or Ginny Gilhooly's death had been weeks ago. If the police were aware of Joe's whereabouts, or if he was still a "person of interest," they weren't telling the press.

That evening I decided I needed to take my mind off the whole mess with a book. I felt I ought to tackle *Trout Fishing in America* again. But in spite of a lovely mug of hot chocolate, reading wasn't helping. The book had clever lines like "Truth is stranger than fishin'." But still no plot.

Buckingham liked to sit on my lap when I was reading, so I didn't feel I could get up for another book. He was mostly a happy kitty these days — thoroughly enjoying Peter's salmon. I'd frozen it in little baggies and served it to him several evenings a week. So, I guess Peter's bizarre visit had one positive outcome. I hadn't heard from him since that first email from Banjul. I wondered if he'd found Fanna Badjie. Or if he was ever going to tell me what happened to Ginny's corpse.

I was almost relieved when Marva showed up again. She was dressed as Margaret Thatcher this time, complete with 1980s helmet-hair.

Buckingham jumped down to greet her.

"Please tell me you've found Joe?" I took her raincoat and hung it on a hook by the door. The evening was drizzly and the coat was quite damp.

Marva shook her lacquered head and spoke in a stagey British accent. "Not a soul has seen him. Some of his friends think he might have headed for the east coast. That's where he's from, apparently. Rhode Island. Quite a long journey for a man who hasn't a penny to his name."

"Joe's an amazing musician. He could probably make enough money for the trip by busking. Did he take his guitar?

Marva nodded. "He did, and that's what worries me. If he starts playing that instrument, the police will spot him immediately. He's significantly more talented than most buskers and the coppers know it."

Buckingham started circling Marva. I don't think he knew what to make of her any more than most people did. Buckingham liked most men and some women. But he was very picky about what perfumes he wanted to be around. Marva smelled strongly of lily of the valley tonight.

"I don't suppose you have a spot of brandy?" Marva sat daintily on the couch. "I believe I'm over the cleansing thing. Chocolate would be good too."

I got out the brandy and a giant chocolate chip cookie from Kat's across the street. I cut the cookie in two and put each half on a little Limoges plate. Marva sat on the couch with her plate, and Buckingham immediately availed himself of her lap. Maybe lily of the valley was an approved perfume after all.

I could tell Marva had something she wanted to talk about, but I wasn't sure how to approach it. But I shouldn't have worried. Marva usually spoke her mind.

"I know Joe's secret," she said in a conspiratorial whisper, dropping the accent. "His name used to be J. J. Tower. You know that 90s hair metal band — Towering Inferno? He was the front man. He was supposed to have died in a fire or something, but he didn't. Some of his friends were killed, though, and he couldn't handle it so he bumped off J. J. Tower and hit the road. And Hobo Joe was born."

She looked as if she expected more of a reaction from me.

"Yes. I sort of knew that. Ronzo told me he was pretty sure Joe was J. J. Tower. He has the same tattoo as Mr. Tower. Ronzo said Joe told him he was once rich and famous, but he hated the person he became."

Marva studied my face. "You knew?"

I nodded. "Not for certain. But Ronzo was convinced." I sipped brandy, wondering how Marva got Joe to reveal his darkest secret. "I guess I should say he *is* convinced. Ronzo's not dead, is he? Just dead to me."

I'm not sure why that came out. Maybe it was the brandy.

Marva gave me a funny look. "Ronzo and you — are over? Well, that's awkward."

"Why? Ronzo's back in Newark. So is his once and future ladylove, Saffina."

"Oh, I saw them on the Kahn show. She's a dreadful phony, isn't she? Joe thought so too. Didn't like her one bit."

It was too funny that Marva, in her campy Margaret Thatcher persona, would call anybody a "phony." But I knew exactly what she meant. Marva was an honest phony. There was nothing deceptive about her drag characters. But Saffina's persona was dishonest.

"You and Joe watched Ronzo on Jonathan's show?"

"Yes. That's what I need to tell you about." Marva sighed and poured herself some more brandy. "That night, Joe told me who he was. He said Ronzo had tried for years to prove he was J. J. Tower, but Joe kept evading him. But now he says Ronzo is one of the few people in the world he trusts, and he'd like to see him restore his reputation and get *Rolling Stone* to give him back his job as a music reviewer."

"Joe is very empathetic. I know he likes Ronzo."

"Yes. In fact, he likes him so much, he wants to come out as J. J. Tower so Ronzo can write about it. The whole story of his miraculous escape from death in that roadhouse fire and his subsequent hobo life. He figures *Rolling Stone* will probably buy it."

Marva said this in one quick breath.

I wasn't quite sure what I was hearing. "Joe wants to go back to being a rock star? After so many years in hiding?"

"No. But he knows if he reveals his true identity, he'll have a better chance of getting the legal help he needs to get the cops off his back."

That made sense.

"So, do you think Joe has gone off to Newark to see Ronzo?"

"I think it's possible. That's why I'm here. I wanted you to warn Ronzo and tell him to prepare for the scoop of his life." She gave me a sorrowful look. "But if you two have broken up, I guess you don't want to contact him. Tell me what's going on. He isn't in love with that simpering idiot, is he?"

I told her I had no idea, then took a rather large gulp of brandy.

Personally, I thought the news about Joe was good. If he had a way to prove his innocence without me, then I didn't have to worry so much about my bag of dubious clues. Or that wandering phone.

Marva finished her brandy and stood, suddenly shaking off her Iron Lady persona. "Hon, I gotta get home and out of this god-awful wig. It's so full of Aqua Net I'm sure it weighs five pounds."

After she left, I sat and finished my brandy and petted Buckingham, who seemed to have decided I was a possible substitute for a man in drag.

My phone dinged. I had a text. From Plant. He apologized for not calling and asked if there was any more scuttlebutt about Ginny's catfish. And if her death had officially been ruled an accident or homicide. He was working on a storyline for the catfish TV series with a character based on Ginny. I wondered if I should tell him about Adriana's discovery of the phone. Of course, he'd only tell me again that I should go to the police. Which I knew. I should tell him Marva's news about Joe, though.

But before I could type anything, Buckingham jumped up, ears twitching. He must have heard something in the courtyard. Then I heard it too. Footsteps. Heavy ones. Probably a man.

Then came a knock on the door. I looked at my watch. Ten o'clock. Not a polite time to come calling. Maybe it was Joe. Please!

I went to the door but didn't open it.

"Is that you, Joe?"

"No," said a booming voice familiar to TV watchers everywhere. "It's Jonathan. Camilla, can we talk?"

# twenty-five

· · ·

## The Swamp Creature

*J*onathan was more handsome than ever. He'd acquired that slick, perfect look of a TV star. Every hair seemed have been arranged with precision, then cemented in place with some kind of light-emitting gloss.

But I was sleepy and not overjoyed to see him. Although of course the Manners Doctor would never let a guest know such a thing.

"Jonathan! Lovely to see you. What are you doing in our little provincial backwater? Would you like some tea?"

Buckingham was already snaking around Jonathan's designer-suited legs.

I put the kettle on and made some peppermint tea. I didn't know what to do about the brandy bottle on the coffee table. Jonathan hadn't been in recovery all that long. But if I grabbed it now, it would be an obvious reference to his alcoholism.

So I asked about the mudslides in Santa Barbara.

I managed to keep the chit-chat to weather and traffic as I made the tea.

When we retired to the living room, Jonathan sat on the couch and I retreated to my usual reading chair. The brandy bottle glinted on the coffee table between us.

Jonathan pretended not to notice as he sipped his tea. Of course, Buckingham immediately jumped onto his lap. Unfortunately, Jonathan wasn't terribly fond of cats. We'd always had dogs when we were together.

"Don't let him bother you. I know you're more of a dog person." I stirred stevia into my tea and wondered what to do with the half-full brandy snifter on the table next to me.

Jonathan's eyes went suddenly misty. "I miss Barkley. What a great dog. I'm going to look in the shelters for another Lab mix like him."

"So you're not living a nomadic life anymore? You're going to settle down and get a dog?"

"Yes." He gave a big laugh. "A dog and a house. I made an offer on a house in Brentwood this week. Not a mansion like the one we lost, but a nice place. I can't wait to show it to you." He took out his phone. "It's got all the things you like: a big kitchen, walk-in closets, dual sinks in the master bath, a nice sized pool and..."

He handed me his phone, where I could see a slide show of a pretty Southern California stucco home with a red-tiled roof and exuberant bougainvillea decorating the entryway. The interior had hardwood floors and lots of light. Jonathan had obviously landed on his feet. I was happy for him.

I gave him back the phone and offered him a warm smile. He grinned back. He was almost like a kid trying to get mom's approval.

"You really are getting your life back, aren't you? I'm very proud of you." I had no idea where this was going, so I sipped more tea.

Jonathan brushed off Buckingham and came over to my chair and took my hand.

"Camilla, I screwed up. I screwed up our marriage. I screwed up my career. I screwed up my life. But I'm getting things back on track. I've been wanting to reach out to you, but I didn't know how. But after I put the down payment on the house, I suddenly realized I needed to come up and talk to you, face to face. So after filming today, I got in my car and drove up here to tell you in person. I'm sorry it's so late. I would have been here before nine, if the damned mudslides hadn't closed the 154."

"You've been wanting to reach out to me? How? You mean that email?" I looked away from his intense gaze. I grabbed my brandy and took a big gulp before I realized what I was doing. I quickly plunked it down and exchanged it for my teacup.

"I mean helping by your friends — Plantagenet and Ronzo and Saffina. I've been trying to do some good now and undo some of the tragic stuff your friends have gone through."

"Are you trying to tell me that you started an anti-#MeToo TV show to help me and my friends?"

Jonathan laughed and sat on the arm of my chair.

"Of course not. I know you're not an idiot." He took the teacup from my hand and put it on the coffee table, then bent down to kiss me. The kiss was warm and sweet and more affectionate than sexual. But the sexual aspect was there. My body responded in familiar ways I didn't want it to. This was way too confusing. What was Jonathan up to?

He pulled away and went on, as if he hadn't discombobulated my entire being.

"The idea for the program came from the producers, and they offered me the job because I'm a fellow victim of cancel culture, still pretty well-known, but cheap. My agent has been selling me as the poor man's Keith Morrison. You know, the sexy older guy from Dateline?" He laughed again and picked up his tea. "Now I'm supposed to be one of those silver fox journalists who make the old ladies get all hot and bothered."

I carefully retrieved my tea and took another sip. All right, if he was going to pretend he hadn't kissed me, I could do that too.

"You are looking very well, Jonathan. You're obviously taking good care of yourself." I had to give him that. "You're brave to dive back into the Hollywood swamp."

He looked down at his teacup. I wasn't sure if he was being bashful or pretending to be. He took a thoughtful sip.

"Yes. I know it's a swamp. And I know you've always disapproved of me working for the network. But I took the job in spite of the political overtones because I thought I could use that kind of show for good. Lots of men are sexually harassed too. By other men and by women."

"But mostly it's been the other way around for, like the past four millennia or so." I wasn't ready to buy the idea that all this was returning to his social justice crusader roots. When I met him, he was editor of a struggling progressive newspaper. But that was a long time ago.

"Sure. But right now, the pendulum has swung so far the other way that innocent men are being hurt. Look at Plantagenet. Anybody who meets him for two minutes knows he's gay. But he had no venue to tell the press that. All they got was that superannuated bimbo's ridiculous lies."

"Kensie really is too old for that bimbo persona, isn't she? Those awful tight clothes. My mother would have called her 'mutton dressed as lamb.'"

Jonathan went to the kitchen for the tea pot.

"Here's the thing." He stood over me and refreshed my cup. "If we believe women are equal to men — which I do — then you have to believe they have an equal capacity for evil."

He refilled his own cup and looked off into the distance.

I had to think for a minute about what he'd said. It sure was true of Saffina in her "Lady Ruffina" days. She'd murdered kittens, for good-ness' sake.

"But Jonathan, you made that psychopathic woman who tried to kill Ronzo look like a princess. And you made them look like lovers — was that doing good in the world?"

"But they are lovers. Anybody can see that. She's bonkers about him."

My eyes stung. Jonathan wasn't saying anything I hadn't seen with my own eyes, but I still hated hearing it.

I stood and looked him full in the face.

"Jonathan, Ronzo hasn't told me that."

He gave me a melty look and put his hands on my shoulders and started to move in for another kiss. But I pushed him away.

"I'm not ready for this. I need time to process. And I'm very fond of Ronzo."

Jonathan reached for me again. He was not reading my signals.

Luckily, we were interrupted by a knock on the door. I'd been too startled by Jonathan's sudden appearance that I hadn't locked it.

In stomped a man. A soldier. In what looked like a Desert Storm uniform. A man I almost recognized.

He wasn't as tall as Jonathan, but he looked tougher than three of him.

"That's enough, dude." The soldier spoke right into Jonathan's face. "The lady is obviously not that into you."

# twenty-six

· · ·

## A Fine Kettle of Fish

"*A*re you okay, Camilla?"

The mysterious soldier had a deep, gruff voice. He looked familiar, but I still couldn't place him.

"I saw that car parked in your driveway and figured something was up. I know you don't usually have visitors at this time of night." He harrumphed. "And I also know your boyfriend's not in town. And he doesn't drive a Tesla." He glanced at the bottle of brandy on the table. "Plus, I happen to know you already had two hefty snifters of that stuff."

So that's who he was. I had to avoid eye contact, or I'd burst out laughing.

"I'm Marvin." He gave Jonathan his hand. "Marvin Skinner. Private First Class. Medical Corps. Ronson Zolek and I served together in Iraq."

Dear Lord. Marva must have seen Jonathan drive up as she was leaving. And she decided to play protector in case something was wrong. She did say she'd been planning to look for Joe after a change of clothes. Well, there s/he was, clothes changed.

Jonathan stared for a moment, then shook Marvin's hand and gave a big laugh.

"I'm Jonathan Kahn. Camilla's ex-husband. I don't intend to steal Mr. Zolek's woman, I assure you. Although I didn't realize she was his personal property." He turned to me with a mocking smile. "That guy has a watchdog keeping track of your love life, Camilla? While that sleaze is back in New Jersey with a new girlfriend?"

I cringed. For Jonathan, for Ronzo. For Marvin, too. And for me. This pretty much defined "a fine kettle of fish."

"Marva-in...um...isn't exactly Ronzo's watchdog. He's..."

I didn't know what to say because I couldn't really define Marvin. I usually interacted with Marva, who was a distinctly different persona. But Marva once had a very kinky encounter with Jonathan, and I feared she was taking a big chance of being recognized.

He/she/they. One of these days, I should really ask Marva what pronouns she preferred.

But right now, this was Marvin, and I didn't need him to be interfering in my love life, no matter how altruistic his motives.

"Thank you so much, Marvin, for making sure I'm okay. That's really kind. But things are fine. Jonathan is buying a new house in Brentwood and wanted to show me the pictures."

I turned to Marvin and gave him a look I hoped let him know it was perfectly fine for him to go. And it would be a good idea to leave before Jonathan figured out who he was.

"Have I met you before, Private Skinner?" Jonathan was scrutinizing Marvin now. "Did I interview you — maybe a while ago? You have a familiar face —"

I did not want this to happen. Marva had tried to blackmail Jonathan back in his drinking days and the last thing I needed was for that to get dredged up.

I took Marvin's arm and led him to the door.

"I promise I won't stay up past my bedtime, Marvin. Thanks for looking out for me."

I stood at the door between Marvin and Jonathan, hoping that they'd both get the hint that it was time to leave. I turned to Jonathan.

"I didn't mean to push you away. I'm simply overwhelmed by all this. I need to sleep on it. And call Ronzo. He and I need to have a serious talk."

Jonathan sighed, then leaned in to kiss me on the cheek.

"Hey, I'm sorry if this was all too much, too soon. I thought you would have broken up with that guy a long time ago. But I'll be staying here a few days for a little vacation. I'm going to check into the Inn at Morro Bay. Do they still have hot tub rooms looking over the bay?"

"They do. They're awesome," Marvin said. He gave me a peck on the cheek too. I could smell lily of the valley. "Are you leaving, Kahn? I need to move my car. My Lexus has your Tesla parked in."

I watched the two of them leave. My ex-husband, who claimed he was still in love with me, and my ex-enemy, Marva/Marvin, who seemed have become my protector.

They were both good-looking men. But I was awfully glad neither of them wanted to stay. I must be getting old. But I needed alone time to process everything Jonathan had told me. He'd said he could tell Saffina was bonkers about Ronzo, but he hadn't mentioned if Ronzo was similarly crazed about her. Maybe Ronzo wasn't all that interested, but he needed to make things look lovey-dovey for the cameras. I knew all those romances on reality TV were faked.

No. I was deluding myself. Jonathan had pretty good instincts about people. If what Jonathan saw was just a woman throwing herself at a guy, he wouldn't have driven all the way up here to spring his Brentwood dream house on me.

I knew Marva wanted me to phone Ronzo and tell him to be on the lookout for Joe. But calling Ronzo after all his silence would be humiliating in the extreme. I didn't want to be a Kensie Wiener type, living in a narcissistic fantasy world. How tragic to spend your life imagining men were attracted when they only wanted you to go away.

So okay, I guess Jonathan wasn't being pushy with his assumption that I'd been dumped. The dumpee is always the last to know.

But why did he think that being single meant I immediately needed another partner? Some people still thought singleness was some kind of disease that needed to be cured.

I poured my tea out in the sink and grabbed my brandy snifter, topped it off, and booted up my laptop. I suppose I was looking for the inevitable break-up email from Ronzo. At this point, I would even welcome it. At least I wouldn't be living in this limbo anymore.

But there was nothing from Ronzo.

There was, however, another email from P. Pelletier. What was Peter up to now?

# twenty-seven

. . .

## Snakes and Crocodiles and Angry Hippopotami

*P*eter had sent a long email this time. Maybe he was finally going to answer my questions about what happened the night he evaporated from my courtyard. I grabbed my brandy glass to provide fortification for a long read. At least Peter's shenanigans would keep my mind off Jonathan and Ronzo.

"Hello Duchess," he wrote. "I hope all is well and Joe is still safe with Marva. Today I managed to get Fanna's assistant in a more talkative mood. It didn't hurt that I took him to a pub in the tourist district for a pint. And that his ladylove wasn't hovering. I did get him to tell me there's nothing wrong with Fanna as far as he knows. He says she's simply suffering from writer's block. But I'm certain he's hiding something. He says he last saw her about six weeks ago, and seems rather cross with her. She's gone upriver to a small village where her aunt lives. But he was vague about the name of the village and how far inland it is.

But The Gambia's a small country — only a strip of land on both sides of the river — so I have hopes I can find her. If she's blocked, I have no idea why she didn't tell Pradeep. He knows the book will be brilliant when she gets it done. He might even help her finish it — even be her co-author. Pradeep's a brilliant writer himself. Of course, there's the bigger question of why Fanna isn't picking up the money in her account. No writer has ever been so blocked they couldn't accept their royalties. And he doesn't seem to know why her advance came back to us. He says she's near skint, since her business manager in Leeds stole everything out of their joint bank account. That's one of the reasons Fanna has gone to her aunt's village, apparently — she couldn't afford to keep her beach house here.

Tomorrow I'm going to catch a ride on a boat upriver to ask around about her. I have a friend from Uni who runs a village school somewhere in the provinces. Used to do some editing work for us. He's mad as a box of spanners, but he might have heard some gossip about Fanna. She's quite a celebrity in this country.

Do let me know what's going on with Joe and Marva. Let's hope your local coppers get their hands on the real culprit."

I wondered if I should tell him about the "evidence" on Ginny's phone. Which was still missing, along with Adriana. He'd also want to know about Joe's disappearance and planned trek to New Jersey. But I decided to wait and see how things played out. Peter and Ronzo had an uneasy truce at best.

Of course, my biggest question was why Peter didn't say why he'd evaporated that night. Or whether he knew how the body got moved.

Was he deliberately keeping me in the dark? Maybe he was off on an adventure he found more interesting than telling me why he disappeared in such a rude way. I shouldn't be surprised. He often disappeared in a rude way. People don't change. No matter how much we want to believe they can.

Which led me to thoughts of Jonathan. Could he actually have turned over a new leaf? Could I let myself believe he had? I didn't have a clue what I should do with the emotions he'd stirred up.

It was easier to focus on Peter. I wasn't in love with Peter. I guess I'd thought I was for a bit back in England, but I was totally over it.

I wondered what he meant about going "upriver." I pictured a scene from the Katharine Hepburn-Humphrey Bogart film *The African Queen*. And a scary river full of snakes and crocodiles and angry hippopotami.

Although, come to think of it, hiding out in an African village sounded preferable to the craziness that was my love life. I might be better off with those angry hippos.

I replied with a light note trying to make the night's dramas sound funny. Marva bursting in on us dressed as a soldier was the stuff of farce. By the time I hit send. I was almost ready to laugh at it.

Until my phone rang.

It was Adriana. She spoke in spoke such a small, weak voice, I couldn't understand the words.

"Oh, my goodness! Are you all right, dear?"

I couldn't hear the answer.

# twenty-eight

. . .

## Oedipus Rex and Catfish

*A*driana's voice was so faint, I had to press the phone to my ear.

"Adriana, it's nearly eleven o'clock. What's wrong? Fish and I have been worried about you all week. Are you all right?"

"I'm fine. Nothing's wrong. But I have to talk real soft so my mom and Britney can't hear. But I had to tell you — I've found the catfish. I'm pretty sure I know who he is. I've been hanging out at the library watching the homeless guys. Sometimes they forget to clear their history, so I jump in and see what they've been up to."

I couldn't help letting out a gasp. This brilliant child really did fancy herself Sherlock Holmes. Which was not a good thing. We were not living in a fictional world with fictional villains.

"You've been stalking homeless men? Do you know how dangerous that could be?"

"You sound like my mom. Do you want to know what I found out, or not?"

"Yes, please. But it's late —"

"His name is Barry Brown. See, that's where the "Brownie" name comes in. He was using the computer today and I went in and sure enough he didn't clear history and right there he'd been Googling

Garth Brooks lyrics. Like Brownie put in the lovey-dovey emails. I'm sure he's the guy."

The child was amazing. Unfortunately, a Google search wasn't exactly evidence.

"Adriana, that's some spectacular sleuthing. I want to hear all about it tomorrow. And I need you to bring Ginny's phone back to the store so I can put it in the safe. It's dangerous for you to be running around with it..."

"My mom's coming up the stairs. Gotta go."

Oh, dear. After my crazy evening, I really didn't need to worry about that girl on top of everything else.

But I had to get Ginny's phone. And take it to the police. Tomorrow.

Tonight, I had to sleep. Or try to. Jonathan's visit had discombobulated me. And I was worried about Joe, too.

Buckingham sauntered in from the kitchen and gave me a look that meant it was past our bedtime.

I had finished brushing my teeth and was getting into bed when the phone rang again. I almost let it go to voicemail. Who would be rude enough to call at this hour?

Finally, I picked up. It was Plant.

"So sorry I'm calling so late. Did I wake you? I didn't realize the time until I punched your number. I'm working such crazy hours."

I mumbled something I hoped was polite.

"The son," he said. "Ginny Gilhooly's son. Moe or Curly or whatever his name is. What if he's actually the catfish? I'm storyboarding Ginny's murder, and I think it's going to work. At first my person of interest was your friend Peter, but most of the time the culprit is somebody in the family."

"You think Larry was romancing his own mother? You're rewriting *Oedipus Rex*?" I couldn't help laughing. "*Oedipus Rex and Catfish*. It might work. Sort of like *Pride and Prejudice and Zombies*?"

At least he was over casting Peter as the villain. Which was absurd. Peter was a smuggler, not a murderer.

"I'm serious, Camilla. Remember how Larry pretended he'd never heard of his mother's unlucky pen-pal lover? And he somehow didn't notice she was giving this guy big chunks of money?"

I had to agree that was odd.

"I didn't buy it then." Plant's tone was scornful. "And I sure don't buy it now. But I would believe he was scamming his mother for all that money. And he might have killed her when she found out what he'd been doing. That was an angry man."

I wondered if Plant and his screenwriting team had been smoking something. His theory was shocking enough for a Netflix series, but not believable enough for the real world.

"That sounds like a great plot for your TV script, but it didn't happen that way. We're on the trail of the real Brownie. Adriana has found him." I didn't want to tell Plant about the phone. I felt guilty enough I hadn't taken it to the police.

"You have proof?" Plant voice was a bit harsh.

"Well, kind of. Adriana has been sleuthing in the library where a lot of the unhoused people hang out…"

"You're encouraging a thirteen-year-old to stalk homeless guys?"

I yawned. I didn't need to argue with Plant. I needed sleep. I wondered if I should tell him about Barry Brown, or Jonathan's bizarre visit, but decided not to.

"Plant, I love you but I'm exhausted. It's been a fierce day. Let's talk another time."

"Of course, darling. But I tell you I'm right. There's some Oedipus stuff going on in the Gilhooly story."

Plant was brilliant at writing stories, but he was a moron at reading people. I did not believe Larry Gilhooly could do any of those things. Besides, Adriana had found the real culprit, a homeless man named Barry Brown.

# twenty-nine

. . .

## Swimming with Sharks

*I* did manage to get to sleep, after some tossing and turning. But I had weird dreams involving Jonathan and Peter and Plantagenet on a raft in a shark-infested ocean. One of the sharks circling us looked like an angry Larry Gilhooly. He tried to flip the raft and we all fell in the water. We were all about to be eaten when I woke up.

After a lot of caffeine and a not-sufficiently-toasted English muffin, I was sort of ready to face the day.

Fish was relieved to hear that Adriana had called. I said she'd been going to the library all week for a school project. Almost true, except the part about school.

But he kept pestering me for more information. I hated having to make up silly lies about a phony school project, since I'd have to brief Adriana about my deception before she talked to Fish this afternoon. Oh, what a tangled web...and all that. I couldn't keep lying to Fish. I liked him and wanted to keep our relationship honest.

So, after our lone morning customer left with a used copy of Fanna Badjie's *Under an African Moon*, I decided to open up to Fish about Adriana's "sleuthing" and how she was trying to prove Joe's innocence. I blurted out the whole story as he shelved some stray books. I told him all about Ginny's phone and my bag of "clues." I also let him know Adriana had been spying on homeless men in the library, which I found awfully upsetting.

"You were that upset but you didn't call me? I could have gone looking for her, you know. I know some of those guys."

"She was calling from home, so I knew she was safe for the moment, but I don't know if she'll be safe today."

"I'll talk to her. She should not go back to that library. She thinks she's playing games, but she's swimming with sharks. Some of those guys are dangerous criminals."

"I think she's figured that out. But she thinks she's found Ginny Gilhooly's catfish here in Morro Bay."

I watched Fish shelve the new James Patterson in the Horror section with an angry shove — I didn't know if that was from ignorance of popular fiction or pure snark — but I didn't give in to my urge to stop him. The issue at hand was more important.

He turned to face me. "So, who is this catfish guy?" Fish's eyes sparked with intensity.

"She thinks it's a homeless man named Barry Brown. Although if he got all that money out of Ginny, I don't understand why he'd be homeless anymore."

"Barry B? He's not what I'd call homeless. He's a van man. He's got himself a sweet vintage Winnebago camper van and moves around to different campgrounds. You think he's a romance scammer?"

"You know him? Barry Brown?"

Fish let out a snort. "Pretty much everybody knows Barry. He's kind of the town drunk. If I've ever seen him sober, I wasn't aware of it. He used to be a stand-up comic who worked the west coast casino circuit — even played Vegas. But now he couldn't remember his own name, much less a punch line. Hard to believe he has the smarts to catfish somebody." Fish paused a moment to reshelve a book that was out of alphabetical order. "Although come to think of it, I wouldn't put it past him. He used to be quite the ladies' man back in the day, to hear him tell it."

"Whether he's Ginny's catfish or not, I need to get that phone to the police. So, if Adriana brings it in today the way she promised, will you hold the fort while I take it to the police station?"

"Cops? Why are you bringing the cops into this? You have some reason to trust Morro Bay's finest? I don't." Fish turned back to the shelf and avoided eye contact.

I didn't know what to say. His distrust of the police was so intense, there had to be a dark story behind it.

I tried to laugh. "They usually treat me like a dingbat and don't believe anything I say, but they tend to solve their cases in the end."

"Well, they won't believe anything I say, that's for sure. I steer clear of the local pigs. If it were me, I'd keep hold of that phone until you know more about what's on it — and more about what Barry Brown is up to. That dude is a slimebag."

And he also was very likely a murderer. I had to keep Adriana out of that library.

# thirty

. . .

## Shrimp Pad Prik

$\mathcal{J}$ was so immersed in worries about Adriana and her dangerous sleuthing that I'd almost forgotten Jonathan had asked me to lunch. I guess I hadn't quite said no. I'd murmured something about having to work, but hadn't been very emphatic about it. It had always been hard for me to say "no" to Jonathan.

Today he had dressed casually in khakis, polo shirt and windbreaker, but he still had the sheen of celebrity about him.

"Money." Fish whispered to me on his way to the mystery section. "That dude stinks of money. Sell him something big. Like that ninety-dollar coffee table job about Formula One racing."

Of course Jonathan didn't really stink. He smelled lovely. The spicy notes of his Paco Rabanne aftershave mixed with his own warm, clean scent brought back a flood of memories. I offered him a quick kiss as he gave me a hug — a carefully chaste hug, but it still had a powerful effect on me. I probably blushed.

"I hope you're taking a lunch break soon," Jonathan said. "Do you want seafood or Thai? I've got the names of some good restaurants in the neighborhood."

"Um, I don't really have time… The store." I didn't want to tell him the importance of being in the store to meet with Adriana. She would be coming in after school and I absolutely had to see her, get Ginny's phone, and explain to the child that she had to stop stalking homeless men. She might be in as early as three and right now it was past one.

"You don't eat lunch? You must have Simon Legree for a boss." Jonathan gave me his movie star grin and took my hand. "A very beautiful Simon Legree, but still, she's a tyrant."

I have to admit part of me wanted to throw myself in his arms and let him take me away for Thai food and a visit to his elegant Brentwood home.

Fish emerged from the mystery section and gave me a big smile. He apparently approved of Jonathan as a suitor, in spite of the "stink of money".

"I got this, Camilla. Go have some lunch. My money's on the Thai. Up at that Elephant place you can get great pineapple shrimp fried rice, so you can have your seafood too."

"Thai Elephant?" Jonathan hooked my arm with his. "That's on my list. So Thai Elephant it is. Right up the street. We'll be back in an hour." He turned to Fish. "Or an hour and a half, tops."

The shrimp fried rice, served in a hollowed-out pineapple, was indeed delicious. I would have liked to have been able to make the decision of my lunch entree myself, and not have it made by two men, but I supposed I had to forgive them. Fish had no idea of my history with Jonathan, and I did want a quick meal so I'd be back in time to talk to Adriana.

While we enjoyed our food, Jonathan confined his conversation to small talk and gossip about celebrities. I supposed it was his way of apologizing for coming on too strong last night.

Also, a group of women in the back were loudly berating the waiter over the amount of heat in the shrimp pad prik. When people are making a rude scene in a restaurant, I always stay as quiet as possible and try to politely fade into the woodwork, to avoid making more work for the beleaguered help.

I gave a light laugh in response to Jonathan's anecdote about Jim Carrey's recent art show and concentrated on my shrimp fried rice. But after a moment, I recognized the voice of one of the rude women.

It was Larry Gilhooly's charming bride-to-be, Crystal, and her bimbo brigade of bridesmaids. Again, Larry sat silently overlooking them, like a large, pink vulture.

Of course. This was June. The brigade was here for the big wedding. I wondered if Ginny were spinning in her grave. And it would be typical of Crystal to order the spiciest item on the menu and then complain it was spicy. A busty woman in a low-cut top waved her blood-red claws in the waiter's face so close I was afraid she'd wound him. Then a big blonde waved an empty water glass, and one with purple hair streaks looked as if she might stab him with her chopstick.

Jonathan asked me for the second time what I'd been up to lately. But the presence of Larry Gilhooly and his tribe filled my head with Plant's Oedipal theories, and of course, worries about Ginny's phone. Not something I wanted to confide in Jonathan. At least not until I had the phone securely in my office safe. Jonathan would of course tell me what a moron I'd been to let the child take such important evidence out of the store.

So, I launched into a lighthearted version of the story of Fanna Badjie's disappearance and how my publisher was off in The Gambia trying to find her.

But Jonathan gave me a dark look of concern. "He's gone to The Gambia? That's not a place I'd choose to be at the moment. I've heard rumors of political unrest and police crackdowns."

Crystal and company, having finished yelling at the waiter, now seemed to be shouting at each other. Larry finally spoke. Not nicely. He told purple hair she could go back to Bakersfield if she was going to badmouth his mother. My goodness. The man had a backbone after all. As purple hair flounced off in the direction of the bathroom, I tried to ignore them and get back to the subject at hand.

"Fanna Badjie's books don't suggest she's into politics. Her stories are all about nasty European sex tourists and evil foreign cartels that exploit African children."

Oh. No. Why did I bring up exploited children? That only made me think about Adriana and the danger she could be getting into.

"And the bad foreigners always get their just deserts." I laughed.

Jonathan gave me a sad smile. "I haven't read a novel in years. Maybe I should get back to reading for fun. I like it when the bad guys lose. It never seems to happen in real life these days." He laughed. "Except maybe on my show. I'm so glad to have a hand in getting your friends' lives back on track. Have you heard from Plantagenet? He seems to be Hollywood's darling again."

I was relieved when Larry and Crystal and their entourage marched out of the restaurant, still in high dudgeon. Everybody in the place looked relieved. That crowd probably brought joy wherever they went, simply by leaving the premises.

I tried to entertain Jonathan with some stories about Plant's new life in Hollywood, but I couldn't help thinking about his news about unrest in The Gambia. It was just like Peter to leave out that uncomfortable detail.

"Do you think Fanna might have been purposely disappeared by political factions or the police?"

Jonathan shrugged. "I don't have a clue. I'm mostly on the domestic celebrity beat these days, not international news. Celebrity stuff pays the bills."

"But things could be bad for her?"

"From what I've heard, yes."

"That's where Peter is right now. Do you think he's in danger?"

Jonathan speared one last shrimp at the bottom of his pineapple.

"Yes," he said. "Didn't you say he has a criminal past? He could certainly be in danger."

# thirty-one

. . .

## Goldfish Bowl

$\mathcal{W}$hen Adriana arrived after school, she didn't look like her usual perky self. Fish and I both rushed over to see what the problem was. The poor girl looked close to tears.

"I have to talk to Camilla," she said to Fish. "It's about my, um, project."

"I know about your sleuthing." Fish took her hand. "Did Barry Brown do something to you?"

She shook him off. "No. No. It's nothing to do with the catfish or Mrs. Gilhooly. Can I go into the office?"

Fish looked a little hurt, but I took Adriana to the back room.

"Is this about Britney? Or her mom?"

"No. I mean, well, partly. Her mom finally started texting her again, but she won't say when she's coming home and Britney's going totally wack. She still thinks it's all my fault." Adriana collapsed into my desk chair.

The girl might be in tears, but I felt a wave of relief. At least Britney's feckless mother wasn't dead. I gave Adriana a hug.

"I'm so sorry, dear. I do hope Shannon will come home soon. Then she can tell everybody the whole truth about her African adventure, and you and Britney can patch things up. It's so hard to be feuding with a good friend. I understand why you're upset."

Adriana pulled away with a sniff.

"That's not why I'm upset." Her expression darkened with anger. "I'm upset because of Willow O'Malley. She's like the meanest mean girl in our school, and she makes fun of the food I bring to lunch because it's pupusas not some stupid peanut butter and jelly. She's also been catfishing Ruben Moreno, which is so gross. He's, like, in college."

This was another reminder that I was dealing with a child. Who got bullied by mean girls, and shouldn't be playing detective around dangerous men.

"Children who are ignorant can be so unkind, can't they?"

"Yeah. Well, today Willow would not let me alone. She and her squad kept following me and calling me names. One said my last name, Garza, means heron and I have skinny legs like a heron bird. And Ruben Moreno will never like me. Like I care. He's just a guy from church."

Adriana went on with tales of Willow O'Malley's misdeeds. It was something of a saga, but obviously she had to unload. I hoped Fish was okay on his own in the store.

"These girls kept coming closer and one of them reached in my backpack. She pulled out the phone. Not mine. Mrs. Gilhooly's phone. But they thought it was mine. They laughed at the green case with the shamrocks and got mad because I'm not Irish and I guess Willow is, so she said it should be hers and she took it right out of my hand." Adriana gave a big sniff. "So it's gone. And I can't find out any more about who killed Mrs. Gilhooly. Plus, I knew you'd be mad."

This was awful news, but I told her I wasn't angry, and everything would be fine. I probably wasn't telling the truth, but I needed to say something. The poor child — bullied in school and her best friend giving her the silent treatment. She was a brave little soul.

I hoped some of her bravery would rub off on me. I was going to need it, because I needed to pay a visit to the Morro Bay police, whether I had the evidence on the phone or not.

I wondered if I should go ahead and ask Jonathan's advice about the whole mess. He had more knowledge of the law than I did. He'd asked me to have dinner with him at his hotel. I felt I should go because lunch had been so short. And dominated by those shouty rude people.

I checked my email before I left and saw there was something from Peter. Apparently, Jonathan had not been wrong when he described Banjul as dangerous, especially for dodgy foreigners.

 Hello Duchess," Peter wrote. "The city is pretty uncomfortable at the moment, with coppers everywhere. All I've had to eat today is a few swallows of baobab juice and a bit of domoda — a dish that consists of white rice and peanut sauce — not my idea of culinary heaven. So I'm going to go upriver for a while."

He said he had hoped for some help from Fanna's less than useful assistant, but apparently the man and his American ladylove had disappeared from their hotel. So he'd decided to take that *African Queen* style river voyage. It sounded terrifying. He said he hoped that if he went inland, he'd be able to get some news of Fanna from villagers. He proposed to visit his friend with the village school — the former editor who was "mad as a box of spanners."

That seemed to be a remarkably iffy plan, since he wasn't even quite sure of the name of the village where his friend was living.

He signed off saying he didn't know whether he would have any internet or phone service as he wended his way along the crocodile-infested river.

 I'm not so terribly afraid of the crocodiles," he wrote. "But it's the hippos. It seems they're the most dangerous land mammal on the planet and have very sharp teeth."

Not reassuring. In fact, I was decidedly less reassured than I was before I read the email. Plus, he had still managed to avoid the subject of Ginny's body and its disappearance from my back step.

When I met Jonathan at the hotel restaurant, the place was filled with noisy patrons shouting over the loud music that blared from the bar. I didn't feel I could talk about such a sensitive subject as the missing phone while having to shout. After all, I had probably broken the law and I'd be admitting it where everybody could hear.

Speaking of everybody, I could see Larry Gilhooly and the awful Crystal sitting back at a corner table with the posse. Were they stalking us? And were Larry and Crystal ever alone? The bridesmaids were a source of a lot of the noise in the dining area. The big blonde was sending her entrée back, and the busty one demanded a dirtier martini. I should have asked Jonathan to go to a less touristy place.

I tried to ignore the noise and enjoy the food and good wine. But about halfway through my entrée — some lovely grilled scallops — I had to deal with something much more dramatic. I guess I'd known it was coming, but I'd imagined I could avoid it a bit longer.

"I hope you've been giving my offer some thought." Jonathan took my hand. "I apologize for doing this wrong last night. Obviously I did, or our old friend Marva wouldn't have jumped in to save you from me."

"You knew that was Marva?" I should have realized her ruse wouldn't work on Jonathan. I laughed and retrieved my hand to grab my wine glass.

He laughed too. "Of course. Not a lot of male GIs wear pink pearl nail polish and lily of the valley perfume. I take it you two are friends now?"

"Sort of. Maybe frenemies. She's tight with Ronzo. They served in Iraq together."

"Marva really was a soldier?"

"Yes. Is that hard to believe?"

"Not really." Jonathan fumbled with something in his pocket and looked distracted. Suddenly his expression changed. He gave me a goofy grin.

"I don't know what the etiquette rules are for proposing to an ex-wife. But...Camilla, will you marry me?"

His eyes got misty and for a moment I was afraid he'd be totally trite and go down on one knee. He didn't, thank goodness, but he did produce a jeweler's box. He opened it and put it on the table in front of me.

"We can exchange the ring for another style if you like. I told the jewelers it had to be perfect, but not flashy."

It was a flawless diamond set in rose gold. Exquisite. Exactly the ring I would have chosen for myself if I were in the market for an engagement ring.

Which I totally wasn't.

But I could see Jonathan had put some thought into it. The box came from a jewelry store in San Luis Obispo, right down the road, so he must have bought it sometime in the last two days. The store was run by two of Plant's friends, George and Enrique.

"It's a perfect ring, Jonathan. Did you tell George and Enrique it was for me?"

"I did. They seem to be fond of you." He paused and took a long sip of his Edna Valley Chardonnay. "So? What do you think? Can I get a do-over? Would you consider marrying me again?"

As I tried to form the words to let him down politely, I sensed a rise in the decibel level of the voices around us. I looked up and saw half the diners in the place were taking pictures of us with their phones.

Jonathan had been spotted. I'd almost forgotten he'd become famous again.

I could see Larry and Crystal and all the bridesmaids gawking at us from their dark corner.

"Oh, go on. Kiss her," a busboy said to Jonathan as he cleared a table near us.

"Kiss!" Somebody called from the back of the room. "Let us get a shot of you two kissing!"

Oh dear.

I didn't have time to ponder, because the crowd started chanting — yes, chanting — as if they were in some athletic stadium.

"Kiss, Kiss, kiss!" They shouted.

Jonathan, ever the showman, got up and came over to my chair. He grabbed my hands and pulled me to my feet and planted a romantic kiss on my scallop-buttered lips. The crowd roared and clapped.

"Put on the ring!" somebody yelled. Echoes ensued.

Still holding my right hand, Jonathan leaned down and plucked the ring from its satin box and slid it on my finger. Of course it fit, since George and Enrique at the jewelry store had my size.

I suppose I should have refused, right there. But it would have been so impolite to make a scene. So I gamely held up my hand to show off the ring to their phone-cameras.

I saw Crystal taking a photo along with the rest of them. I wondered what she'd do with it. What any of them would do with it. Probably try to sell it to the press. The press. Damn. This was not going to be good.

"This will all be on TMZ in a matter of hours, won't it?" I whispered to Jonathan through my phony smile.

"Oh, yes. More like minutes." Jonathan put an arm around me and waved to the crowd.

I whispered in Jonathan's ear "Get me out of here."

He whispered back, "you didn't say yes."

"That's right," I said. "I didn't."

# thirty-two

. . .

## A Whole New Can of Worms

After Jonathan drove me home, I made him take back the ring, lovely as it was. I told him it would be safer with him, and I couldn't give him an answer now because I needed to "sleep on it."

He smiled, but I could see anger flash in his eyes. He took it out on poor Buckingham, who slithered around his legs as we stood in the doorway. Jonathan pushed Buckingham away with an annoyed foot and the poor kitty ran outside, even though it was time for him to come in for dinner and some snuggles.

The problem was that Jonathan had all sorts of lovely plans for blissful domesticity, but they didn't really involve me. They involved a Camilla who no longer existed — the fashionista who would be his arm candy in public and endlessly supportive at home.

I didn't know that woman anymore. I had my own plans for the future. Okay, that future had until very recently involved a rock and roll guy from New Jersey. But it also involved a bookstore.

I gave Jonathan a quick kiss and sent him on his way. He didn't talk about plans for the next day and I was grateful. I simply didn't know what to tell him.

So I called Plant. It was only about nine. Early for him in his new Hollywood life.

I started to give him a recap of the last few days with Jonathan.

"I know, darling," he said. "You're trending on Twitter. Looks like a nice ring."

Good lord. I went to the fridge and got out my open bottle of Chardonnay, and poured myself a large glass.

"Well, that's annoying. I guess some of those people taking pictures of us must have posted to social media right then and there. Probably Crystal's bridesmaids."

Plant laughed. "The bimbo brigade was at the Inn at Morro Bay? Isn't that a bit pricey for them?"

"I'm sure Larry was paying. It was sort of their rehearsal dinner, I think. Which the groom's family is supposed to pay for. I'm not sure he has any more family, but he must be rather well off now he's inherited Ginny's money — I think there's a lot of it."

"Of course. I told you he's your murderer. He has the best motive. Even if he's not the catfish."

I didn't want to have this conversation. I'd have to tell him about Ginny's phone and that would be a whole new can of worms.

"Do you believe they're going ahead with a lavish wedding in spite of Ginny's death? Such a breach of etiquette."

Plant laughed again, but his laugh sounded forced.

"So, are you going to do it? Marry Jonathan again?"

I took a large gulp of wine.

"I haven't got a clue. That's why I phoned you. Is it a stupid idea?"

"Yes. But that's never stopped you before."

"That's not helpful, Plant." He seemed to have taken a course in Hollywood rudeness. "I guess this is a problem I have to work out by myself."

"Darling, I'm sorry. I know Jonathan is sober now and things may be very different."

Okay, Plant's tone said he was firmly in the "don't marry him" camp.

"I told Jonathan I'd sleep on it, and I guess that's what I need to do."

Of course, "sleeping on it" only works if you actually fall asleep and stay there, and that eluded me. I kept thinking about Ronzo. If

Jonathan and I were trending on Twitter, Ronzo was sure to have seen something. If he was in a serious relationship with Saffina, he'd be relieved, but if he wasn't, he'd be devastated. This went around in my brain with all my mixed thoughts about Jonathan. I had to admit part of me was not averse to resuming the kind of comfortable life I used to have. But the man had broken my heart.

And Ronzo was breaking my heart too. Maybe what I needed was to have no men in my life for a while so my heart could heal.

I finally got to sleep at about three, which meant I overslept in the morning.

Well, that and the fact my furry alarm clock wasn't on the job. I'd forgotten to call Buckingham back to the house after Jonathan had so rudely evicted him. When I woke up and realized Buckingham was missing, I yanked myself out of bed, threw on my robe, and ran to the door. The poor little guy had to be starving. I called his name, but he didn't appear. I called again and was relieved to see a rustling in the growth of bushes by the fence where he often hung out.

But something much bigger and less furry emerged from the bushes.

# thirty-three

. . .

## Sardine Time

*E*merging from the bushes behind my cottage was Britney, dressed in her favorite pink hoodie and trendy knee-less jeans.

She rushed over to me, looking equally sad and angry.

"Where is she? I know she's here. She's hiding in there." She pointed at the living room behind me and sniffed back tears.

"Britney, who are you talking about and how did you get in there?" I looked at the overgrown bushes — some kind of mallow that grew like a weed here. I had no idea a human could hide in there.

"The fence posts are all falling down behind those bushes. You should really fix that. It looks slummy. That's what my mom said. Anyway, I couldn't get into the store. The sidewalk in front is full of tourists, and it didn't look like you were open anyway, so I came around to the alley." Britney put her hands on her hips and looked right past me into the house. "Addie? Adriana, I know you're in there! Your mom is hella mad. You're supposed to help her with the computer today. She's hoping for an email from my mom."

"Why are you looking for Adriana?" I stepped aside and motioned for Britney to come in. "You have to tell me what's going on. Would you like some tea? I'm a little slow getting started this morning. I overslept."

Buckingham bounded in behind Britney. She leaned down to pet his furry black head.

"You're just getting up? It's like nine-thirty." Britney peered into my bedroom to check it out before sitting at my kitchen table. "Are you sure Adriana's not here?"

I put on the kettle and stuck two English muffins in the toaster oven.

"I'm absolutely sure. Have you checked the library?"

Buckingham gave me a curt meow to let me know I was shirking my cat-mommy duties. I went to fill his bowl.

"Duh, people aren't allowed to spend the night in the library." Britney sounded as if she still thought I was lying.

That's when my sleep-addled brain finally understood what was happening. It made my whole body go cold.

"Adriana is missing? She didn't go home last night? When did you last see her?"

"Yesterday morning. Friday. On the bus to school. She's been trying to act all nice for the last couple of days because she knows I can't deal with my mom ghosting me while she's over in Africa with her supposedly 'cute' boyfriend."

I could see Britney's lower lip tremble. The poor child. Her mother had a lot to answer for.

But right now, I needed to find out about Adriana.

"So, you sat together on the morning school bus — you and Adriana?" I put a cup of tea, butter, and a toasted muffin in front of Britney, but she didn't show much interest.

"Yeah. We sat together on the bus. We didn't sit together for a couple weeks because I was mad at her. But we kind of made up."

"What did you talk about yesterday morning?"

"Well, she'd already told me all about how she's been doing that Sherlock Holmes thing with you. And how she found this phone that has a bunch of clues on it for solving the mystery, but Willow O'Malley and them stole it. So, on the bus yesterday morning, Addie got all puppy-dog-sweet and asked me, pretty-please, to ask Willow to give it back. Just because my locker is next to Willow's. Like Willow O'Malley would do something for me. Her squad always calls me Basic Britney. They say I'm basic because I watch *Friends* with my mom." She gave an appropriate eye roll.

"And where did she go when you got to school?" I put out almond butter and some jam, but Britney still didn't seem to be interested in the muffin.

"She had to get something in her locker, and I went straight to homeroom. That's the last time I saw her. And we don't usually take the school bus home together on Friday, because I usually have junior cheerleading, so I didn't notice she was missing until dinner."

"So, Luisa hadn't seen Adriana either?"

"No. And she was real mad Addie didn't show up, because she made fish tacos just for her. I don't even like fish tacos, but I had to eat three so Luisa wouldn't feel bad. Then Addie didn't show up to fight over what Netflix to watch on the big screen TV like we always do. She has her own room in our house, and sometimes she likes to be alone to read, so I didn't think that much about it. But this morning Luisa woke me up pounding on my door asking where Addie was. I tried to tell her I don't have a clue, but now Luisa thinks Addie is out hooking up with a guy and I'm covering up for her. As if."

I tried to look calm as I finished my breakfast. But I was increasingly afraid Adriana had got herself into some deep trouble. She could so easily have been kidnapped by that Barry B person. Why hadn't I stopped her from spending time in the library with homeless men who looked at porn on the Internet? Any one of them could have followed her and done.... I couldn't bear thinking about it.

I tried to swallow my last bite of muffin, but it wouldn't go down.

Somebody banged on the front door.

I opened it and there was Fish.

"So, you planning on opening up the store today or what, boss lady?" His tone was light, but there was an undertone of irritation. "They're banging down the door. I never saw people jonesing for books like that before."

146

I tried to laugh at his weird joke and looked at my watch. 10:15. I'd never been this late opening the store. I quickly gave him a recap of what Britney had told me.

"I'm going to scramble into some clothes and then call the police," I said. "I hope you don't mind opening up? I'm terrified for Adriana. I think her sleuthing has let her straight to a murderer. Do you know where they can find Barry Brown?"

"No." Fish gave me a look I'd never seen before. Equally hostile and frightened. "I don't know where he is, and I won't open the store if you're going to call the cops. I can't stand them. Pigs. Every damned one of them. They'll figure I'm guilty and never look for whoever really has the kid."

I took a deep breath. Fish's reaction was scary. His fear of the police was over the top. I thought of Marva's first reaction when she heard Fish lived in the camp where Ginny died. Could he be some kind of killer? Ginny's killer? I didn't have time to think about it.

"Will you let me get dressed at least? Open the store and I'll make myself respectable and then we can discuss what to do."

"Are you going to let me in on the discussion?" Britney chimed in from the kitchen. "Because I vote for no cops too. On account of Luisa doesn't have a green card. If they show up, they're going to want to talk to her and — bam! Luisa's back in El Salvador where the gangs are going to kill her. And me, I'm an orphan because my stupid mom is off having her tropical romance fantasy and forgot she has a kid. And Adriana will be an orphan too and they'll put us in the foster system and we'd have to hang out with lowlife delinquents and turn into hardy criminals by the time we're eighteen."

I had to stifle a laugh at "hardy" criminals, but the girl had a point.

However, right now the point was I needed to put clothes on, I was freezing to death in my bare feet and nightgown.

"See you both in the store," I said. "I have to get dressed now or I'll scream."

Actually, I thought I might scream anyway. And I did, kind of, into my closet as I looked around for something clean to wear.

But I should have saved my screams for later. After I threw on some clothes and applied minimal make-up, I rushed in the back door of the store without even touching my hair with a curling iron. It was looking positively witchy.

And the store was packed. More than packed. It was sardine time. People were squished against the shelves and more were lined up outside. Fish hadn't been joking about jonesing book people. Except they weren't book people. They were gossip journalists. With cameras rolling.

And oh, dear, there was CNN.

# thirty-four

. . .

## Sardine Time

*I* tried to keep my cool as the TV people pushed microphones at me and the looky-loos took phone photos of my sleepy-saggy face and Broom-Hilda hair.

"Are you going to remarry Jonathan Kahn?"

"Have you forgiven Jonathan for all his womanizing?"

"Does Jonathan still visit sex workers?"

I put on my Manners Doctor smile and kept saying "I have nothing to say at this time," as I pushed my way into my store.

I was grateful to see Fish's face emerge from the sea of people. He reached for my hand and pulled me behind the counter with Britney. The counter offered us a barrier from all that flesh. I could see Buckingham crouched in a dark corner under the desk. Poor guy. This was not a safe place for somebody with a tail.

"Uh-oh." Fish tapped my shoulder. "It looks as if we're going to have a swine management problem after all."

I stood up to see him pointing over the heads of the crowd to the street outside, where a police car rolled slowly by.

The car pulled into my driveway beside the store. A few minutes later, I could see two of Morro Bay's finest marching toward the front door. I don't know when I've ever been so glad to see the boys in blue.

But Fish didn't share my elation.

"I don't know what kind of drama you've got going on here, Camilla. Nobody told me you were some big fish in our little pond, or I would have asked for more pay. But I'm outta here. I'm seriously allergic to pigs. I've been talking to Britney here, and I've got some ideas of where Adriana might be. First, I'm gonna look up old Barry B. I might have an idea where he is after all."

"Can I come with? I promised Adriana's mom I'd find her." Britney probably felt trapped behind the counter. I sure did.

"Not a chance, girly. There's some dangerous dudes where I'm going. You be cool with the po-pos now, okay? Don't want you landing in juvie."

He disappeared into the sea of faces as the two officers cleared themselves a path through the crowd.

The taller officer informed me I had a public nuisance going on that was blocking sidewalk traffic. Trying to communicate with him took some doing, since several journalists kept trying to interview me at the same time, but I finally got both officers to understand the public nuisance was not of my making. I let them know I'd be eternally grateful if they could ask everybody to vacate the premises.

The tall officer broke into a grin and, in bullhorn voice told everybody to leave the store.

I grinned back. His nametag said "Dwayne Pilchard." He had a friendly face. Maybe I could talk to him later about Adriana.

Adriana. Good Lord, I had to hope that girl was all right. All I could do was hope Fish would rescue her in time.

Officer Pilchard and his partner were civil but firm with the crowd, herding the journalists and looky-loos out the door like so much livestock.

I grabbed the front door key and followed them, repeating my thanks and gratitude. I was going to have to lock up. I didn't want any of the crowd sneaking back in once they saw law enforcement was gone. Losing a chunk of Saturday income wasn't going to be good for my bottom line, but I needed a moment to breathe. And try to figure out what to do about Adriana.

But before I had time to think, what was left of the crowd got noisy again as a gleaming Tesla pulled into the spot the police car had left. Voices got even louder as my ex-husband stepped out into the sunlight, looking elegantly casual in an open necked shirt and Armani blazer. It looked as if he was going to give the crowd a Hollywood show. He spoke to each of the local television stations in turn, before giving his full attention to the woman from CNN. Crowds terrified me, but he seemed totally at ease. For which I was grateful. I knew he was entertaining the troops so I didn't have to. He did care about me. I could tell that.

But I wasn't sure that was enough. Anyway, I had more important things to think about. Like finding a lost little girl. And reassuring my cat. I bent down to pet him and could feel him shaking.

Britney kept glancing out the window at Jonathan's impromptu press conference. Maybe it was good her mind was off Adriana for a moment. But I needed answers. I called her back to the counter.

"I need to know — did Adriana say anything to indicate her plans after school yesterday? Did she say anything about somebody named Brownie or a man named Barry B?"

"She didn't say much besides asking me to talk to Willow and ask her to give that phone back, which I told her was bananas. The more important something is to you, the more Willow wants it. It's like she takes mean girl lessons. Then Addie tried to talk me into looking for the stupid green phone in Willow's locker, but I told her no way. Geez. I'm supposed to be a burglar now?"

She pulled out her own phone and started scrolling. I supposed she was hoping for word from Adriana.

"So you talked about Willow the whole time? She didn't mention any plans?"

Britney let out a snort. "No. Adriana doesn't plan anything. She can't even remember to charge her phone. She had to ask to borrow mine to send a text to her mom because her phone was at less than one percent. Who lets their phone go down to one percent?"

"How about the library? Did she say anything about the library?"

"Nope. She's been going there a lot, though, and Luisa hates that.

She thinks Adriana is meeting up with Ruben Moreno. He's cute, but me and Adriana are not into old guys. He must be, like, nineteen."

The crowd outside started to disperse, so I picked up Buckingham and took him back to my cottage. I gave him a couple of kitty treats and filled his water bowl. I hoped he'd survive the day's disruptions.

Back at the store, a few celebrity-seekers were still milling around outside the front window. I wondered if I should send Britney home. There wasn't much for her to do here but worry.

I was doing my share of worrying too. Noon came and went and I hadn't yet heard from Fish.

"You haven't had a text from Adriana?" I asked Britney.

"Na. Nothing." Britney wasn't paying much attention to me as she kept her eyes on her phone. "And there hasn't been a call from Fish. I thought I saw him out there, but it was some other old hippie."

I looked out the window and saw Jonathan in the thinning crowd, peering into the shop. He held a bag from Kat's Cafe. I signaled to him to tell his fans to stand back, and opened the door half-way to let him squeeze through. Maybe he'd be able to help us find Adriana.

He gave me a chaste sideways hug and handed me the bag.

"Oh God, Camilla, I'm sorry. I didn't have a clue that would happen. I thought the tabloid press might come to the hotel, but not your little store. What a nightmare. Are you going to be able to open for business?"

"Maybe later, but we've got a bigger problem. Our little friend Adriana is missing, and I'm terrified. Fish is out looking for her. I've been waiting until your fan club was gone to decide what to do.

The bag held two coffees and two Danish pastries. They looked a lot better than the dry English muffin I'd had for breakfast, but I wasn't particularly hungry. I put the bag on the counter.

"And who's this?" Jonathan beamed his movie star smile at Britney.

"I'm Britney, Mr. Kahn." She put on her grown-up lady smile and extended her hand to shake his. "I'm Adriana's best friend. She's been missing since after school yesterday."

Jonathan looked back at me. "A little girl is missing? Have you called the police?"

Britney sniffed. "She is not little. She's thirteen and a half. And we can't tell the police because Luisa didn't get her green card renewed because of some kind of technical difficulties and Fish is allergic to pigs."

Jonathan looked as if he were about to laugh and then got serious again. He grabbed the lattes and handed me one. I gestured to him to give a Danish to Britney.

"How long has your friend been missing?" He handed her the pastry with a wad of napkins. His tone was light. I could tell he wasn't taking this seriously enough.

Britney and I filled him in on the details as she devoured the Danish. Between bites, she added that Adrianna did say on the bus yesterday morning that she had found some more clues to some mystery she was "sleuthing." I wished she'd told me that earlier. It was amazing how Jonathan could get people to tell him things simply by looking at them with those deep blue eyes.

"What mystery are we talking about, Britney?" Jonathan's investigative reporter instincts were kicking in. That could be a good thing or a bad thing. I wasn't sure which. I also couldn't tell if Britney knew the "mystery" involved the death of Ginny Gilhooly. I had a feeling Adriana had been cagey about that.

"They're playing Sherlock and Watson — Adriana and Camilla." Britney seemed to think this was a perfectly normal thing for a forty-year-old bookstore owner and a thirteen-year-old to do with their time.

Jonathan gave me his signature raised-eyebrow skeptical look.

"Really? So, which is which? Are you Sherlock Holmes, Camilla? Tired of being the Manners Doctor?"

Britney snorted. "Of course not. She's Doctor Watson. Adriana has to be, like, the alpha. She's always been that way. Which is why she never tells me where she's going. It's like I'm not supposed to ask. But before this, she always came home for dinner. And she never has a sleepover anywhere. Her other friends are either nerds or homeless. So that's why I'm feeling so pressed. I don't even know what to tell her mom, who thinks it's all about Ruben Moreno. That's so stupid.

Ruben probably doesn't even know who Adriana is. Not Willow O'Malley either, even though Willow has his picture on the inside of her locker."

Jonathan's expression changed from smug to worried. I could see I needed to talk to him about this alone. No need to stress Britney any further.

"Britney, could you keep an eye on the store? If people try to come in, wave the "closed" sign at them. Jonathan and I have some things to discuss."

Britney gave me a silly grin. Still thinking matchmaking thoughts, apparently.

I took Jonathan back to my office and gave him a short recap. He stopped me right after I told him about Adriana haunting the library in search of the browsing history of the homeless men who hung out there.

He gave me a fierce look and grabbed my desk phone.

"We're calling the police. I don't care who killed your customer. This child is in danger."

I put my hand on his.

"Wait. We need to think this through. Remember what Britney said about Luisa's green card. That's Adriana's mother, and Britney's mom is off traveling in Africa. These kids will end up in foster care if we bring in the police."

Jonathan stared at me for a moment, his jaw clenched.

"You think foster care would be worse than whatever that man is doing to your missing thirteen-year-old?"

Loud knocking on the office door stopped us both. I let go of Jonathan's hand and opened the door.

There was Fish, looking as if he might jump out of his skin.

# thirty-five

· · ·

## Drinking Like a Fish

*I* could see Fish was having trouble catching his breath. I gave him a bottle of water and motioned for him to sit down in my office chair.

He glanced at Jonathan with skepticism. "Is it safe to talk around Mr. Armani, or whatever his name is?"

"Of course," I said. "Jonathan is as concerned about Adriana as I am."

Fish gave a snort. "Well, I found out where Barry B lives now. He's got his camper squatting in a turnoff on Highway 41. Right past the hardware store. So, I guess he's run out of money again. His turnoff isn't far from the camp people have made up there. They kicked him out because he fell off the wagon and he's been drinking like a fish. A couple of the guys said he had a girl out there last night. Kinda young Hispanic girl. Could be Adriana."

I prayed that it wasn't. "Did you get any other description of this girl?"

Fish shook his head. "Nothing solid, but we gotta check it out. I figure it might be better if I didn't go after him on my own. You don't have a gun on you, do you, Mr. Armani?"

I laughed at the idea of an anti-violence guy like Jonathan having a concealed weapon.

"I have a little Smith and Wesson Bodyguard 380 in the car if you think we need it."

A chill went through me.

"You have a gun, Jonathan? Right here on my property? Now?"

Jonathan nodded. "Teslas tend to be targets for carjackers. One of the techs at the studio got his Tesla jacked by a skinhead who jumped in at a stoplight and pushed him out of the car. Guy broke both legs. As soon as I heard, I bought a weapon."

"I hope you don't have to use it," was all I could say.

This was getting way too real. What if that man had done something horrible to Adriana? If he had, it was my fault. I'd let myself forget what a child she was. I should have put a stop to her library "sleuthing" as soon as she told me about it. I could have called Luisa. The poor woman. What a load of responsibility had been dumped on her by Britney's feckless mother.

Fish cleared his throat. "Okay, we could stand here all day debating the second amendment, or we could go save a smart little girl from a drunken lowlife. What do you say?" Fish extended his hand to Jonathan. "By the way, I'm Fish."

"I'm Jonathan Kahn."

"You some kind of movie star? Those are some crazy fans you've got."

Oh, no. I'd been so rude.

"I'm sorry, Fish. I forgot to make introductions. Jonathan's a television journalist. Jonathan, this is Morris Fishman. We call him Fish."

How could I have forgotten to properly introduce them? The gun thing discombobulated me. And the sheer terror I was feeling for poor Adriana. I turned to Jonathan. "Fish is my right hand here at the bookstore. Where are my manners?"

"We can't go in your fancy-ass car, Kahn. All those media vultures will follow us. But I got a '92 Toyota pick-up in the alley out back that runs pretty good."

Jonathan nodded at Fish, then grabbed my shoulders and looked me in the eye with his "I'm dead-serious" face.

"Camilla, I'm going to phone the police if there's the slightest hint of a crime going on here. I'll let you know if this drunk has the little girl. If we can get her without law enforcement, fine, but they may need to be involved. Maybe you should call her mother and ask what she wants to do. She's probably so insane with worry, she's not thinking about the ICE guys."

I followed the unlikely duo as they dashed down the hall and out the back door — wiry little Fish with his long braid and tie-dyed shirt leading the tall Armani-clad Jonathan.

But I was surprised to see that after he got his gun from the car, Jonathan followed Fish away from the driveway, which was the only way out.

I called to him.

"How are you going to get past the crowd? The entrance to the alley is around the corner."

Fish headed for the same bushes where Britney had emerged this morning. Buckingham meowed from behind the screen door, obviously annoyed they were violating his private hidey-hole.

"There's a couple of fence posts missing here," Fish shouted over his shoulder. "Makes a cool shortcut when I'm late for work. But you're a big guy, Kahn. It's going to be a tight squeeze."

Jonathan seemed to manage the squeezing.

As I watched them disappear, I had a realization. I felt like one of those cartoon characters with a lightbulb over my head.

A shortcut to the alley.

That had to be how Ginny Gilhooly's body disappeared that night. Probably Barry B had dragged the body into the alley. If he had a car out there, he could have loaded her in, driven out to the highway and dumped her body near the homeless camp. At three A.M. he might have escaped notice.

Except by Peter Sherwood. How could Peter have not seen somebody dragging Ginny's body across my courtyard when he was right there? It had been a dark night, but he should have been able to see from the kitchen window.

I needed to write Peter about that. I needed answers. I went to my office to compose an email. I hadn't checked my mail this morning, with all the worries about Adriana. And there was a message from Peter that had come in last night.

 Duchess — I have solved the mystery of Fanna Badjie's disappearance. She doesn't exist. That's right. She never did. Those bestsellers have been written by my old friend Neezer — the bloke I've been visiting here. Neezer was catfishing everybody at Sherwood. His full name is Ebenezer Hack. Bad name for a writer. Because he's White, and decidedly not African, he decided to send Sherwood Ltd. a picture of a village woman who agreed to pose as the author for a few quid. He used her name, too. He thought 'Fanna Badjie' had a nice exotic ring to it.

And this is where things started to go pear-shaped. It seems the actual Fanna's 'fame' went to her head, and she teamed up with a vacationing con woman from Leeds who talked her into joining up with her as a 'business partner,' and flew her back to the UK. Pradeep was ecstatic she was there to promote her latest book, so nobody noticed or cared that the two women were siphoning off all the royalty payments we'd been sending. Neezer never saw a penny.

After that, the picture gets murky. Neezer has no idea why Fanna never signed for the advance, or where she's got to. But at least the money is still in our account to pay Neezer. Finally. He's been starved for funds for nearly a year, while Fanna and her girlfriend enjoyed their ill-gotten profits in all the hotspots of Leeds."

Oh dear. One more complication in the already complex world of

Sherwood Ltd. And obviously I was not going to find out what Peter saw the night of Ginny's death any time soon.

I went back to the counter in the store feeling lightheaded and dizzy. It was all too much — worrying about the drunken Barry B and Adriana and trying to take in the complexities swirling around Peter. Part of me wanted to go back to my cottage and do some drinking myself. But I probably should phone Luisa first. And tell her…what? That my ex-husband was going to try to rescue her girl from a drunken pedophile with a gun he probably didn't even know how to shoot?

Britney appeared at my elbow.

"Breathe, Camilla," she said in an authoritative voice. "Deep breaths. In and out." She demonstrated, putting her hand on her abdomen and pushing in and out.

I followed her directions and did feel a little better.

I had to admit I probably hadn't taken a real breath in the last ten minutes. I felt like an idiot. Here was a child telling me how to take care of myself.

"There's too much crazy going on," Britney put on a grown-up face. "When there's too much crazy, my mom always says, 'Don't forget to breathe.'"

I looked down at her sweet face. How could I tell her that I might be responsible for her best friend's kidnapping — or worse?

I couldn't tell her anything. Not until I had some facts. I took another breath.

"You're totally blissed on that guy, aren't you?" Britney gave me a knowing smile. I didn't smile back. I didn't want her — or anybody — to think I was feeling that way about Jonathan. Time for a change of subject.

Food would be good. I was suddenly ravenous.

"So did anybody eat that second Danish?"

# thirty-six

. . .

## A School of Piranhas

As soon as I'd swallowed a few bites of Danish and fortified myself with coffee, I phoned Luisa. The poor woman had to be going crazy with worry. I told her that Britney was with me, and we were looking for Adriana.

I wasn't prepared for her reaction. "You find that Reuben Moreno! She's with him — swear to God. She's same like my niece down in LA. Too smart for her own good. So she goes off with a college boy who knocks her up and leaves her, and now my sister — she is stuck with the girl and her baby in a dump off Michigan Avenue. Rats, it has. Bigger than cats. This is going to happen to Adriana. I told her stay away from that boy. He is in college!"

Here Luisa went off into Spanish and lost me.

"That sounds like a terrible situation for your sister," I said finally. "I'll call you if we hear anything about Adriana."

"And Britney. She is no trouble for you?"

"No. In fact Britney is going to work for me today, if that's all right with you? My clerk has been, um, called away."

I wished I could feel as calm as Luisa sounded. I asked Britney if she thought Luisa could be right, and Adriana was off with some boy.

That in itself would be a problem. Especially if the boy really was in college.

Britney gave me a look of intense scorn. "Excuse me? Have you met Adriana Garza? Nerd on a stick? Would not know lip gloss if it bit her in the butt? Reuben Moreno was the captain of the football team at Morro Bay High and now he's a big star at Cal Poly. He's about as likely to want to hook up with Addie as Zac Efron is going to want to hook up with me."

Zac Efron. The *High School Musical* actor supposedly lived around here. I wondered if Kensie Weiner really had a friendship with him. Or a movie deal. At least she wasn't harassing Plant anymore

The crowd finally dispersed outside when they saw Jonathan wasn't going to emerge. I almost wished they hadn't gone. I'd been able to fantasize Adriana would emerge from the crowd with some plausible explanation for her disappearance.

But now the sidewalk and the store were horribly empty. So around two, Britney and I re-opened the store, and I rescued Buckingham from his exile in my cottage. I hadn't heard from Jonathan or Fish. I was getting more than a little annoyed with Jonathan. He had to know I was going batty with worry.

Britney's phone kept dinging, and every time, we'd both perk up, hoping for something from Adriana.

Buckingham, now giving himself a wash on the easy chair, looked up with every ping, as if he knew we were waiting for a call.

But Britney would make a face and put the phone back in her pocket. "Spam," she said after the third ring. "Some troll keeps texting me weird stuff. I'm sure it's Willow O'Malley. I hate that girl. I really do."

A customer looked over with a disapproving scowl.

Britney pretended not to see and gave me a shrug as she clicked off her phone.

"I'm not apologizing. Willow is horrible. I'm turning the phone off for a while, okay? If Addie was going to text me, she would have done it by now."

I was pretty sure Adriana had the store number, so she could call me if she was able to get in touch. But the longer she was missing, the worse the danger something really awful had happened. I wished I could think of something else I could do. I'd be happy to close the store and go out hunting for her. If I had any idea where to hunt.

We had a lot of new customers who seemed to have been drawn by our earlier drama. One bought an expensive coffee table book of celebrity photographs, and another bought a stack of about 20 sci-fi paperbacks. Another bought a hardcover of Fanna Badjie's most recent book, *Under the African Sky*. It was good to be busy. It took my mind off Adriana. A little.

Britney ran around being an efficient little whirlwind. I guess being busy helped with her anxiety, too.

But as the afternoon wore on, the worry about Adriana — and increasingly, about Jonathan and Fish — took up most of my consciousness. I must have seemed a little zombified to my customers.

Luckily, they were all charmed by Buckingham, who was a better host than I was today.

After a couple of hours, I had to take a powder room break, and hoped Britney would be able to maintain things on her own. My phone buzzed while I was there, and I grabbed it, even though I've always thought it was rude to speak with somebody while engaged in bathroom activities, but I so hoped it was Jonathan. Or Ronzo. But it was only a text from Peter, so I figured I'd deal with it later. I didn't need his drama on top of everything.

When I returned to the floor, I was surprised to see Britney chatting with a cluster of other middle-school girls. She flipped her hair and kept giving a phony laugh. My efficient little worker had morphed into a teenaged caricature.

The landline phone rang and I ran to answer it. Let it be Adriana.

But it was Fish. His voice sounded even raspier than usual. Almost a whisper.

"I'm lying low. I don't know when it'll be safe to go back to the store."

Safe? That was ominous in this context. Was he that afraid of the police, or was something else going on?

"Where are you, Fish? Is she with you? Did you find her?"

"Nope. Our girl isn't with Barry B. His camper is clean. But he could have hidden her somewhere, so I'm going to have a look around the camp up there."

"Is Jonathan going with you? Can you put him on?"

"That would be a negative. Your Mr. Armani might be in the hoosegow. Dammed Barry B called the cops on us because of Kahn's gun. I split, but Mr. Armani didn't seem to mind a run-in with the law. He's probably got good lawyers, right? You haven't heard anything about Adriana on your end?"

I told him I hadn't, but my voice came out almost as raspy as his as I choked back my anxiety. How could they arrest Jonathan? That made no sense. Fish's deadpan delivery didn't help..

"There's nothing we can do? That poor girl is probably in terrible danger."

"I've got a few friends who sometimes hang with Barry B. Usually too wasted to make much sense, but it's early in the day. Gonna check out their campsite. They might know something."

I took a breath. There was no point in being angry with Fish.

"I will hope for your friends' relative sobriety." I tried to mimic his flat tone.

Fish seemed to be my only hope at this point. But I wasn't sure I could trust him. I wondered if I should call the police station to find out if Jonathan was actually in custody. Fish was right that Jonathan had good lawyers, but he could be spending some uncomfortable hours.

But I could hardly hear myself think. Britney's middle school friends were not using their indoor voices. Very inappropriate behavior for a bookstore.

"Are any of you here to buy a book today?" I set down the phone and gave them a stern look.

A tall one with spikey hair dyed a bizarre shade of orange gave me a defiant grin.

"No. We're here to see Jonathan Kahn. We heard that Jonathan Kahn was here. From the TV show?"

"But nobody's here but Basic Britney!" Another girl piped up in a whiney voice.

Orange spikey hair walked up to the counter and pushed her face way too close to mine.

"You let a thirteen-year-old girl run your store? Ever heard of child labor laws, lady?"

"And you must be an idiot to hire Basic Britney!"

"Basic Britney! Basic Britney!" The whole group joined in the nasty chant.

"Basic" seemed to be a dreadful insult to these children. Britney was doing her best to keep a professional demeanor, but I could see tears welling as her lower lip trembled.

Dear Lord. The scene reminded me of my first week at boarding school. Hell on earth. Thirteen-year-old girls can be the cruelest people on the planet. Especially when in groups. This gaggle of mean girls had to be the notorious Willow O'Malley and her squad.

Hard to believe these were school children. A school of piranhas, maybe.

I grabbed the nearest hardcover book and slammed it on the counter. Buckingham jumped off the chair and ran to the relative safety of the remainder table.

But the noise seemed to get the girls' attention.

"Leave, children. Now. Or I will call the police. You are creating a public nuisance. Not to mention embarrassing yourselves."

"Public nuisance" was the first thing that came to mind. Thanks, Officer Dwayne Pilchard.

Three or four of the customers who had been browsing came over and stood by me for solidarity. At least I think it was solidarity. Maybe they were checking to see if I was a child abuser.

As the mean girls started to leave, the orange-haired Ms. O'Malley spoke to Britney over her shoulder. "Too bad your friend Adriana is such a dweeb. She found out what happens to dirty Mexicans who steal."

What happens? Did this child know something about who took

Adriana? I felt like jumping from behind the counter and strangling her. Instead, I tried a dignified posture.

"What do you know, Willow?" I stood right by the phone, so I could call the police if she had any news. "What happened to Adriana Garza?"

"Sorry, lady. I don't have a clue." Willow flounced out the door with her entourage following behind her like obedient little ducks.

"She's not Mexican," Britney shouted at their backs as her tears started to flow. "She's Salvadoran, you morons."

"She's toast now," the last duck in the line called over her shoulder. "And you'll never find her."

An icy chill went down my spine.

"Wait, girls. Wait! What do you know about Adriana?"

But I got nothing but giggles as the little sociopaths ran out onto the street.

# thirty-seven

. . .

## Jail Bait

*A*fter the mean girls sashayed out of the store, Britney burst into noisy sobs. "I'm sorry," she said. "I'm so embarrassed. I... I hate them!" She ran toward bathroom.

Poor Britney. I wanted to comfort her, but I also wanted to run out in the street and get those awful girls to tell me what they knew about Adriana. Had they watched her abduction and jeered? I could see they were still loitering on the corner down from the store.

I had no customers at the moment. The nasty scene had probably driven them away. I flipped the "Closed" sign, shut the door and ran out to the sidewalk.

"Girls! What do you know about Adriana? Where is she?"

One of the squad turned to make a rude sign with her middle finger. They all laughed. So did the few looky-loos who had been milling around the sidewalk in front of the store. I wondered if any of them were reporters. All I needed was for the scene to make it onto *Entertainment Tonight*.

Willow led her nasty entourage across the street to the bus stop. I knew I'd never get an answer out of them. Maybe they were making things up to be cruel. Cruelty seemed to be their main reason for being.

When I was in boarding school, I'd seen girls persecuted the way they were doing to Britney. Old feelings of rage and helplessness made my eyes sting as I made my way back to the store. I felt somebody coming up behind me. Probably a reporter. I so much didn't want to talk to the press right now.

"Are you closed? Please don't close, ma'am." A remarkably handsome young man tapped me on the shoulder. He didn't look like a reporter.

"Please open the store, ma'am. I need to talk to you."

He looked truly distressed, so I let him in, although I didn't want to put off talking to the police just because some kid needed a copy of a textbook he'd failed to buy before finals.

A couple of customers came in behind him and disappeared behind the shelves.

"Do you remember me?" The young man walked up to the counter. "I bought some of my psych textbooks here last fall."

I had to admit I didn't. Maybe Plant had waited on him. I thought I would have remembered such a good-looking young man. Buckingham emerged from his hiding place under the remainder table and rubbed the young man's leg. Obviously, he liked the man's looks too.

"When I was here, there was an older lady named Mrs. Gilhooly. She talked my ear off about the importance of an education for Latinos like me."

Oh, how awful. I could picture Ginny, thinking she was being helpful, blabbering away at this boy with unconscious racism. I tried to be diplomatic.

"Yes. Ginny Gilhooly spent a lot of time here. It's so sad she passed away."

The young man looked at me as if I were slightly senile. "She's not dead, ma'am. She's sending me text messages. I don't know why, but she seems to be in major trouble. The only time I met her was here in your store. She asked for my phone number so she could text me about some book she thought I should read. I don't remember getting the text, but she's in my phone. I thought maybe you could get in touch with her, since she doesn't pay attention to my texts. She seems hella stressed."

One of the new customers emerged from the romance section with the new Nora Roberts and gave the young man a superior look.

"A little bit more than stressed, hon." The woman gave a harsh laugh. "Ginny Gilhooly was murdered back in March by some homeless man. Don't you ever see the news?" She gave an unfunny smile and made a "woo-woo" sound. "Maybe you're getting messages from the Great Beyond."

As I rang up her book, the young man's face reddened.

"What are you saying? Mrs. Gilhooly was murdered? I don't follow the news. Too busy studying. I gotta get my grades up to keep my football scholarship. That's why I can't handle these crazy texts."

He turned to my customer. "You really think these messages could be coming from a ghost?"

Football. Some puzzle pieces fell into place in my head as I became aware of Britney sliding silently behind the counter with me. She looked up at the young man with a mix of adoration and adolescent angst.

"Hi Ruben," she said in a babyish whisper. "Do you remember me? I'm Britney. We met at the middle school when you gave your talk about stick-to-it-iveness."

"Hello, Britney." I could tell he didn't remember her, but he gave her a nice smile. "It was awesome to meet all of you!"

So this was Ruben Moreno. No wonder Luisa thought a young girl might run off with him. When I was a young girl, I might have run off with him myself. He was beautiful. But was he also some kind of psychic? Very odd to think that Ginny Gilhooly might contact him from beyond the grave. Not that I really believed that kind of thing.

The customer obviously didn't either. She left the store shaking her head as if she thought we were all lunatics.

Britney's phone started dinging frantically. "I guess I should take this," she said to Ruben in that same baby voice. "I had my phone off because somebody keeps sending me bogus texts. I think it's Willow O'Malley."

"Willow O'Malley? That little bi — um, witch who's trying to catfish me?" Ruben made a face. "If you know her, tell the kid to lay off. My coach says she's jail bait, trying to get me in trouble. And I remember her from my presentation at the Middle School. She doesn't have a shape like that porn star she stole her profile picture from."

"Yeah. Willow's like, totally flat-chested." Britney grinned happily, but her phone dinged again. "I guess I should..." she studied her phone and gave a little yelp. "You know, these stupid texts say they're from Mrs. Gilhooly too. So that's what's going on with you too, Ruben? I think we're both being trolled by Willow O'Malley. She stole the old lady's phone from Adriana. It must still have minutes on it from before the lady died."

"Willow stole a phone from a dead person?" Reuben looked at me. "That kid is more psycho than I thought."

"Actually, she stole it from a classmate — " I tried to explain.

But Britney interrupted with another yelp and Buckingham ran back to his hiding place. "No! Oh, God. It's not Willow. It's Adriana texting from Mrs. Gilhooly's phone. She says she's locked in a shack. The spider shack!"

Good Lord. I had trouble catching my breath. Adriana was a prisoner. And she'd been trying to contact us.

"That means something to you? The spider shack?" Reuben pulled his phone from his pocket. "That's what Ginny Gilhooly is talking about in these texts."

Britney gave Ruben a frustrated look. "It's not Mrs. Gilhooly. It's Adriana, my friend who's missing. It's a shack down behind the school. It's so scary, kids pee their pants if they go in there."

Had Adriana been locked in a shack all this time while we callously went about our business? I felt awful. Had Barry B stashed her there?

"Britney, do you know where this place is? This shack?" I was going to have to shut the store again and go look for her. I wished Fish were around. Or Jonathan. Yes. I needed Jonathan. And his gun, God help me. But apparently he was in jail. Could Fish possibly have been right about that?

Now Britney was literally jumping up and down while she looked at her phone. "Yes! We gotta get there. She's been sending these texts for hours. And I ignored them because I thought it was that disgusting Willow."

The poor child. We had to go find her. Now.

But three middle-aged women banged open the door and marched up to the counter. "You are a Badass," said a tall one with one of those fashion-victim haircuts, shaved on one side.

"What did you say to her?" Ruben sprang to my defense.

"I'm afraid we're closing," I said. "Family emergency."

"We'll only be a minute," a darker one said. "Do you have it or what?"

I took a breath and told the woman we did indeed have *You Are a Badass* by Jen Sincero. I led them to the self-help section, moving way too fast. I felt like screaming when I heard another customer come in, but the amazing Britney greeted her brightly.

"We're closing now, ma'am, but we'd love to see you tomorrow…"

"I have no intention of doing business with a child," the customer said. "I want to speak to Plantagenet Smith. Now."

Oh my. I'd know that voice anywhere. Sidling up to Ruben Moreno, in all her hot pink glory was Kensie Weiner.

I tried to ignore her as I rang up the book for the three women. I could sense Ruben's discomfort as Kensie whispered something to him and flipped her hair to better show off her cleavage.

Britney grabbed Ruben as he tried to make his escape. Britney spoke to him intensely, but I couldn't hear her over Kensie's blathering about how much she hated Plantagenet.

"Plant doesn't work here anymore, Kensie." I tried to keep my voice pleasant. "He's down in Los Angeles working on a Netflix series."

Kensie's gaze followed Ruben's well-toned derriere as he and Britney moved toward the door.

"So you've got children working in your store now?" she said. "Is that even legal?"

"Actually, Ruben isn't a child." I couldn't help delivering a little snark, since I knew she was talking about Britney. "He's a student at Cal Poly. But definitely too young for us." Kensie turned and looked at me, her eyes flashing anger. I gave her a big smile. "I'm so sorry we're closing up early. Family emergency. Do come back another time. I'd love to hear all about your movie."

Britney waved goodbye to Ruben and jumped from one impatient foot to the other.

"We gotta go," she said in a semi-whisper.

But Kensie wasn't going to budge. "As if you didn't know what happened to my movie deal! Your friend Plant destroyed it. But he's going to have to get me another one. Where is he?"

"I honestly don't know Plant's LA address." I waved her away as I took the cash drawer out of the register. "We're going to have to close up, and I need to put this in the safe."

Kensie's face hardened as she reached into her purse for something.

A gun. A pink and black Beretta Nano. Like the one Count Juan Carlos gave my mother for their first anniversary.

Unfortunately, Kensie was aiming hers right at me.

# thirty-eight

. . .

## The Sand Bar

*I* tried to keep my face bland as I stared at Kensie Weiner's pink Beretta. I didn't believe she intended to kill me, but the silly woman could easily trigger the gun by mistake.

"You probably told Plantagenet to wreck my career on purpose." Kensie's voice got shrill. "He's probably real tight with Zac Ephron. You've always been jealous of me. And you know where Plant is. Tell me. Now."

I tried for a nonchalant laugh. "The last I heard he was staying with a friend in West Hollywood."

"But he's only visiting down there while he works on his Netflix thing. He has a 'husband' here, so he must come up a lot." She made some snarky air quotes when she said the word husband. "But he's not at his house. I've already been there. I'm sure you know where he is."

"Not a clue." I kept the smile on my face, but my eyes stayed on the gun. I hoped poor Silas hadn't been confronted with it. Kensie had harassed him in the past.

"Well, where's Jonathan Kahn? I know he was here this morning. I saw it on TV." Kensie gave a petulant pout.

I took a breath. "Jonathan is in jail. For a gun violation, as a matter of fact. Maybe you'd like to go point that little thing at the Morro Bay police so you can join Jonathan in his cell. The police station is just around the corner."

I knew immediately I shouldn't have said it. Kensie looked positively homicidal. She had the Beretta in a white-knuckle grip.

But little Britney, apparently oblivious to the danger, came running up to the counter and held up her phone.

"We gotta go! I haven't had a text from 'Ginny Gilhooly' for over an hour. Last one I read, Adriana was eating a sand bar. And dreaming about fish tacos. She's starving."

Good Lord. Eating sand? We had to rescue that child immediately, Kensie or no Kensie.

Britney let out a squeal. She seemed to have noticed Kensie's gun for the first time. But instead of showing fear, she gave Kensie a big smile.

"That is so cute! I've never seen a pink gun! I want one. That would totally shut up Willow O'Malley! I dare her to call that gun basic. Do you want to help us rescue my friend? We could use somebody who's armed. We have to go right now. She's almost out of water, too."

Kensie stared at Britney as if she were some species of talking dog or a maybe a space alien. But she lowered the gun.

"I'm Britney." She offered Kensie her hand as if she were at a tea party. "I've seen you in here before, but I don't remember your name. I help out in the store sometimes."

I couldn't have been prouder of her. She had disarmed a crazed gun-person with nothing but impeccable manners.

Kensie sniffed and put the gun back in her purse.

I picked up the cash register drawer. "I'm going to put this in the safe and then we're on our way. Britney, you know where this spider shack is?"

"Down by the creek behind the school. I've only been there once and it was hella scary. But I think I can find it."

Unfortunately, we might also find Brownie / Barry B, if he was responsible for holding Adriana captive in that shack. In which case, Kensie and her pink gun might actually be helpful.

"Does Adriana say whether it was Barry B who locked her in the shack? Or did she mention anything about somebody named Brownie?"

Britney jumped from one foot to the other. "She didn't say anything about Brownies or Girl Scouts or anybody. Except Willow O'Malley, who she hates even more than I do. Most of the texts I got before said that she's hungry and needs to be rescued. And she wants fish tacos. But she hasn't sent anything for over an hour. Maybe the phone went dead. We have to go!"

Poor Adriana. Dehydrated, eating sand, crawling with spiders, and God knew what else.

"Let's go out the back to avoid those people." Loiterers still lurked on the sidewalk out front. "They might be reporters."

"You're going to close your store in the middle of the afternoon? What about your customers?" Kensie didn't appear to be willing to move.

"They're all gone. Here. I'll make a sign!" Britney grabbed a piece of paper from under the counter and wrote with a pink sharpie, "Closed Do 2 Family Emerginsee."

I didn't even have time to laugh at the hilarious spelling. I grabbed the keys and a piece of tape. I stuck the sign to the window and locked the front door.

"How do I know you're not sneaking off to warn Plantagenet?" Kensie reached a threatening hand into her purse. "How do I know you're not making this stuff up?"

I decided to ignore her. She was too ridiculous.

"So which way do we go to the shack, Britney? Is it nearby?"

"It's down by the creek behind my school." Britney shouted over her shoulder as she ran to the back door. "You can park in the school parking lot. Hurry up, you two. And bring that gun."

Kensie followed us into the driveway where my Honda was parked. Was she really going to join us? Normally, getting into a car with Kensie Weiner would be at the top of my list of Things Not to Do. But right now, I figured an extra person might be a help. Especially if that person had a gun. I had no idea what we'd encounter 'down by the creek,' but if it was Ginny's murderer, a weapon would certainly come in handy.

"So, are you going to come?" I turned to Kensie when we got to my car.

"Not if you won't open this car door." Kensie was always in character.

I unlocked the back door and let her in while I asked Britney to sit up front with me so she could navigate.

The school parking lot was pretty empty, since it was Saturday. A few cars were scattered in the spots closest to the classrooms, sporting bumper stickers like "Discover Wildlife, be a Teacher." But no camper van. Or any car that looked as if it might belong to a homeless man known as the town drunk.

I parked, locked the car, and followed Britney down a steep incline toward a stand of willows by a dry creek bed. Kensie seemed to keep up better than I did. In spite of her stiletto heels.

"There it is!" Britney ran toward a ramshackle shed that looked as if it might have held maintenance equipment before it started to biodegrade. She called toward the shack, "Adriana! We're here! Hang in there!"

We followed as fast as we could. As we approached, I could see a padlock hanging on a big rusty hasp on the door. How were we going to get that thing off? I'd been an idiot not to bring some tools.

"Come on, gun lady," Britney called "You can shoot the lock off this door."

Britney pulled at the door and we were astonished to see it open easily as the padlock fell to the ground. I wondered if little Britney had somehow managed to break it, but then I saw the loop of the lock had been cut right through.

That was more than a little odd.

"Addie! Adriana! Come on out!" Britney now had the door wide open, but Adriana did not emerge.

Kensie tottered down and peered inside.

"There's nobody in there, ladies." Her voice dripped scorn. "You got the wrong shack, morons."

"Are you sure?" I followed, slipping a bit on the ice plant that covered the hill. "Maybe she's passed out. Dehydration can do that."

"Fine. You go in there and hang out with the spiders." Kensie was already making her way back up the hill.

I stepped inside. There were indeed a number of spiders on the ceiling. On the walls, too. Way too many for my comfort zone. Poor Adriana. Had she really spent the night in here? And who got her out? Barry B wouldn't need to cut the lock. One could presume he had the key.

Britney seemed less intimidated by the spiders than I was. But it was obvious her quest was futile. She rummaged around in the rusty buckets and discarded paint cans as if she might find a magically shrunken Adriana behind them.

"Kensie is right, Britney. Adriana's not here. Are you sure this is the right shack? Maybe there's another one around here."

But Britney gave out one of her squeals. "Look!" she said. "Look! I found a sand bar wrapper! See? It's from a Probiotic Chia Seed bar. Nobody buys these but my mom. They're like eating sand. Adriana will eat them, but I don't know anybody else who does. She had to be here. Look!"

She handed me the brown and silver wrapper. It did look as if it had been discarded recently.

"That proves she was here, doesn't it? Nobody else eats sand bars."

Britney sounded triumphant, but I felt nothing but increased anxiety. What had happened to the poor girl? If Brownie / Barry B had kept her trapped here all night and then he'd come to get her, what was he doing to her now?

"Do you think somebody took her?" Britney's tone changed as she picked up on my anxiety. "Is she getting murdered or something?" Her lip trembled.

"We'll find her," I said. "Or the police will. I'm going to call them as soon as we're back at the store. If we call from a cell phone it goes to the Highway Patrol instead of police dispatch, and we'll have to wait here forever."

Britney made a sour face, but she nodded in agreement.

Back at the car, Kensie had apparently been building up a head of angry steam while she scrolled through her phone.

"It's about time, you two. I told you there was nothing to see down there. I have to get back to your store. I saw on the TMZ website that Jonathan Kahn didn't get arrested. The guy who called the cops on him did. He's some homeless guy who was camping illegally. I'll bet Jonathan is heading back to your place. I'm going to give that creep a piece of my mind."

A piece of her mind seemed considerably less dangerous than whatever Kensie had intended to do to Plantagenet with that pink gun, but I didn't look forward to a confrontation. And had Barry B really been arrested? Fish did say he'd been camping on the side of the road.

But if Barry B was in jail, who had Adriana now?

# thirty-nine

. . .

## Other Fish in the Sea

The store looked deserted when we pulled into the driveway. The looky-loos from this morning were gone and there were no eager customers waiting for us outside. Certainly not Jonathan. I did hope he was all right. He'd probably had an unpleasant time at the police station, even if he hadn't been actually arrested.

I wondered how much he'd told the police about our missing Adriana. I needed to phone him as soon as I could get some privacy.

I opened the front door and took down Britney's "Emerginsee" sign while Buckingham snaked around my leg and yawned. He probably hadn't even been aware we were gone. Everything seemed perfectly fine except of course that Ronzo hadn't returned my call, Adriana was still missing, and I felt like punching something. Preferably Kensie Weiner.

"Jonathan Kahn isn't here," Kensie spoke in a tone that implied this was somehow my fault. "You and your little friend are a total waste of time. I'll bet that kid wasn't even in any shack. The two girls were probably yanking your chain."

Britney and I watched her mince back to her own car, parked across the street in front of Kat's Café.

"Buh-bye." Britney put on a large fake smile as she watched Kensie out the window. "We won't miss you." She plunked herself in the reading chair and busied herself with her phone.

I laughed and retreated to my desk to check my landline voice mail. I so hoped for a message from Jonathan. Or Fish. Even Ronzo. Somebody who had some good news. Any kind of news.

But two customers came marching in, clad head to toe in shiny new L.L. Bean fishing gear, complete with matching multi-pocket vests and bucket fisherman hats. They wanted the travel section. Britney sweetly walked them there, but she gave me a funny look over her shoulder and pointed at her phone.

As soon as they were safely planted amongst the fishing and sailing books, Britney came rushing back to the counter and squealed. She held out the phone to me.

"I got another text! She's not murdered. But Mrs. Gilhooly's phone is dying, and Adriana's talking about fish tacos. And Ruben Moreno. Plus, she has a message for you. Kinda. Sounds bananas."

I read the text on her phone, "Phone dying. Trying 1 more. Ruben Moreno (heart emoji) fish tacos. Tell Camilla Brownie is…"

I started to ask Britney if she had a clue what it meant, but the fishermen marched up to the counter demanding a guidebook I knew was out of print. But they insisted it wasn't. Not what I needed — annoying customers who weren't going to buy anything.

Britney's phone dinged again and she rushed to grab it. I tried to read over her shoulder while the cranky amateur fishermen called me an incompetent moron. The fact my attention was elsewhere made him even angrier.

I had no idea what to do. What did Adriana mean by, "Brownie is…" Was she with him? Was he "grooming" her by taking her out for fish tacos? What was up with Ruben Moreno? I really had to call Jonathan and find out what the police knew.

"*Going Coastal SLO.* Are you going to get it for us, or do we have to go to Barnes and Noble?" The taller fisherman shouted through his scraggly beard, as if his words had trouble fighting their way out.

"There's a lovely Barnes and Noble in San Luis Obispo," I told them.

Then three more fisherpersons stomped in. A man and two women. All wearing brand new L.L. Bean gear.

Oh, joy.

"Do they have it?" A woman in the second group wanted to know. "This place is a dump. They probably don't. Look. Half their books are used."

I gave them all my Manners Doctor smile. "No, we don't have that title. But Amazon is excellent for finding out-of-print books. You might also find it on E-Bay."

"It's not out of print!" Scraggly beard was not going to let this go. He turned to one of the women. "This bimbo is a total moron."

"Ask to see the manager," the other woman said. "A bimbo like her can't be running the place."

It had been a while since anybody called me a bimbo. I suppose I should try to take it as a compliment. And now more customers were streaming in. The late afternoon crowd, looking for books to read in the evening.

I looked over at Britney for help, but she was texting fiercely. I wondered why. Unfortunately, if Ginny's phone was losing power — or had simply run out of data — Adriana wasn't going to get the text. I felt rising panic, then took a deep breath. I had to call Jonathan — and then the police. I knew it was rude, but I turned my back on the customers and punched his number.

The sound of his voice gave me a little relief.

"Oh, Jonathan, are you all right? Do you know anything about Adriana? We found out she'd been locked in a spider-infested shack near the middle school, but she's gone, and we don't know if Brownie has her. That awful Kensie and Britney and I went to...where are you, anyway?"

"Right here." Jonathan himself stepped from behind the squabbling fisherpersons. He gave me that grin that shows his dimples.

"And I'm here, too. That awful Kensie." Yes, there she was. For some reason with her arm hooked in Jonathan's.

Jonathan disentangled himself from the arm and rushed to give me a hug. "I'm sorry if you were worried, Camilla. There was a mix-up at the Morro Bay PD. But everything's all right now. Well, sort of. I have some troubling information…"

He gave the fisherpersons a get-lost look I knew well. It used to chill me right down to my toes. I was glad to see it still worked as they scurried out of the store, whispering to each other about entitled celebrities.

Unfortunately, most of the other customers filed out too. They must have thought I was closing because of the fisherperson exodus. Fine. A few lost sales was nothing compared with the anxiety I was feeling about our missing girl. I looked at Jonathan.

"You've got information from the Morro Bay police? About Adriana?"

"Sounds juicy." Kensie slithered up to Jonathan and grabbed his arm again as if she owned him. "And you promised me a selfie. Remember?" She pulled her phone from her purse. "Smile!" She made a pouty fish face as she looked adoringly up at her phone.

"This is important, Kensie. I need to talk to Camilla in private."

"Yeah. They're, like, engaged." Britney could be counted on to stand up for me, even if she was misguided about the reasons. I could tell Jonathan didn't have anything romantic on his mind. He looked seriously worried as he steered me toward my office.

"I'll keep an eye on the store," Britney called to me. "Kensie, Mr. Kahn is Camilla's boyfriend, so they need to be alone to kiss and stuff. Don't you have somewhere to be?"

"Of course I do. I have a meeting with my movie people. I only wanted Jonathan's photo for my website. Personally, I don't find him that attractive — all that white hair. Besides, there are other fish in the sea. What was the name of that dishy guy who was in here earlier? Ruben something?"

"Ruben Moreno is, like, nineteen years old, Kensie." Britney seemed to have a little mean girl in her after all.

I could hear Kensie's stiletto heels making furious clicks out the door. Good. There were no customers left. Britney should be all right on her own.

I peeked down the hall. I could see the girl at the counter, texting somebody again. I hoped she understood Adriana would not be able to read any texts.

Unfortunately, Adriana seemed to be lost to us again.

# forty

· · ·

## A Suspicious Fish

*J*onathan closed the door of my office. I didn't like the look on his face.

"What's this information from the police?" I leaned against my desk, trying to brace myself for bad news. "Is it Adriana? Does Barry B have her?

Jonathan shook his head. "Barry Brown seems to be a harmless drunk. He's in custody now and I hope somebody will try to get him into rehab, but he doesn't have your girl. And I'm not sure he has the brain cells to pull a romance scam."

That was odd news.

"So who does have her? We went to the shack where she'd been locked up and she was gone. Adriana had been sending texts to Britney with Ginny Gilhooly's phone, but Britney thought the texts came from some mean girls who had been bullying her. Then it turned out Ruben Moreno was getting the texts too. So, he came here looking for Ginny and I had to tell him she's dead. But we finally figured out Adriana had Ginny's phone."

Oh, dear. Maybe that hadn't made much sense.

"Britney mentioned that name. Who is Ruben Moreno?"

This was going to take a while. I hoped Britney would be all right on her own in the store. I cracked the door open and heard a male customer talking to her in there. I hoped it wasn't another angry amateur fisherperson.

I went back to perch on the desk and motioned for Jonathan to sit in the desk chair as I explained that Ruben was a college football star and all the middle school girls seemed to have a crush on him. And apparently, Ginny Gilhooly had developed a crush too, since she had his number in her phone. And that's why Adriana had been able to text him as well as Britney. Lucky, since Britney thought the texts came from the mean girls. Ruben thought they came from Ginny and they disturbed him enough he came to me.

"You said you went to the shack? Did this Moreno guy go with you?"

"No. He left as soon as he found out why Ginny Gilhooly's ghost was texting him. He had to study for some exam. Your friend Kensie went with us, though. Not that she was terribly helpful, but she had a little pink gun we thought might come in handy."

I could hear Britney chattering away with the male customer. Something about Buckingham. She sounded a bit intense. I hoped she didn't need to be rescued.

Unfortunately, Jonathan kept asking questions instead of telling me what was on his mind. He sat in my chair and leaned back.

"Why were you so sure it was Barry Brown who killed Mrs. Gilhooly? Didn't your sleuthing come up with any other suspects?"

"Barry B seemed to be the catfish — that is, her fake 'Texas oilman' boyfriend who had been conning her for months. The night she died, she'd just found him out. That makes him by far the most likely suspect to me. The police suspect Joe, of course, but I know he didn't do it."

"You know? How?" Jonathan sat up straight and looked me in the eye. "Because he's your friend?"

I did not need one of Jonathan's TV-interviewer interrogations. And I really needed to get back to the store. It was time for him to get to his big revelation. He did love to stretch things out for dramatic effect.

"I know Joe didn't like Ginny. None of the homeless people did. But people don't commit murder because they dislike someone. If they did, there would be five dead amateur fisherpersons out in my store right now."

Jonathan ignored me as he seemed lost in thought.

I could hear Britney still talking with the customer. They sounded more relaxed now and seemed to be talking about tacos.

"And you're sure this catfish has Adriana?" Jonathan was in full interviewer mode.

"Of course not. I don't know anything for sure. Except that Adriana said the catfish lives in Morro Bay and used the library computer. Today, she texted Britney and Ruben to say she was locked in that shack, and we could tell she'd actually been there, because she left a granola bar wrapper, but — somebody had taken her. The lock was broken and she was gone. We thought Barry B had taken her."

"But obviously he didn't. He's totally innocent in all this." Jonathan gave me one of his fierce looks. "But I'm afraid I know who kidnapped her. The police are on the lookout for him now, and I'm expecting a call from an Officer Pilchard soon."

I didn't need for Jonathan to draw out the suspense any longer. This wasn't his TV show.

"And who is it...?"

"It's Fish, Camilla. Your friend Morris Fishman is a convicted sex offender. A pedophile. He could be your catfish, too. And Gilhooly's murderer. He's served prison time." Jonathan's voice was cold. Professional. "It makes sense to me that Ginny might have found out about his record, so he eliminated her."

I felt a chill as I remembered Marva's reaction when I first mentioned Fish lived at the camp where they found Ginny's body.

"That can't be true. I didn't even hire Fish until months after her death." I did not want to believe a word he was saying. Maybe that pedophile stuff was about a different Morris Fishman.

I could be fierce too. I looked Jonathan in the eye.

"You're wrong. Fish is an odd duck, and he's terrified of law enforcement, but there's no way he's a murderer. And no way was he

Ginny's catfish. Those "Brownie" emails were practically illiterate. Fish is an educated man. And he's a good person, Jonathan. Quiet and well-mannered. I can't believe he'd hurt children."

"That's the thing about pedophiles. They're always quiet and well-mannered. That's why nobody suspects them."

Now it was Jonathan I wanted to punch.

# forty-one

. . .

## A Wayward African Fish Eagle

onathan was wrong about Fish. He had to be wrong. But I didn't want to keep arguing with him.

"I'm going out in the shop to see if Britney's doing all right."

Jonathan gave me a small nod as he pulled his phone out of his pocket. He didn't seem to understand how much his news about Fish had upset me.

The chatty male customer was gone, and Britney didn't look all that stressed. In fact, she gave me a big smile, looking more relaxed than she had in days.

"You just missed him," she said. "Some guy who came here right from the airport. He says he's your friend. He's gone to the Taco Temple, but I think he's coming back."

"My friend? Someone who arrived in a plane? Did he say where he flew from?" All I needed was one more mystery. Had Peter returned? I really didn't want to deal with him right now. Especially since Jonathan obviously disliked him.

"No, but I could tell he'd been here before. Buckingham seemed to know him, and really liked him."

That didn't mean much. Buckingham liked pretty much all males.

"He didn't tell you his name? Was it Peter?"

Britney shook her head. Of course, who knew what Peter might be calling himself now.

"Did you tell this person I was in the office? Why didn't he wait?"

"I told him you were in an important meeting about my missing friend and couldn't be disturbed. I didn't think I should tell him you were back there with Mr. Kahn, since I didn't know if you were being romantic or what. Did I do okay?"

The poor girl. I gave her a reassuring shoulder pat.

"You were fine. But don't worry. Jonathan and I aren't going to be doing anything embarrassing in my office, I promise. That would be very bad manners."

She gave me a lopsided grin.

"Well, actually, it kind of backfired. I shouldn't have talked about Adriana because then he wanted to know all about my missing friend. When I told him about Adriana being locked in the spider shack all night and sending me those texts, he got real worried. I showed him her texts and he kind of went bananas. He suddenly asked where to get the best fish tacos in town. I told him Taco Temple and he ran out of here like the place was on fire. But I'm sure when he comes back, he'll explain everything."

"What did he look like?"

"Nice looking. Casual clothes. Super polite. He had a funny accent."

It had to be Peter. His northern English accent was strange to most Americans. Especially if he was still trying to sound Canadian.

"Super polite? Maybe it's somebody looking for Plantagenet Smith," Jonathan walked in, his tone dismissive. "Didn't Plant work here before he got his big break with Netflix?" His gave a smug smile. He knew Plant owed his new job to the #MenToo interview. "You know, tacos sound really good. I'm starving. Is anybody hungry?"

Food. He was going to go eat after dropping that bombshell about Fish.

"They have pretty good tacos at Kat's across the street." I gave him a big smile I hoped didn't look too fake. It would be better if he didn't meet Peter. anyway. Or whoever my visitor was. Could I re-marry a man who would ask about a missing child, call my friend a pedophile and then run off to eat tacos?

Jonathan asked if we wanted anything, but I couldn't imagine eating at a time like this. What if Fish was the catfish — and the murderer — and Adriana had figured it out. Then she'd be in terrible danger.

Britney said she wasn't hungry either. She seemed relieved to see Jonathan rush off to the restaurant across the street.

I guess I was too. I had too much information to process. The dreadful news about Fish, and — what if Peter really was here? He had sent me a couple of texts and a long email I hadn't had time to read. I needed to go look at them now.

"Britney, can you hang on here a little longer? I need to go back to my office. I might have a message from your mysterious stranger."

Britney gave me a bouncy smile. How could she suddenly be in such a good mood with her best friend still missing?

Peter's texts hadn't suggested he was planning to leave Africa. But things had sounded pretty dire for him there. I fished his email out of my inbox where it was buried in mountains of spam that offered to give me billions of dollars and cast magic spells to enlarge my penis. Sometimes Peter seemed as shady as they were, but he was my publisher, so I had to be pleasant. Especially if he had flown all the way from Africa to see me.

Hallo Duchess!" the email began.

"I'm still alive. Barely. It's been one adventure after another on the river. We met a couple of very large crocodiles and a terrifying mother hippopotamus trying to protect her child from our evil riverboat. But the worst hazard was a wayward African Fish Eagle who kept trying to take our supplies. These things have a wingspan of nearly two meters. But we survived.

So far, no joy in locating Fanna, but I'm finally at my mate Neezer's village school. I'm using his laptop here.

He's not been particularly helpful. Whenever I mention Fanna, he clams up as if I'd asked a rudely personal question. Otherwise, he's quite hospitable.

The school is fairly make-shift, and but it's got a new roof. Apparently the previous roof blew off during a storm last September, so they raised funds for months to replace it. But then someone broke into Neezer's hut and stole all the roof money. So, he had to go a-fundraising all over again. He says he has a colleague in Banjul who's a bit shady, but raised the donations they needed."

This was all sounding weirdly familiar. Didn't Adriana say Shannon's catfish asked for money for a school roof?

The email went on.

> Neezer does indeed live in a hut. With a dirt floor. A far cry from his digs at Oxford. But he seems to be thriving. And so is his pet goat, which sleeps in his bed like a lapdog. He says his last goat died in childbirth, which was a great tragedy for his little pupils. He seems devoted to the youngsters."

A pet goat. Shannon's catfish had complained about a goat. This was sounding spooky.

> Neezer has a guest hut where I'm staying. Formerly inhabited by the fundraising colleague who has recently left for the UK. The colleague had a lady friend who contributed some civilized touches, including small bottles of shampoo and lotion from some tourist hotel. Neezer is being kind.
>
> Which is why I'm especially dismayed at his lack of forthrightness about Fanna Badjie. It's obvious he

knows something about her and her whereabouts, but he refuses to say a thing.

I hope Joe is still safely wearing dresses and hiding out at Marva's abode. Let me know if you hear anything more about the mysterious disappearing corpse."

So. The disappearing corpse was a mystery to Peter, too? That was disappointing. I'd clung to a small hope he'd know something that would exonerate Joe. And now Fish, too. I so much didn't want Fish to be a monster.

But there was nothing in the email that suggested Peter had been thinking of flying to America. Of course, you could never know, with Peter. Maybe he'd decided to hitch a ride with the wayward African fish eagle.

# forty-two

• • •

Fish Tacos

$\mathcal{P}$eter's email had been sent three days ago. I suppose he could have got a riverboat, then a taxi to the Banjul airport and flown to the US in that amount of time, but it would have been a squeeze.

I heard a commotion out in the store. Britney gave a high-pitched squeal.

I rushed out, then froze.

There was a beaming Adriana. With the beautiful Ruben Moreno. Britney hugged them both.

And behind them both was — Ronson Zolek. Yes. He was right there, grinning at everybody. That meant my mysterious visitor was Ronzo, not Peter. Ronzo's New Jersey accent would probably have sounded "funny" to a Californian. And his Nana had raised him to be extraordinarily polite.

I stood rooted to the floor for a moment, not sure whether to hug Adriana or Ronzo first. Adriana solved my dilemma by running to throw her arms around me.

"I'm so sorry Britney didn't get my last message," she said. "Ginny's phone died and Ruben's needed a charge. I texted that Ruben had found me in the shack and took me to Taco Temple because I was starving. But it was hella crowded and we had to wait forever."

I looked over at Ronzo, trying to catch his attention. But for some reason he was avoiding eye contact.

"I'm sorry we took so long," Ruben gave us all a big grin. "Looks like my work here is done. I gotta run. If I fail this exam, I am so screwed."

As I watched him sprint out the door, I was having trouble breathing. I turned to Adriana.

"I'm so relieved. Have you told your mother? Why did Ruben bring you here instead of to your mother? She's got to be going crazy with worry."

Ronzo stepped up. "That was my fault. I wanted to bring her to Britney first, since I promised I would."

"You promised Britney?"

Ronzo still wasn't looking at me.

But Britney was beaming. "I showed him Adriana's texts and he said he thought he knew where she was, and promised to bring her back. But I didn't want to get your hopes up."

My hopes. What a sweet girl to be worried about my feelings. I turned to Ronzo again.

"You're brilliant! How did you figure out where she was?"

He gave me an adorable smile and I ran over and enveloped him in a hug. Buckingham emerged from hiding and rubbed against his leg.

But Ronzo showed no interest in our little family reunion. He stood still, barely moving. Then he retreated and picked up the cat, never looking at me.

"I am a detective, you know." He spoke in a monotone as he scratched between Buckingham's ears. "Licensed again, for real. After I read all of Adriana's texts, and got Britney's story, I thought she might have been rescued by Mr. Moreno before you got to the shack. And then there were all those texts about tacos, so I figured he might buy her some. Probably at the best place in town."

"But — what are you doing here?" I felt like crying. I wanted him to either hug me or hate me.

Instead, he gave me a cold smile. "I figured congratulations were in order. I understand you're getting married. I saw you get engaged on TMZ last night."

I could see pain in his eyes, although he kept smiling. Given his meager income, he wouldn't have flown here if he weren't seriously upset by Jonathan's proposal.

I'd hurt him terribly.

So there he was, petting Buckingham, surrounded by the beaming girls.

Ronzo had figured out where Adriana was in a matter of minutes. He was amazing. And he looked good too. His hair was shaggy again, but it made him look rock and roll instead of homeless.

I tried to touch his shoulder, but he shook me off.

"I'm not engaged, Ronzo. Not really. I gave Jonathan the ring back. I wanted to talk to you first..."

Ronzo kept petting Buckingham.

I had to do something to keep from screaming. Things were okay, I told myself. Adriana was safe. And she didn't seem to have been harmed. And Fish was not involved. This was all good.

Except Ronzo hated me.

I turned to Britney, who was eagerly whispering to Adriana.

"You look so happy," I said. "Did your text to Adriana go through? The one you were sending when Jonathan and I went to the back room? You looked like you had a lot to say."

Britney's grin widened. "Oh, I wasn't texting Adriana. That shamrock phone was totally dead, and Adriana hasn't had a way to charge her own phone for days. I was answering a text from my mom."

"You heard from Shannon? Thank goodness. Is she all right?" That was good news. I had to concentrate on being happy for Britney and Adriana and let the awful stuff with Ronzo go for the moment.

"She's fine. And she's coming home real soon. She promised. She had to go to England first, but she's safe there and then she's flying back to California." Britney couldn't have grinned any wider. I gave her a hug. Adriana hugged me too. Their joy rubbed off a bit.

"That's wonderful news! Shannon is in England? Why hasn't she been texting you?"

"I guess Derrick's hand got injured by some huge eagle that was trying to steal his tuna sandwich when they went on a river cruise. So they got stuck in some village where he went to get bandaged up. And her charger doesn't work with the Chinese solar electricity they had in the village."

"That's why we haven't heard from her? Because she doesn't have the right phone charger?"

Britney lowered her voice. "It's more than that. My mom says this totally all secret and hush-hush, but she and her boyfriend had to smuggle a thumb drive out of the country, and now they have to get this secret drive to a publishing company in a place called Lincolnshire. Doesn't that totally sound like Hobbits live there?"

Lincolnshire. Peter's company, Sherwood, Ltd. was in Lincolnshire. His employees were sort of like Hobbits. But this was all very strange.

That's when Jonathan walked in, with a bag of Kat's famous chocolate chip cookies. He gave Ronzo a startled smile. Hella startled, as the girls would say.

So. This was going to be awkward.

# forty-three

. . .

## Lady Catfish

"*L*ook, Mr. Kahn!" Britney jumped up and down like a small child. "This is Adriana. She's saved! Rueben broke her out of the shack and took her for tacos and then this guy found them at the Taco Temple."

Jonathan gave another stiff smile in the direction of "this guy," but turned back to Adriana. He offered the girls cookies, which they took eagerly.

Ronzo seemed detached from the whole scene, and stood silently with Buckingham in his arms. I still had no idea why he was here in California. He looked wonderful — healthy and well fed. Saffina must have been taking good care of him.

"What happened, Adriana?" Jonathan gave the girl his serious-reporter face. "Were you really locked in a shack overnight? Why did you wait until this morning to text someone?"

Adriana chewed her bite of cookie while Britney took hers over to the reading chair. Britney was probably exhausted from worry — plus working in my store all day. I had to remember to pay her. Breaking child labor laws again.

"My phone was down to 0%," Adriana said. "Totally useless. And I didn't even know the other phone was there on the floor of the shack

196

until this morning. At first it was dark, and I didn't realize they threw Mrs. Gilhooly's phone after me when they locked me in. I guess they couldn't figure out the password so they were over it. But sometime in the morning, light came through the knotholes in the wall and I saw the sparkling shamrocks. The phone was almost fully charged from when I was sleuthing, so I decided to see if it still had any minutes. I started sending texts but it seemed like nobody got them. I guess Ruben read them, but he thought I was Mrs. Gilhooly since he didn't know she was dead."

"And I thought you were Willow's squad pretending to be Mrs. Gilhooly's ghost. I'm so sorry!" Britney looked teary.

Adriana gave her a forgiving smile. "Well, anyway, Ruben said he came here and together you guys figured out what was happening. So, everything is okay, kind of. Except I want a shower soooo bad."

I still didn't completely understand what had happened.

"But who locked you in that shack, Adriana?" It was odd that the girl seemed so calm after such an ordeal. "Was it Barry B? Or Brownie? Are they the same person?"

"No." Adriana made a scornful face. "I wasn't even doing any sleuthing. It was the squad. They caught me trying to get Mrs. Gilhooly's phone back after they stole it from me. So they kidnapped me and decided to 'teach me a lesson' by locking me in the spider shack. But they didn't know that I'm kind of into spiders. The nice ones. I knew there were no Black Widows in there, because Widows don't hang with other spiders. It was mostly Daddy Longlegs and they're fine. It's an urban myth that they have the deadliest venom known to man, but fangs that are too short to bite you. Longlegs just eat bugs and stuff. Some mice were in the shack too. I talked to them to keep from getting bored. A mom and a baby, so I called them Mary and Jesus. They're real cute."

Britney laughed, and so did Ronzo, but Jonathan gave Adriana a dark look.

"Adriana, if somebody kidnapped you and locked you in a shack overnight, that's a serious crime. You need to press charges against this 'squad.'"

"You mean go to the police? No. No. I can't do that." A look of real terror came over the girl's face. Losing her mother at the age of thirteen would be pretty terrifying. I hoped the Morro Bay police wouldn't report Luisa to ICE.

Jonathan harrumphed. "Did Morris Fishman have anything to do with this?"

Of course he had to jump in with that.

"Are you talking about Fish?" Adriana gave a dismissive wave. "Mr. Fishman from here in the store? What would he have to do with anything? He doesn't even know Willow O'Malley. Look, I should go home and let my mom see I'm okay and get cleaned up." She looked at Britney and gave a big laugh. "And I can tell her Mary and Jesus stayed with me all night."

I said a little prayer of my own, thankful that Fish was not the total villain Jonathan imagined.

Britney petted Buckingham where he snuggled in Ronzo's arms. But the cat wasn't interested. He rubbed his face against Ronzo's cheek as he purred loudly. After all, Bucky was Ronzo's cat. I guess I always knew Ronzo might take him back. Maybe that's why he was here. To rescue his cat from me.

Was he going to take Buckingham back to New Jersey to live with him and Saffina? I suppose he had the right.

Jonathan was going into newsman mode again.

"You need to talk to the police, Adriana. Otherwise, the people who kidnapped you will hurt other children. There have been accusations of child molesting. And even murder. We need to hear exactly what happened."

Adriana gave one of her eye rolls.

"Willow O'Malley isn't a child molester. She's, like, a child. Well, sort of. She's thirteen. She's a heinous person, but she isn't a molester. And nobody's been murdered. Except Mrs. Gilhooly. I'm pretty sure I know who did it now — or at least who was catfishing her. All I had to do all that time I was in the shack — while I was waiting for you morons to answer my texts — was read Mrs. Gilhooly's phone messages and emails, so I got more clues."

I wanted to return Adriana's eager smile. But I knew it was time to let the police have a look at that phone.

"I'm glad you got some sleuthing done, but you're going to have to turn over that phone now." I gave Adriana a look she must have seen on her mother's face many times. "It needs to go to the police. So we can exonerate our friend Joe, you know?"

Adriana gave me a look of sheepish defiance.

"Fine," she said after a moment. She slid off her backpack and took the phone out. "Here. I guess you have to. But I haven't read everything. There's a lot of messages on that phone. It was hard to read while I was sitting there in the dark, starving, with nothing to eat but that sand bar. Britney's mom has terrible taste in granola bars."

Britney laughed. "But you still eat them, Addie. I can't even."

I handed the phone to Jonathan. "Didn't you say you were in touch with Officer Pilchard?"

Jonathan nodded. "What did you find on this phone, Adriana? Anything I can tell the officer?"

"I found out Mrs. Gilhooly had a lot of enemies. A whole lot. I mean people who emailed her death threats. And that's besides the catfish — those romance emails were so lame — even though you can tell she totally bought into the scam. But I can tell the catfish isn't Barry B. So, I don't think he murdered her."

Jonathan jumped in. "I agree. Barry Brown did not seem like a guilty party when he phoned the police about my gun. He had the outrage of an innocent man. In my job, I learn to read people pretty well."

"Mr. Kahn is totally right." Adriana gave an exasperated sigh. "I figured out the real Brownie isn't one of the homeless guys. I think the real Brownie is a regular person with a house who uses the library computers so the messages can't be traced to their home."

"Who is this Brownie they're talking about, Camilla?" Ronzo finally put Buckingham down and joined the conversation.

Britney immediately picked up the cat, and amazingly, he didn't seem to mind.

I was glad Ronzo was talking to me about something, so I turned to him with a big smile.

"We don't really know anything about Brownie — except that the day Ginny died, she'd figured out her unlucky boyfriend who called himself Brownie was two-timing her. With some woman named Tiffani." I tried to keep my voice bright and detached. "But it had been obvious to the rest of us that this man was catfishing her. You know, doing one of those online romance scams. He got a lot of money out of her with outrageous stories of getting his pocket picked in Naples or Greece or somewhere. But Adriana thinks he lives right here in Morro Bay and uses the public library computers."

"I don't *think*. I know." Adriana gave an epic sigh. "And it's not a he. It's a she. I'm pretty sure the catfish is a lady."

# forty-four

. . .

Catfish vs. Catfish

*J* stood behind the counter watching the drama unfold. I was impressed by Adriana's resilience. She was an amazing young woman.

But as Jonathan let up on his interrogation, Ronzo leaned down to look the girl in the eye.

"Are you saying you know who murdered this lady? The one with the phone?" He sounded as much like an interrogator as Jonathan.

Adriana looked annoyed at all of us as she shook her head.

"No. That's not what I said. I said I know who was writing the catfishing emails. I should have realized it earlier, but when I read the emails again, I could tell it was a lady. There was so much girly stuff in there. Brownie's emails talk about how beautiful and well-conditioned Ginny's hair looks in her selfies and how 'he' likes women with nice, long, polished nails in warm colors. I never heard a man talk about warm colors in my entire life. Do you talk like that?"

Ronzo smiled. "Nope. Not a dude thing to say."

Jonathan nodded as he ate his cookie. "I don't talk like that, but decorators do. The guy could be a decorator."

Adriana gave a snort. "Well, he gets super-sappy romantic — you know, like Hallmark channel romantic — so I don't think Brownie is any kind of a guy. He also never talks about this oil rig he supposedly lives on. The one in his Facebook profile."

This was all fascinating. Ginny had started getting her nails done about a month after her husband died. She started going to a new salon down on the Embarcadero, I remembered, and then her drab gray hair turned a sparkly silver. Maybe Brownie had already been working on her.

"This woman met her scammer on Facebook? You've seen his page there?" Jonathan was back to doing his interviewer thing.

"I've seen it too," I said. I hoped I could take the pressure off the poor girl. "Brown David Jack is what he called himself. A tanned Adonis. Wearing nothing but a hard hat and cut-offs. Totally buff. His profile picture looked like the cover of a steamy romance novel. When I checked, he had six friends. All his posts are photos of roses and puppies."

Jonathan laughed. "I'm sure he's related to the ladies like Emily Brandi and Parker Sue, who constantly ask to be my Facebook friends. Their pages show a whole lot of boob, and not much else."

"The dude sure sounds dodgy," Ronzo said. "But you don't think he's a dude? Or a murderer?"

Adriana shook her head.

"I think Brownie stole the page from another catfish. If you do a search for Brown David Jack, he has another profile that's exactly the same, with more friends. So, I think Ginny's catfish cloned the first catfish's profile. I should have checked it out earlier. It explains a lot."

"Whoa!" Ronzo was thoroughly involved now. "A catfish hacked another catfish?"

"You don't have to actually hack into a person's personal data to clone a page." Adriana was obviously proud of her tech nerd credentials. "Just copy it and paste the data in a new page. Then you can send messages and it looks like they're from Brown David Jack."

"Can you do this stuff, Adriana?" Britney had been following the conversation like a spectator at a ping-pong game. "You know how to clone somebody's Facebook page? Maybe we could do Willow O'Malley's page and then send nasty messages to all her friends, and they'll think it's her so she'll have no squad."

Adriana burst out laughing and gave Britney a hug. "Brilliant. That would be fire!"

"Girls, I think it's time for you to go home to Adriana's poor mom. She's got to be worried sick." I looked over at Jonathan. "Could you take them home? Then maybe contact Officer Pilchard and tell him what's happened." I picked up the sparkly green phone on the counter in front of me. "And tell him we've got Ginny Gilhooly's phone."

Adriana gave me a lopsided smile. "You need to at least check out some texts and emails while you're waiting to give it to him. Look at the stuff she says about Crystal's friends. She hates two of those ladies and tried to get them kicked out of the wedding party. I'll bet they hate her back."

"Ooooh. We get to ride in a Tesla!" Britney was all smiles. Her whole body had been radiating good spirits since she'd heard from her mom.

Ronzo picked up Buckingham again.

Jonathan gave me a pointed look as he ushered the girls toward the door. He knew he was leaving me alone with Ronzo and that the scene would be awkward.

As Adriana trailed out the door behind Britney and Jonathan, she called to me over her shoulder.

"Look at what she says about Betty Boobs and the Barracuda. She really hates those ladies. Maybe they could have killed her."

Jonathan laughed. "Because of a wedding invitation? That's pretty unlikely."

Britney laughed too. "Adriana has a great imagination."

Adriana gave them a fierce look as she followed them out of the store.

As soon as they were gone, Buckingham meowed, jumped from Ronzo's arms and scurried over to hide under the remainder table. Even he wanted to avoid the painful conversation that was about to happen.

I walked out from behind the counter, but didn't attempt to touch

Ronzo. I needed to use my best Manners Doctor communication skills. He must want to talk to me. He'd come all the way across the country. In spite of his ailing grandmother.

I started by filling him in on the story of Ginny Gilhooly and her disappearing corpse. And how the police suspected Hobo Joe. Then I explained Adriana's "sleuthing" and my fears it had led to her kidnapping.

"But it turned out to be some school kids that locked her up?" he said. "It's amazing how cruel little girls can be."

All I could think of was the cruel girl he was now dating. Saffina had been horrible to him when she was with Mack Rattletrap's band. The silence between us was more than awkward. I needed to say something.

"It really is wonderful to see you," I said finally. "Is your grandmother on the mend?"

He stared at me through another painful silence.

"No." He looked at me steadily, but his voice had gone whispery. "No. Nana died last week. The funeral was yesterday. I came home and turned on the TV, and there you were. Getting engaged to Jonathan Kahn."

# forty-five

. . .

## Other Fish to Fry

*R*onzo and I stared at each other, both of us holding back tears. I don't know when I've ever felt so guilty and miserable. The person Ronzo loved most in the world had died and I hadn't been there for him. I'd been worried about my own petty jealousies. So what if he was with Saffina now? He was still my friend.

"I'm so, so sorry about your Nana, Ronzo." I wanted to say some more soothing words, but they weren't there.

"Me too." He stepped forward and gave me a hug. Tentative at first, then a full-on bear hug. Then I heard a sob.

I squeezed him close and let my tears fall too.

Part of me wanted to kiss him — to tell him I forgave him for leaving me for Saffina. And let him know I understood why he needed somebody more geographically appropriate.

I looked at his tear-stained face, but there was still something cold in his eyes. No. He would not have welcomed a kiss.

I heard the bell on the door jingle, and looked up to see Officer Pilchard. His face had turned pink.

"Sorry. Your sign says open. I came because Mr. Kahn said…"

I was probably blushing too. I stepped forward and shook his hand. "Thanks so much for coming, officer. Mr. Kahn told you we found the little girl?"

Ronzo scooped up Buckingham from under the remainder table and sat in the reading chair petting him, politely pretending not to be there.

"Yes ma'am. I guess it was a middle school prank gone wrong. He said she's home safe with her mother now." He harrumphed. "He also said you had some evidence in the Gilhooly case?"

I'd been hoping I'd have a few minutes with the phone to check out Adriana's enigmatic remarks about Betty Boobs and the Barracuda, but Jonathan had been right to mention it to Officer Pilchard when he gave him the news about Adriana. I went behind the counter and got the phone from the drawer where I'd stashed it. The shamrocks glinted in the late afternoon light. I wondered if I should go back to my cottage for my bag of "clues."

"This is the victim's phone? How did you come by it?"

This was going to be tricky. I didn't want to say anything that might incriminate Adriana — or me.

"As far as I know, the phone was found by a child up in the homeless camp off highway 41, shortly after Ginny's death in that area last spring. Then several children fought over it and one of them threw it at Adriana when they locked her in the shed last night. Adriana got into the phone by using the password Brown David Jack, which she knew was the name of Ginny's online boyfriend. When she was alone in the shed, Adriana read Ginny's old emails, and she says there are some clues on there that might indicate who wanted to kill Ginny."

There. Some solid information, leaving out the part where the phone was illegally in my custody for several weeks.

Officer Pilchard looked me up and down and then over at Ronzo before he fished a baggie out of his pocket and dropped the sparkly green phone inside.

"Clues? This little girl thinks she's Nancy Drew?" He studied the phone through the plastic, but didn't show much interest.

"She thinks she's Sherlock Holmes, actually." I gave him a smile. "I hope your people can get something out of it."

"I doubt it," He set the phone back on the counter as he took out an iPad and booted it up. "The coroner still thinks the death could be accidental, so we're waiting on lab results from LA before they'll assign anybody to investigate. Those guys are so slow. It's not like on TV where the lab gets them results in a matter of hours. Try months, especially with the huge backlog they've got right now."

My goodness. They still didn't know if Ginny's death was accidental. That should be good news for Joe.

"The homeless musician — the man who calls himself Hobo Joe — is he still a suspect?"

"He's a person of interest, yeah, and our detectives want to talk to him, but we gotta wait on those lab results. Have you seen him? Joseph Torres?" The officer looked at me, and then over at Ronzo. Ronzo had on his inscrutable face. I wondered if he'd heard from Joe about his big plans to bring J. J. Tower back from the dead.

"Joe hasn't been around here for months." I tried to keep my face a bland mask. Joe hadn't been around, exactly. Only Josephine.

I saw the Tesla pull up in front of the store and Jonathan rushed in to greet Officer Pilchard.

"Sorry I wasn't here to meet you, Officer. The girl's mom needed to be reassured that nobody was going to kidnap Adriana again. She kept trying to blame the Moreno kid. I hope I convinced her he was the rescuer not the perpetrator. But it had to be a frightening time for her as well as the child."

Officer Prichard. who had been typing away on an iPad. looked up at Jonathan.

"But, Mr. Kahn, you said on the phone that this kidnapping was only a childish prank?"

"Seems it was. The girl and her mother are vehement about not pressing charges. But there's a group of middle school bullies who gang up on the nerdy, smart kids like Adriana. A tale as old as time. I got stuffed in a few lockers when I was a skinny little ninth grader. But this group's bullying got seriously out of hand. Still, probably not worth taking police time. These are kids — twelve and thirteen years old."

Officer Pilchard nodded.

Jonathan went on. "But I said she needed to report the incident to the school, so I'm going to take her into the principal's office first thing on Monday."

"Great idea, Jonathan." I was impressed he'd given up on getting Adriana to report her kidnapping to the police, since that certainly would have put Luisa on ICE's radar. "A celebrity newsman walking into the principal's office will certainly make the school pay attention. Those girls are dangerous. Something needs to be done."

"Ruben Moreno says one of them has been catfishing him, pretending to be eighteen." This came from Ronzo. I was surprised he'd joined in the conversation. "The guy is terrified she's going to get him in trouble. He's nineteen, so he's the one who would be blamed. Maybe you should have him on your show, Kahn."

Jonathan brightened. "Not a bad idea, Zolek. In fact, I'll look into doing that."

I was glad to see Jonathan remembered his manners and finally acknowledged Ronzo's presence.

"Mean girls can hurt a man at any time in his life." Jonathan spoke as if he had personal knowledge of the subject. I hoped he wasn't referring to me. "It's what my show is about, most of the time. And that Moreno kid sure is telegenic. He'd make good TV. My producers like that."

So even Jonathan had noticed Ruben's looks. He could probably make the boy a star. If Ruben wanted to be one. I guess it might help his football career.

"The kid might be willing to go Hollywood," Ronzo said. "But I think right now he has other fish to fry. He mentioned a girlfriend he was meeting for a study date."

Buckingham jumped from Ronzo's lap to greet Jonathan, but Jonathan seemed to be on the run again. He glanced at me and said he had a Zoom meeting in fifteen minutes.

"So, are we done here, Officer Pilchard?"

The officer nodded as Jonathan ran off, without even a goodbye kiss. It had to be an important Zoom meeting. Strange that he hadn't mentioned it earlier. Maybe he had other fish to fry, too. I kind of hoped so.

Officer Pilchard gave me a nod before taking off, still occupied with his iPad.

Ronzo and I were alone again and I didn't have a clue what to say to him.

# forty-six

. . .

## Teach a Woman to Fish...

*R*onzo said nothing as we both watched Jonathan's Tesla pull away.

Then he turned and looked me in the eye.

"Do you love him? I get it if you do. You have history and he's sobered up now. Got a great new career. Flying high."

I stepped forward and took Ronzo's hand.

"No. I don't think I love him. I did once, so I have strong emotions around him, but no. I don't love him. Not the way I love you." Yes. I said it. I hadn't meant to leave myself so vulnerable, but the words tumbled out.

Ronzo gave me a penetrating look, and I could see his eyes glisten with tears.

"You love me? You still do?"

"Yes, God help me. Even though you've left me for Saffina. But I'll get over it."

"Saffina? You think I'm dating Saffina?"

"You, well, seemed to be together."

"You mean on Kahn's show? That was all to make 'good TV' like he calls it. To please his producers."

"But I phoned and you were about to go out on the town with her..."

"Out on the town? She was taking me to a club to meet the band I was going to review. That's all. I've been way too busy with Nana and work to think about dating or anything else. Nana needed care 24/7 for the last couple months. I had to hire a caregiver to go hear a band. I didn't break even. That's why I've renewed my detective license. I've been doing research from home. A whole lot of tracking people is done online these days. People have no idea how little privacy they have with a smartphone."

Wow. I'd been such an idiot. And Jonathan was such a liar.

I gave a stupid giggle. "Well, we certainly could have used your skills here. Adriana and I haven't been very successful at our detective work. Too bad I don't still have that phone. You could probably..."

"You mean this phone?" Ronzo walked over to the counter and picked up the plastic-bagged green phone. "I think your policeman forgot it. He didn't seem to have a whole lot of interest."

"Oh my! That's... It might be serendipitous. Maybe you can do some detective work with it. At least we can figure out what Adriana meant about Betty Boobs and the Barracuda."

He put the phone down again. "Okay, but you have to feed me first. I haven't eaten a thing but airline pretzels since nine this morning."

"How about some fish and chips? Remember the place down on the Embarcadero with the calamari and chips you like?"

Ronzo grinned. "As I remember, they deliver, don't they? I don't suppose you got any wine in that little place of yours?"

He leaned forward and gave me a kiss. A lingering kiss. A kiss that said food wasn't the only thing he was starving for.

Buckingham meowed.

"I think he's starving too."

But it wasn't hunger Buckingham was meowing about. The door opened and in stomped two of the rude fisherpersons. The two women. Another couple of customers followed them. It never failed when I was about to close up the store.

"I want to speak to the manager," a fisherperson said. Her voice was whiny and shrill. "I know you must have that guidebook. Nobody even tried to look for it when we came in earlier, and my boyfriend is very upset. He taught me to fish just so we could go on this trip and now we don't have the guidebook."

I felt my face heat up as I clenched my teeth and tried to imitate a smile.

The woman walked up to the counter and slammed her hand down on the stack of tide charts we gave away as freebies. The charts went flying everywhere.

"I want her fired!" The woman's beefy hand came down on the counter again, this time perilously close to Ginny's phone.

I moved toward her, not sure what I could say. Mostly I wanted to rescue the phone. But she shoved me out of the way and stomped up to Ronzo.

"Are you the manager? I want you to fire that bimbo."

We were all silent for a moment. I focused on Ginny's phone and tried to figure out how I could keep her from knocking it on the floor.

"What bimbo? This bimbo?" Ronzo gave me a grin and grabbed Ginny Gilhooly's phone with one hand and my left wrist with the other. "Here." He handed me the phone. "You're fired. And your little phone, too." His accent went from Tony Soprano to Wicked Witch of the West. "For the next fifteen minutes. Don't worry. I remember how to close up, boss lady."

I escaped to my office with the phone as the two fisherpersons stood in front of the counter, looking confused and fearful as Ronzo went back to his Tony Soprano New Jersey thug accent.

"What was it youse guys wanted?" He picked up some of the tide charts and tossed them in their direction. "You like throwin' stuff on the floor? Is that what people do where you come from? Cause it seems kinda rude to me. You know what I mean?"

I clutched Ginny's phone and ran back to my cottage. I figured Ronzo could take care of himself against two middle-aged ladies from the Valley.

I ordered the fish and chips, opened a bottle of chardonnay, and plopped down in my reading chair. Time to go to work on Ginny's phone. Officer Pilchard might show up asking for it at any minute.

But now I had to find out about Betty Boobs and the Barracuda.

# forty-seven

· · ·

## Fish and Chips

Ginny's texts were even more revealing than her emails. Short and brutal, they showed a woman who pretty much rubbed everybody the wrong way. Sure enough, right before her death, she'd been sending texts to Larry complaining about "the Barracuda," who had done her nails all wrong. And there was someone she called Princess Golddigger, who had been Ginny's hairdresser until she cut Ginny's hair too short and left two little bits that kept sticking up.

I remembered those bits. They looked like horns.

Both Princess Golddigger and the Barracuda were Crystal's bridesmaids.

I sipped chardonnay and hoped Ronzo wouldn't mind that I was starting without him. I put a Lalique wine glass next to the bottle for him.

I took the wine into the living room and explored Ginny's phone. Adriana had been right. Ginny made even angrier complaints about a couple of other bridesmaids. She especially hated one she called "Betty Boobs." Apparently, Betty Boobs had complained about the bridesmaid's dresses in such nasty terms that Ginny had asked Crystal to remove her from the wedding party. As I scrolled up, I could see lots of complaints about the Barracuda and Princess Golddigger, and how she wanted to kick them out too.

I tried to think of any situation where it would be good etiquette for the mother of the groom to ask for someone to be removed from the wedding party. I couldn't think of one.

I went over to Ginny's Facebook messages and could see that the Barracuda was supposed to be the maid of honor. She seemed to be named Tiffani. The tall, busty one named Ruby-Lee might be Betty Boobs. The big blonde, Harley Goldman, was probably Princess Golddigger.

Ruby, Ms. Goldman, and Tiffani. No wonder Ginny disliked jewelry-related names. They seemed like awful people, from what I'd seen in the Thai restaurant and later at Jonathan's hotel. Maybe we needed a new term for attendants of Bridezillas. Bridesmonsters, maybe?

But I didn't see anything in the emails that would add up to a motive for murder. The text exchanges were simply bad manners and squabbles. The bridesmaids probably didn't even know the nastier things Ginny said about them to Larry.

Adriana had picked up on the drama, but I didn't think a bunch of obnoxious bridesmaids could have anything to do with Brownie or Ginny's death.

A few minutes later, Ronzo came sprinting across the courtyard with Buckingham trotting right behind him.

"I finally got rid of those terrible women." He bounded in the front door. "I got them to buy some book called *Trout Fishing in America*. It didn't look like it has much to do with fishing, but who cares? Why does everybody have such bad manners these days? My Nana would have slapped them."

I laughed out loud at the idea of those women trying to read Richard Brautigan. I jumped up to give him a hug. He hugged me back, then gave me a kiss. The kiss might have developed into something more if we hadn't been interrupted by the Grubhub girl with our fish and chips.

While I poured Ronzo a glass of the wine, he spread our meal on the coffee table, with the condiment packets scattered about. I usually ate at my little dining table, but I could see Ronzo was too hungry for that.

As we ate, he asked me what I'd found on the phone. I told him about the bridesmonsters with jewelry-related names.

"But you don't think any of these bridesmaids she hated had a motive for murder?" He dipped a French fry in tartar sauce.

"Not that I can see. That doesn't rule them out, but there was no violence threatened on either side. Ginny only called them silly names. I suspect a lot of people do. They're awfully unpleasant. Sort of like your fisherwomen out there. Rude." I picked up a fry. "Are these really good with tartar sauce instead of ketchup?"

"Try it." He pushed the tartar sauce container toward me. "What about the bride? Does she have motive?"

"Sort of. With Ginny dead, I assume Larry has inherited Gil Gilhooly's ill-gotten gains, so when Crystal marries him — or maybe she's married him already; I think the wedding was today — anyway, she'll be a lot richer. Plus, she won't have a hostile mother-in-law to deal with. So yeah. Crystal had a motive. But she's tiny. She could not have carried Ginny's body across my courtyard."

Ronzo's eyes sparked. "That's one hell of a motive. Maybe she got somebody to help her move the body. Like the groom?"

"Larry has the heft to do it, but I honestly don't think he killed his mother. He adored her."

"From what I've seen, love can turn to hate pretty fast if money is involved. Maybe it was the two of them. Bound together in holy murder." Ronzo picked up a French fry, dipped it in the tartar sauce and put it in my mouth. "Dinner," he said. Let's stop sleuthing and eat."

The fry was remarkably good.

# forty-eight

· · ·

## A Fish Out of Water

*W*e hadn't quite eaten all the fish and chips before we rushed into my room, fell onto my bed, and tore each other's clothes off.

But in our defense, we had run out of tartar sauce.

It was bliss having Ronzo back home and in my arms. We even managed to shut the door before Buckingham came slinking in, hoping to make it a threesome. We could hear him scratching at the door at occasional intervals, letting loose his most plaintive meows.

But suddenly his scratches got louder. And his whimper morphed into a human voice.

"Camilla! Camilla darling, you can't be asleep at this hour. Are you all right?"

Ronzo rolled off me, his face dark with anger.

"Kahn! We're a little busy here, man. She may be your ex-wife, but she's my girlfriend, and it's been a while…"

I switched on the light as Ronzo sat up and pulled the blankets over his lap.

The door burst open and there was Plantagenet. He was even more beautifully dressed than usual, with his normally silvery hair now a pale blonde, cut in an impeccable up-to-the-minute style.

"Plantagenet!" I said, partly to let Ronzo know our intruder was not Jonathan. "You're visiting from LA?"

"Camilla darling! And, um, Mr. Zolek. I am so sorry. I… I wasn't expecting you. How rude of me. I'll go now…"

I heard the door click behind him.

I gave Ronzo a quick, reassuring kiss. But the mood was gone for both of us.

I called toward the door. "Plant, don't go. Help yourself to wine. We'll be right out."

Ronzo laughed as we scrambled into our clothes.

"To be continued at a later hour." He gave me a quick kiss on the cheek.

Plant did look fantastic with his new hair color and trendy clothes. He sat on the couch sipping chardonnay and munching French fries.

"I am so sorry, darling. I had no idea Ronzo was even in town." He hesitated a moment. "May I say how relieved I am to see it isn't Jonathan Kahn?"

'Yeah. You can say that." Ronzo grinned as he stepped forward and shook Plant's hand. "Good to see you again, Plant."

"I didn't know you were planning a visit up here, Plant," I said. "Is the project going well?"

"I have no idea. We're on hold at the moment. We lost a gaffer. The union won't let us film without a replacement, and gaffers are apparently rare as hen's teeth at the moment. So, I figured I'd come home for a bit. Well, Silas insisted."

"But he let you come over to surprise me? That's very sweet," I retrieved my wine glass and poured myself some more. I needed a little fortification to keep my polite smile in place. I love Plant to pieces, but this wasn't the right moment for a big reunion. "You look fantastic. How does Silas like the hair?"

Plant shrugged. "He'll get used to it."

Ronzo went to the kitchen for a glass of water, while Buckingham snaked around his legs. Ronzo leaned down to pet the kitty and refreshed the water dish. A better pet-parent than I was. Of course, I still didn't know if he intended to take Buckingham back to New Jersey.

"Silas knew I was eager to see you, darling." Plant squeezed the last bit of ketchup from a packet and gave me a nervous smile. "We need to talk. Well, actually, I guess I need to talk to Mr. Zolek, but I thought you'd have to relay the message to him for me." He looked over his shoulder at Ronzo. "I had a visitor last night who really wants to see you."

"Me? Somebody in Hollywood wants to talk to me?" Ronzo was all attention now as he sat in the chair opposite Plant.

"Well, he's not exactly a Hollywood type. In fact, I think he's terrified of my West Hollywood neighborhood. He's very much a fish out of water. Joe Torres. Hobo Joe."

"You've seen Joe? Is he all right?" This was strange news. "Marva will be relieved. She hasn't heard from him in a while."

"Yes. It seems Joe has been off everybody's radar. He's all right now, but he's been dealing with an injured leg. He tried to hop a freight train, but he's not quite the athlete he used to be. He didn't make the jump, fell and tore a couple of ligaments. He ended up in a homeless encampment outside of Dallas. A nice tiny home village, apparently tended by a very compassionate lady."

"What was he doing in Dallas? I thought he was heading for New Jersey to see Ronzo." I sipped wine, wishing I had another bottle. It sounded as if this might be a long story.

"Hobo Joe was looking for me?" Ronzo had Buckingham on his lap now. He turned to me. "I thought you said Joe had been accused of murdering Ginny Gilhooly. Why was he in Hollywood, anyway?"

Plant laughed. "That's where the first ride out of Dallas took him, I think."

Fierce knocks on the front door interrupted us.

"Cameella! Open zis door. You must vake up! It ees too much early for sleeping."

There seemed to be a German woman outside with an urgent need to get into my house. I froze, but luckily Plant jumped up and opened the door.

In walked Angela Merkel, complete with fashion-free haircut, dowdy blue suit and sensible shoes. She carried a businesslike brief-case, from which she extricated her iPad.

She clicked something on the tablet and waved it at us all. "Have you seen zis? Zey say dat Gilhooly voman vas murdered after all and zey say it is our friend Joseph who has done it."

Plant took the iPad and showed us the headline of tomorrow's paper. "Lab Results Prove Gilhooly Death a Homicide." It was accompanied by an awful photo of Joe looking his most unwashed.

Marva reached into her briefcase and pulled out a bottle of brandy she put on the coffee table.

Then she looked at Ronzo and did a double take. Her whole demeanor changed. "Soldier! I didn't expect to see you here. How the hell are you, man?"

"Dude!" Ronzo stood and gave our visitor a bro-hug. I knew he and Marva/Marvin had served together in Iraq. It was amazing how fast they fell into their military personas. Ronzo invited Marva to sit and join us while I got out some brandy snifters.

"What's this about Joe?" Ronzo said.

Plant handed Ronzo the iPad. He looked it over, then handed it to me while he poured brandy all around.

It seemed the very slow LA lab had finally sent their findings to the Morro Bay Police. They said Ginny had taken an overdose of sleeping medication and later was hit on the head with a blunt object in two different places: first on the forehead, then the back of the head. The first killed her and the second was inflicted post-mortem. The prime suspect was the homeless man who had supposedly threatened her earlier that day, the man who called himself Hobo Joe.

"Damn," Ronzo took a sip of brandy. "I guess we'd better go back to our detective work. I still think the happy couple did it."

Plant nodded. "I agree. At least I'm sure the son had something to do with it. That guy is so tightly wound he could crack any time."

"First we need to find Joe and warn him," Marvin said. "But I got no idea where to find the guy. He cut off all communication about a month ago. The dude could be dead for all I know." Marvin turned to me. "I hoped maybe your friend Fish might know where he is."

Fish. I wondered if he was ever planning to come back, or if his fear of police had driven him away for good.

"Joe is fine," Plant said with a grin. "He's got a sore leg from an argument with a box car, so he limps a bit, but he's alive and kicking in West Hollywood. At my apartment, as a matter of fact. I told him he could stay while I took some time off up here."

Even under all the make-up, I could see Marvin's face relax.

"What's he doing at your house?" Ronzo looked at Plant.

"Hoping for a visit from you," Plant said. "He has a story he wants you to write for your old friends at *Rolling Stone*."

I could see Ronzo's jaw drop. "Is J. J. Tower going to come back to life?"

"Yeah. With your help," Marvin said. "He figures the cops will be more likely to believe he's telling the truth about Ginny if he tells the truth about who he is."

"Really?" Ronzo gave Marvin an intense look. "Well, I think the best plan for Joe would be for us to find out who really bashed Mrs. Gilhooly over the head. Twice."

# forty-nine

. . .

## The Nature of Catfish

*J* woke to hear Ronzo showering. I lay back in the sheets and relaxed when I realized it was Sunday and we could have the whole day together. After all this time apart, I would be content to spend the day with him right here in this bed. Outside my window the sky was gray with Morro Bay's signature "June Gloom" fog, and I didn't feel like budging. I hoped he wouldn't either.

Last night Marva and Plant had urged Ronzo to drive down to LA to interview Joe as soon as possible. But today shouldn't be "possible." He'd only just arrived.

I couldn't hide my disappointment when he emerged from the bathroom, already dressed, and looking ready to face the world.

"You're not going to drive down to West Hollywood to talk to Joe, are you? Can't you rest here for at least one day?" All sorts of abandonment issues flooded in. I cared about Joe, of course, but if Ronzo left again so soon, it would break my heart.

"West Hollywood? God, that's what — a five-hour drive in good traffic? And rental cars cost a fortune. No way." He came and sat on the edge of the bed and gave me a kiss.

"I'm not sure about this whole thing of Joe letting the world know he's J. J. Tower." He smoothed back my hair. "Tower has been dead for almost twenty-five years. Fans may not welcome him back. Joe hasn't dealt with the age of social media. They could crucify him for hiding out all this time. Also for the guys in the band who died. He's an emotionally fragile guy. I'm not sure he could take it."

"I hadn't thought of that. You're right. Some people will be glad to have him back, but there are always the haters on social media. And Towering Inferno never amounted to anything after J. J. Tower died. Plus, I suppose some people will blame him for the fire he supposedly died in. There were fatalities in the audience too, as I remember. The band used crazy pyrotechnics, didn't they?"

Ronzo took my hand and kissed it, but he stood up, launching those abandonment fears again.

"Yeah. And Joe blames himself. It could be a disaster for him. What we gotta do is prove he didn't kill Ginny Gilhooly so he can stay safely dead."

"We've kind of been trying to do that. Without much luck. What are you planning to do, oh great detective?"

He laughed. "First, I'm going to search that phone of hers before the cops come back to get it. I'm sure they will now that they know the Gilhooly woman's death was definitely a homicide."

Now I realized what was happening. Ronzo was always thinking.

"Good idea. I'll make us some breakfast." Maybe we could have some romantic time later in the day.

Ronzo perused Ginny's phone while I fed Buckingham and made coffee and French toast.

He let out a sudden laugh.

"I'm not finding much here about Mrs. Gilhooly's catfish, but these ladies are hilarious." He accepted a steaming cup of coffee with milk and sugar — 'regular,' as he called it. "I can't believe the pranks they pulled on this poor old lady. They invited her to a bridal shower somewhere off in the boonies, but there was no party. She drove all that way and landed in somebody's cow pasture."

I put a plate of French toast in front of him and offered him the syrup.

"That's a terrible thing to do to anybody. What did Ginny do?" I sat down with my own plate.

"She seems to have ordered the ringleaders out of the wedding. The ones she calls Betty Boobs and the Barracuda."

"Oh really? She actually banned them from the wedding? That's such a breach of etiquette, although I sympathize with the poor woman." I dug into my own breakfast. "But you know, all the bridesmaids seemed to be part of Crystal's entourage this weekend. Jonathan and I ran into them in two local restaurants."

At my mention of Jonathan, Ronzo winced a bit. He gave a rough laugh.

"Well, Ginny's gone, so Crystal could have whatever nasty bridesmaids she wanted." He went back to scrolling through the phone. "Ginny here had reason to be mad. These crazy ladies wanted her to refund the money for their bridesmaid's dresses. This is like an episode of *Real Housewives*."

It did sound dreadfully melodramatic. Not to mention that it would be another colossal breech of etiquette. But Ronzo was letting himself get distracted. I had to convince him to search for the catfish. My idea of the most likely suspect.

"That's all great fun, but you'd better scroll back and look for something from the guy who calls himself Brownie. The catfish. I still think he's our culprit. He didn't kidnap Adriana, but that doesn't mean he's not a murderer."

"Didn't Adriana say she thought Brownie was a woman?"

"Male, female, or whatever Marva is — Brownie could have been anybody. That's the nature of catfish. But we do know they sent their emails from right here in the Morro Bay library — which means they had easy access. And Brownie had been dumped by their source of illicit income because of the Tiffani revelation, so there was motive."

"Now who's the 'great detective'." He laughed and grabbed my hand and kissed it before going back to scrolling the phone.

Buckingham rubbed against his leg and begged to be picked up, but Ronzo kept scrolling.

"Sorry, Buck, but we gotta find us a catfish. Camilla says so."

I cleared the table and washed up the dishes. I hoped Ronzo's detective skills would turn up something useful.

"Here it is!" He looked up at me with a grin. "Here's the email she sent to Brownie to tell him it was all over. Ginny could use some salty language. And wow, she threatens to get him arrested, and even kill him. His other girlfriend, too. This old lady was hopping mad."

"She threatened to kill him?" I knew Ginny was angry, but not that angry.

"Well, she says she has her husband's Glock and she knows how to use it." He looked up at me. "But the email two days before says she loves him and she's going to be sending him a gift. What happened in between?"

"That had to be when she got that email. The one signed 'Tiffani.' A lovey-dovey message like the ones from Brownie."

Ronzo was silent for a moment as he scrolled.

"Oh yeah. Here's another thread. "Dearess, I think about you all the time. I can't wait till we can be together agin. Thanks for sending the PayPal. It will help my poor mother recover. Luv you baby. I ain't never luved someone. Not the way I luv you." It's signed Tiffani with an 'i.'"

I turned and looked at him. "No wonder Ginny was angry. That last bit is a misquoted line from a Garth Brooks song. That was how Brownie wooed her — with Garth Brooks lyrics. He must have been wooing Tiffani the same way."

"Except he's sending *her* money. For her poor mother. Sounds like she's the catfish."

Ronzo looked up from the phone and gave me a funny look.

"The strange thing is — this email has the same IP address as Brownie's. This Tiffani must have been living with him or something,"

"All Brownie's emails were sent from the library, according to Adriana."

"Then Tiffani must have been at the library too. This isn't making sense." Ronzo looked intently at the phone, tapping and swiping, obviously looking for more info on the address.

"If Brownie was scamming Ginny to pay Tiffani, that would

explain Ginny's over-the-top rage. Maybe she was angry enough to kill." I remembered Ginny's crazed anger when she phoned me about returning the book.

"Wait! I think I've found something else," Ronzo looked excited as his thumbs typed something into the phone.

Loud knocking on the front door announced the only thing that kind of knocking could mean. Law enforcement had arrived.

Ronzo groaned.

"I'll get it." He stood and went to the door with the phone.

A good idea, since he was dressed and I was still in my nightgown and robe.

"Officer Pilchard! I'll bet you're here for this." He handed the phone to the officer. I couldn't see Officer Pilchard's face, but he must have been in a bit of trouble with his superiors.

Ronzo wished him a cheerful good morning, but his face was dark as he came back to the table.

"Well, I screwed that, didn't I? I could have found out more about Ginny's catfish, but I wasted time on the *Real Housewives* stuff. And I didn't find one suspicious thing on her son Larry, although he's still the most obvious suspect." Ronzo laughed. "Besides. I was almost going to find out who Tiffani is."

"One of the bridesmaids is named Tiffani." I gave him a hug. "Who knows, maybe the bridesmaids were catfishing Brownie while Brownie catfished Ginny. As I said, it's the nature of catfish to be as different from the person they pretend to be as possible."

"But I'm not sure it's their nature to murder people. What they do best is disappear. Sons who are going to inherit a buttload of money, on the other hand, are more likely to kill." Ronzo kissed my forehead. "But without that phone, there's not much we can figure out, Babe. What do you say we worry about all this later?" He gave me a lovely kiss and led me back to the bedroom.

# fifty

. . .

## A Fishy Fingernail

*B*y Monday morning, I'd I finally talked Ronzo into considering the idea Brownie might be Ginny's killer, and her son might be innocent. Innocent of murder. Of course I still considered Larry Gilhooly guilty of being terribly rude.

Ronzo sighed as he put down his coffee cup. "Thing is, searching for Brownie is going to be impossible without Ginny's phone. I have no leads — and still no idea who Brownie is. I can't stake out the library hoping somebody suspicious is using a computer. All homeless people look suspicious, because they're trying to pretend they're invisible. I sure did when I was homeless."

"I think we're going to find Brownie. I still haven't heard every-thing that Adriana knows." I gave him a kiss on the top of his head as I took his breakfast plate away. "Maybe she'll come into the store after school. By the way, I'm going to need your help in there today. My clerk may have disappeared permanently. Jonathan said Fish evapo-rated when Barry B called the police. And that may be just as well."

I still didn't know what to do with Jonathan's information about Fish's scary history.

"Well, if I get to spend the day with you, I guess it won't be wasted." Ronzo took my hand and pulled me toward him.

"I really need to go open the store." I gave him a quick kiss and took the plate to the sink.

"Uh-oh. Somebody's coming back here." Ronzo went to the door, and in came Liza Minelli, complete with outrageous eye make-up and a feather boa. She was carrying a small suitcase and a large tote bag.

"I decided to get my best drag on for West Hollywood." Marva batted her false eyelashes.

"You're going to West Hollywood? — To see Joe?" Marva's ways were always inscrutable to me.

"Well, I'm taking Ronzo to see Joe. He doesn't have a car — am I right?"

Ronzo looked flummoxed. "Um, yeah. I got an Uber from the airport."

"Well then, pack a bag. No way am I driving down there and back in one day, so bring your toothbrush and PJs. Plant said there are enough places to sleep for all three of us if somebody sleeps on the couch."

Ronzo's smile was friendly, but I knew he didn't want to go.

"Marvin, I don't think it's a good idea for Joe to come out of hiding. I'm not going to do an interview. I think it would do more harm than good."

"More harm than being indicted for murder?"

I could see those two were gearing up for a heated discussion, but it was nearly ten, and I had to open the store. I gave Ronzo a kiss and Marva a little wave and took off.

Maybe Fish would surprise me and show up for work.

He didn't, but about 15 minutes later, Ronzo appeared, wearing his backpack.

"Marvin talked me into it. He says I need to talk to Joe, even if I don't do an interview for *Rolling Stone*. I guess Ginny's murder even made the *LA Times*, so he's scared. We'll be back tomorrow." He gave me a quick kiss and was gone.

I felt a bit forlorn. It was a Monday morning, so there were very few customers. That meant I didn't really need help. But I was awfully pleased when around eleven, Plantagenet appeared.

"I thought you might need some help in the store today. Jonathan told me your assistant has vanished, and I know Marva has whisked Ronzo off to join Joe in my apartment."

I gave him a big hug. "I'm so glad you're here. How would you like to clean up the self-help section?"

As Plant re-organized the books, I realized that I hadn't resolved things with Jonathan, and probably owed him a phone call. Or at least an email.

I opened my email program on the old office computer and sure enough, I had a couple of emails from Jonathan. There was also one from Peter Sherwood. Of course that was the one I opened first.

Duchess, I'm afraid I've got in a spot of bother over my passport, so I'll be leaving The Gambia tonight for Senegal with some dodgy but sociable smugglers. I'll probably be French this time, since my contact in Dakar is French-Senegalese.

Don't worry about dear old Sherwood. It looks as if Fanna is back here in The Gambia and willing to continue to pose as Neezer — or at least his co-author — for a bit longer.

It seems that Derrick, the man I met in Banjul, actually has been Neezer's assistant all along, and was secretly in contact with Fanna, which is why he was so cagey with me. Fanna had left the UK, terrified of her former accomplice, who planned to steal the advance for Neezer's next book.

Fanna had given this partner access to the Sherwood email account. The dreadful woman planned to steal the new title and publish it herself under Fanna's name.

So Neezer hadn't been able to send the file to our office for fear of Fanna's former partner. But somehow Derrick got his ladylove to pay for airfare to the UK, so he could hand-carry the book to Sherwood Ltd. It should be safely with Vera now. When that's sorted, she can free up the advance for Neezer, Pradeep can edit the book, and Sherwood can stay afloat another year.

And now I must run. Literally. Next time you hear from me, I'll be Pierre Forêt or something."

Okay. That explained a lot. Fanna had disappeared because she'd been running from her former business partner. The advance was never picked up because Fanna left after refusing to sign it over to the crooked partner. Meanwhile Neezer couldn't get the book to Sherwood because the partner had access to their email account.

"This is strange," Plantagenet said from the self-help section. "Some customer has been browsing rather energetically. She's left a fingernail inside. I'm not sure you can sell this book as new."

"A fingernail? Like an acrylic one? What book?"

"*Grit* by Angela Duckworth. It's got an inscription in it that might interest you: 'To Brownie, with all my love, Ginny.'"

I rushed over. How had I been stupid enough to re-shelve that book without noticing the inscription? I'd have to sell it as used. The fingernail was weird. Ginny seemed to have been shedding nails all over the place.

"Where's the nail — is it green, with shamrocks on it?"

"No." Plant held up the nail. "It's red."

Yes. It was very red. Revlon's Cherries in the Snow, if I wasn't mistaken. But Ginny could not have got a new manicure in the short time from when she bought the book until she died. Besides she still had on the green ones when she landed on my back step — one of which was safely in my bag of clues. I took the book and the red fingernail back to the counter and wrapped the nail carefully in some of the book kitty gift wrap.

I could swear that nail wasn't Ginny's so it probably belonged to her killer. Maybe Adriana was right, and we were dealing with a lady catfish after all.

# fifty-one

· · ·

## Catfish Stories Everywhere

*a* s soon as I got back to the store after stashing the mysterious fingernail in my bag of clues, the bell on the door jingled and Jonathan came in, followed by another man I didn't know. The man was wearing a good suit — way too big for him. And his hair and much of his face were hidden by a baseball cap with an otter on it.

"Sorry I'm late, boss lady," the man said. "I was afraid the po-pos might come back, with all that talk about Joe in the media."

It was Morris Fishman. With Jonathan. Very strange.

"I've talked with Adriana's principal," Jonathan said. "I think that gang of bullies who kidnapped her are in serious trouble."

"Is Fish wearing your suit?" The Armani suit was sadly wrinkled, but he looked rather handsome.

"Yeah. Mr. Kahn was kind enough to loan it to me. It doesn't exactly fit, but I thought it was a good disguise. Nobody's seen me in a suit for twenty years." Fish looked proud.

"So do you want to take over, Mr. Fish?" Plant wheeled over the book cart he'd been using for the mis-shelved books. "It's about time for me to take off for lunch, anyway."

Plant was halfway down the street before I realized I hadn't told him about Peter's story. It was such a juicy one: Fanna Badjie didn't write Fanna Badjie's books, and she had a criminal girlfriend who had been stealing the real author's money. I'd have to tell him after lunch.

I wondered if I should tell Jonathan the story. He'd only had one encounter with Peter — and that was in a sleazy Bangkok bar when he was still drinking. He probably wouldn't want to be reminded. Besides, Jonathan seemed to be in a hurry to leave.

"I have an appointment with Ruben Moreno," Jonathan said. "I think he has a good story to take on my show. Catfished by a thirteen-year-old. That Willow O'Malley is quite a piece of work. People don't believe this stuff goes both ways. And I look forward to getting you on the show, too, Mr. Fish. You've got the best catfish story of all."

Fish on Jonathan's show? He had a catfish story? This was getting weirder and weirder. And Jonathan was practically out the door. Did he want to avoid me that much?

"Good-bye, Jonathan." I called to him as he went out the door, but I'm not sure he heard me.

A flood of customers came in as he left. I was grateful to have Fish to help me. There wasn't time to talk, and I had a feeling he didn't want to explain his bizarre appearance or Jonathan's mention of his "catfish story." Had he been catfished? Funny he and Jonathan had become friends. Not a likely duo.

It was late afternoon when Plant came back.

"I drove up to Big Sur for lunch at Ragged Point. Some cool sea breezes to blow the LA out of my system. Say, have you had any thoughts about that mysterious fingernail? Do you think it's a clue?"

"Yes." I spoke *sotto voce* as I finished gift-wrapping a big coffee table book for an impatient customer. "I put it in my clue bag."

When the customer was gone, I whispered to Plant, "If Brownie is a woman, which is what Adriana thinks, that nail must belong to her. And I think we've got our killer."

"Or maybe Larry likes to do a bit of cross-dressing?" Plant was not taking this seriously. "I'm still convinced the devoted son did it. That's some inheritance he's come into. I Googled around and found out the Gilhoolys owned at least thirty properties on the coast alone."

I sighed. "Well, I think that now Ginny's death has been ruled a homicide, I should take my bag of clues to Officer Pilchard. At least it might take some attention off Joe."

But Plant wasn't even paying attention. Some commotion was going on outside our window.

Adriana ran in, followed by a bouncy, smiling Britney.

"Look, Camilla!" Britney pointed at the door. "It's my mom! She came back! She's fine!"

Shannon appeared at the door, tanned and radiant. She was accompanied by a Hobbit. Or somebody who looked a lot like a Hobbit. He was a good head shorter than Shannon. She was a big woman, but he couldn't have been taller than five foot six. He had shaggy hair and a cute, boyish face.

"Camilla! I hear you've been babysitting our girls while I was gone. I'm very grateful." Shannon seemed changed. More confident, more worldly. She was dressed elegantly in what looked like an Italian suit. She turned to her Hobbit friend. "This is Derrick," she said. "He's my catfish."

Adriana looked stricken.

Derrick the catfish. He had to be the man Peter met in Banjul. "Fanna's" assistant.

Shannon laughed. "Don't worry, Adriana, I know you called him a catfish and that's what he was, wasn't he?"

Derrick looked sheepish. "I'm afraid I was rather fraudulent in my fundraising for our village school after Fanna Badjie's friend in Yorkshire started nicking our royalties. I grabbed a fake profile on Facebook so I could pretend I looked like Benedict Cumberbatch in a hard hat. My Gambian friends say that's the best way to raise funds in an emergency."

"It would have been so much easier if you'd just asked me," Shannon put an arm around him.

"Are you telling me you wouldn't have missed my love letters?" Derrick looked up at Shannon with adoration.

She laughed and gave him a sideways hug.

Derrick extended a hand to me. "I bring greetings from Vera and all the blokes at Sherwood, Ltd. We took Fanna Badjie's new book to them, secretly, so Fanna's former girlfriend couldn't get her claws on it."

"Totally James Bond," Shannon said. "Everybody there was so nice, and I loved Lincolnshire. Derrick says he'll take me back there soon."

She leaned down and kissed him.

"So you were working for Neezer, Derrick? Ebeneezer Hack?" I hoped that was all out in the open by now.

"Of course," Derrick said. "He's secretly the author of the Fanna Badjie books. He was my tutor at university, so I went down to The Gambia to assist him and have an adventure or two. Didn't Peter Sherwood tell you?"

"Peter's emails tend to be a bit sketchy."

"Oh, he had a message for you." Shannon opened her Kate Spade tote bag and pulled out a crumpled envelope. "I've been carrying this around since Africa. He says he owes you an apology."

I opened the envelope gingerly. The note, written on stationery from the Sheraton Gambia Beach Hotel, was definitely in Peter's handwriting.

 Duchess, I must apologize for leaving you with that body on your doorstep last spring. I'm glad Derrick's friend can deliver this in person. Law enforcement reads all our email. That night, I couldn't take the chance of the local constabulary scrutinizing the Canadian passport. It's one of my dodgier ones. So, I simply ran off and hid out at Marva's for a few days. I admit when I found the gap in your fence, I escaped down the alley like a craven coward. I contemplated waiting in my rented motor until the police drama was over, but some young women in the alley spotted me and started giggling. A late-night hen party, I assume. So it was time for me to scarper. I felt guilty leaving you to deal with the police alone. But the next morning, Marva told me the body had disappeared, so I suppose I might have stayed. In any case, I'm sorry."

So that's what happened. Peter didn't even know Ginny's body had disappeared until the next day. He must have driven directly to Marva's looking for a place to avoid the police.

"Are you all right?" Shannon gave me a worried look.

I nodded.

Shannon brightened again. "I must get down to the Embarcadero for my mani-pedi." She waved a hand at me. "Aren't my nails a disgrace? You wouldn't believe what it was like living in that African village while Derrick's hand healed. He was injured by this giant eagle that tried to steal his tuna sandwich when we were on the Gambian riverboat. African eagles are huge and they love fish."

Shannon took Derrick's arm and headed for the door. "I'll be back in about an hour, girls," she said over her shoulder. "Don't cause any trouble for Camilla."

I motioned for the girls to come behind the counter. I needed Adriana's sleuthing skills. I wondered if that giggling "hen party" could have anything to do with the disappearance of Ginny's body.

"Adriana," I whispered. "Plant found another clue. If you're sure Ginny's catfish was a woman, I think we can prove she's the murderer."

# fifty-two

. . .

## Fishing for Compliments

*a*driana leaned on the check-out counter and gave me a big smile.

"I'm so glad you found a clue. Did you see on the news that the police are sure Mrs. Gilhooly was murdered now? But the idiots think Joe did it. What's your clue? You really think it comes from the catfish?"

Britney heaved a dramatic sigh. "Are you going to go all Sherlock-Holmes-y again? I should have gone down to the Embarcadero with Mom. I'm so tired of all this stuff about Mrs. Gilhooly's murder. That's how you got in so much trouble last time. You want to get locked in the spider shack again?"

Adriana looked over her glasses at Britney as if she were a naughty child.

"Didn't you hear what Mr. Kahn said? Willow O'Malley isn't going to be bullying anybody for a while. The principal is going to suspend her, so Mr. Kahn says she's probably going to have to repeat the eighth grade."

Britney giggled. "Sweet! I'll bet her squad won't know who to torture without Willow to boss them around."

I wanted to get back to the subject of my clues.

"Do you think Brownie might have had acrylic fingernails? Maybe painted bright red?"

Adriana took a quick intake of breath.

"OMG yes! At least Brownie's emails were all about hair and nails and stuff like that. Girly things. That's why I think Brownie is a girl. Of course, Ginny sent selfies where she showed off her manicures, so I can't be sure if maybe Brownie was just a guy being polite."

"She sent her lover photos of her manicures? Talk about fishing for compliments!" This was an odd habit. It would never occur to me to take a selfie of my hands, much less send it to a lover. Maybe when my face gets wrinkly, I'll feel differently.

"Yes. There was one email where she said her husband never appreciated all the things she did to look nice for him, but she loved that Brownie did."

Fish came over to the counter. "Britney, do you want to help me shelve the new shipment while these two detectives do their sleuthing?" He gave me a wink. "Do good work, ladies. I'm as worried about Joe as you are."

Britney grinned. Adriana usually monopolized Fish, so Britney was finally getting her turn. I had to hope the story Jonathan had heard about the man was bogus.

Now Adriana and I could go back to my cottage to examine the new fingernail.

Buckingham came trotting after us as we crossed the courtyard. I wondered why he didn't stay with Fish. Maybe he thought he'd get an extra meal.

When I opened the door, Buckingham didn't run to his dish. Instead, he made a bee-line for my bed. Ronzo's scent must have drawn him, poor little guy. He did adore Ronzo. I suppose it would only be right for Ronzo to take him home with him. But I'd miss that furry little face.

I grabbed the bag of clues from my dresser drawer, brought it back to the living room, and dumped the contents on the coffee table so Adriana could examine them. I hadn't showed any of these to her earlier because they seemed so inconsequential compared to the phone.

Adriana picked up the red nail, and then the green one. She seemed most interested in the backs of them.

"Bad glue," she said. "These acrylics shouldn't come off. They're supposed to be, like, cemented on the lady's real nails. But a few months ago, I remember Shannon had a nail come off and she was furious. She went back to Tiffani and demanded her money back. I guess Tiffani had got some bad glue and everybody's nails were falling off."

"Tiffani? Is that name spelled with an 'i' at the end?" Could she be Brownie's other lover?

Sudden bangs on the door startled us both. Britney shouted at us.

Adriana opened the door.

Britney rushed up to me. "You gotta come. Back to the store. Fish is gone."

I felt guilty I'd left her alone. "He simply walked out the door in the middle of his shift?"

Britney shook her head. "Not out the door. Out the window. I was watching the store when he went to the men's room. But he didn't come back. So I'm pretty sure he climbed out the window in there. It doesn't have a screen or anything, and it's pretty big. A police car came and parked out in front of Kat's across the street. Fish totally freaked and ran to the bathroom."

Now I was freaking. I headed for the door. "Nobody's watching the store now?"

"Nobody but Mr. Kahn. He said Ruben cancelled, so he wants to talk to you. He probably wants to know why you chose Ronzo over him. You should be nicer to Mr. Kahn. He's very rich."

Good Lord. Nobody in the store but Jonathan. That could be worse than nobody at all. I pushed open the door.

"I'll put these back in the bag, okay?" Adriana carefully put my clues back in the plastic baggie. I wondered if they meant anything at all.

"Then can we go down the Embarcadero?"

"Okay, I guess." Adriana gave me a questioning look.

I nodded my blessing, put the clue bag back in my dresser, and locked the house. When I got back to the store, sure enough, Jonathan was talking up a book to a star-struck customer.

"If you recommend this, Mr. Kahn, I'll buy it," the customer said. "My husband and I never miss your show."

It was a book by a political pundit that was supposedly a bestseller, but I hadn't moved one in the past two months.

When the woman left, I put my arm around Jonathan and gave him a big kiss on the cheek.

"Thanks for moving that turkey of a book," I was glad to see he wore a genuine smile. "I don't know how it got to be a bestseller."

"Super-PACs." Jonathan laughed. "They buy up thousands of these political books the first few days they come out. Then they give them to donors, or pulp them. But it gets the books on the *New York Times* bestseller list."

"Do you think these authors realize nobody's reading their books?" I looked at the cover, graced with the familiar smug face of one of Jonathan's colleagues.

"Nope. There are some people who are sure they are brilliant in spite of all evidence. Give that guy a few compliments and he'll spend an hour telling you he's a literary genius. Fishing for more compliments, of course."

I laughed. "I won't fall for that again. No reason to order books that won't sell."

Adriana and Britney came running in, giggling. "We're going down to the Embarcadero now." Britney was all smiles. Thank goodness her wandering mother had come home.

Adriana smiled too as they rushed out the door. She had her friend back. All seemed forgiven.

But that left Jonathan and me alone in the empty store.

The silence turned awkward. I knew it was up to me to apologize. If Peter could apologize to me, I certainly could apologize to Jonathan. I'd abandoned him as much as Peter had abandoned me.

# fifty-three

. . .

## Fish Story

*J*onathan and I stood side by side behind the counter of the empty store. The silence felt heavy and sad. I knew I had to say something.

"Jonathan, about Ronzo — I didn't know he was coming. When he was suddenly here, I felt off-balance, and I didn't have time to talk to you —"

"No need to explain." He patted my hand. "I'm the one who screwed up. I wanted you back. I thought your boyfriend had moved on. I was wrong. That's all. Not your fault."

I kissed his cheek. "Thanks for understanding. And thanks for taking over the store when Fish evaporated."

Out in the street, a policeman came out of Kat's Café, eating a giant cookie and carrying a takeout bag. He got into the police car and took off.

I sighed. "I have no idea why Fish is so paranoid. Britney said he escaped out the window. That policeman was probably picking up lunch and some of Kat's famous chocolate chip cookies. Nothing to do with Morris Fishman."

"They're great cookies." Jonathan spoke in a flat voice, as if he were thinking of something else.

"Is Fish really a convicted sex offender?" I sat in the cashier's chair. It was the only chair behind the counter, so that might have been a little rude, but I didn't want to keep standing up there, so close to Jonathan.

"Yes. And it's a sad, sordid story." He turned to face me and leaned on the counter. "Catfishing 101. Mr. Fishman was teaching at a community college up in the Bay Area, and he caught a gang of girls cheating. They had each plagiarized their writing assignments from one of the short stories of Flannery O'Connor."

"Flannery O'Connor? They thought they'd get away with that?" Poor Fish. I'd probably give up teaching, too, if I had to deal with such brazen cheating.

"Apparently. This was in the heart of Silicon Valley. So the students were entitled, pampered rich kids. Fish said most teachers let the bad behavior slide, because the parents donated so much money to an otherwise underfunded school. But he didn't care. He flunked them all."

"So they got him fired?" I could imagine Willow O'Malley and her minions doing something like that.

"Yes. He lost his job — and a whole lot more. A couple of days after the incident, he started getting romantic emails from the hot new secretary in admissions. He'd flirted with the woman a bit, and he says she flirted back. After a couple of weeks, the emails heated up. Then he got one with a bunch of attachments. She said they were photos of herself in new lingerie."

"Uh-oh, I hope he wasn't at school when he opened them?" The flirtation didn't sound like Fish, but I could imagine an awkward man like that wouldn't quite know what to do if an attractive woman sought him out.

"No. Mr. Fishman waited until he got home to open the email attachments, which of course didn't come from the secretary. And you're so right. It was an 'uh-oh' moment. There were no glamour shots of the object of his affections. Each one showed disgusting child pornography. Opening them loaded the videos onto his hard drive. He tried to delete them, but he's not computer savvy. A half hour later, the cops showed up. Alerted, he's sure, by the mean girl brigade as soon as they saw him leave for home with the laptop."

"And I suppose he was fired and blackballed from teaching?" My heart went out to poor Fish. No wonder he was cagey about his past.

"Not only that. He was arrested and convicted of having kiddie porn. He spent three years in prison and has to register as a sex offender for the rest of his life. Can't live near a school or a play-ground or church. Which often puts him in a homeless camp. Tragic story. I'll bet he was a damned good teacher."

I sat speechless for a moment as I took this in. I have to admit my eyes stung. The mean girls' revenge was so simple. And so cruel. They had utterly destroyed a life. And had probably gone on to destroy other lives. Entitled monsters like that were hard to stop. I'd gone to school with some myself.

"So the police still harass him? Because he's supposedly a sex offender?"

Jonathan nodded as he leaned down to wipe my tear away with the elegant pocket square he always wore in his jacket.

"Some people destroy their own lives with alcohol and cheap sex," he said. "People like me. But this poor guy — he did nothing wrong but believe a catfish. Well, a school of catfish." He gave an unfunny laugh.

"So that's why you're going to have him on your show?"

He gave me a wry smile as he nodded. "I don't know if it will help clear his name, but at least he'll get to tell his story after all these years."

I stood and gave Jonathan a hug. Finally, I could see how his TV show might be doing some good. He looked at me with those fierce blue eyes and I saw the man I'd married — the fearless journalist who spoke truth to power.

"Thank you," I said. "Thank you for doing something to help Fish. He's a good person and a hard worker. He didn't deserve any of it. Nobody does."

The bell on the door jingled. Two middle-aged women walked in.

"Oh, my heavens!" one said. "Is it really —?"

"Yes! It's Jonathan Kahn!" said the other. "From that TV show!"

Yes, it was Jonathan Kahn. The man I married. Essentially a good man. Who was getting his life together. Part of me would always love him.

# fifty-four

· · ·

## The Barracuda

*A* surge of customers arrived as I was closing up the store for the evening. As I rang up their purchases, I was surprised to see Adriana waiting patiently in the line.

I motioned for her to join me behind the counter.

"Where's Britney?" I asked. "You two didn't fight again, did you?"

Adriana shook her head as she helped me bag the books. "Nah. I just don't want to hear any more of her mom's stories about that stupid bird in Africa who steals tunafish sandwiches. Shannon keeps talking and talking and you might as well not even be there."

I rang up the last purchase, steered a straggling customer to the bestseller table, and turned back to Adriana with a laugh.

"Shannon managed to talk for an hour and a half about African Sea Eagles?"

"Well, except when Tiffani was talking about how much she hated Mrs. Gilhooly and was glad Joe killed her. She talked over me when I said Joe didn't do it, and it was some catfish called Brownie. She totally gave me the evil eye."

This was interesting.

"So, Tiffani the manicurist hated Mrs. Gilhooly? But Ginny was one of her best customers. She had her nails done for every holiday. I'm sure she said it was at that salon down on the Embarcadero. Now is that the Tiffani who was one of Crystal's bridesmaids?"

Adriana nodded. "Yeah — until Mrs. Gilhooly tried to kick her out of the wedding. Tiffani acts all fakey-sweet to customers, but she hates most of them. And she really hated Mrs. Gilhooly."

"Because Ginny wanted her out of the wedding party?" Being stuck with an expensive, probably hideous bridesmaid's dress would make a lot of people feel a bit hostile.

"No." Adriana shook her head. "Tiffani hated her before that. Last year Mrs. Gilhooly evicted Tiffani's mama from her apartment and the old lady had to move in with Tiffani. Sounds like her mom was real traditional, like mine, and she made Tiffani go to mass and stuff and wouldn't let her boyfriend stay overnight, even though she's old. Like twenty-five or something."

"Oh, dear. That sounds like a recipe for disaster."

"Yeah. It was. I guess there was a big fight and Tiffani kicked her mom out, and two weeks later her mom died of a heart attack in a homeless camp. And it was all Mrs. Gilhooly's fault. According to Tiffani."

Well now. That was a major chunk of information. This Tiffani had to be the one Ginny called the Barracuda. And she certainly had a motive for murder — and for dumping Ginny's body in a homeless camp. I was dying to bounce this off Adriana, but I didn't want to say anything about the murder while a customer was still in the store.

"What a soap opera." I decided to say. "Sounds like you really got an earful down there."

Apparently, the customer at the bestseller table had heard enough, too. She left without buying anything.

Adriana checked her phone. "It's after six o'clock. Should I switch the sign from 'Open' to 'Closed'?"

I nodded. She'd given me a piece of the puzzle we hadn't had before — a murder motive for one of those bridesmaids Ginny hated. A much more believable motive than a wasted bridesmaid dress.

Adriana turned the sign and I locked the door.

"Adriana dear, I think you may have solved our mystery. Tiffani has to be the Barracuda. And I think she's probably Brownie the catfish, too."

Adriana nodded as my brain kept gathering puzzle pieces.

"All the selfies Ginny sent of her manicures — they make Brownie sound more like a manicurist than a guy who works on an oil rig, don't they?"

Adriana gave me one of her eye-rolls. "That's what I've been telling you all along. Brownie is a lady. And that last email she sent — she could have just signed 'Tiffani' without thinking — instead of 'Brownie'. And there never was any 'other woman'."

"Do you think Tiffani could bash one of her clients over the head?"

"Totally! And she'd lie about it. She's so fake, she's scary."

"Does she do her own nails a bright red?"

Adriana dismissed my question with a wave. "Nah. She's always got purple nails. It's like her brand. The whole salon down there — it's totally purple since she had it redone a couple of months ago. Shannon doesn't know where Tiffani got the money, since she used to be broke all the time."

Hmmm. My puzzle pieces didn't quite fit together. But Tiffani's mother's death gave her a strong reason to want revenge on Ginny. And if she was the Brownie who had conned Ginny out of all that money — it would explain why she could afford to redo her salon. Plus, she was obviously into nasty little schemes. She was one of the bridesmaids who sent Ginny to that non-existent party.

Adriana's phone jingled.

"It's Britney," she said. "She says my mom has made a huge taco feast and there's fish and shrimp and homemade frijoles and empanadas for dessert — like a welcome home for Shannon. So, I have to go home right away."

"Do you need a ride? The bus won't come for fifteen minutes."

"Nah. Shannon's coming to pick me up. She's going to pick up some of the ladies from the salon, too. I guess she invited everybody

— even Tiffani. But it's okay. My mom always cooks a boatload of food."

Oh, dear. The girls were having dinner with the Barracuda. Even if she wasn't our killer, I was pretty sure that woman was dangerous.

# fifty-five

. . .

## Fisherman Jack's

*I* finished closing up for the day and was about to head for my cottage when I got a text from Jonathan.

"Wonderful to see you and your store thriving. I'd never have pictured a New Yorker happy in small town CA, but here you are. I'm heading back to LA. Mr. Fishman is coming with me to give an interview for the show. He's saying he might stay there. He's got a cousin in Van Nuys who might accept him after the interview. He wants me to tell you thanks for everything. I thank you, too. All my love."

"All my love." That had a tone of finality about it. I guess that made sense. He'd come up here to get a wife for his new home and I'd turned him down. So now he was leaving.

Why did that make me feel so empty?

Even Fish was gone. Typical of Jonathan not to think about what I would do without Fish's help in the store. But I should be happy for Fish. He might finally get his life back.

When I got back to my cottage, I fed Buckingham and cuddled with him as I phoned Ronzo. I wanted to hear if Joe was all right. Plus, I needed to hear from Ronzo himself. I wanted him back here. To remind me why I let Jonathan go.

But Ronzo didn't pick up.

So I phoned Plant. I wanted to talk to him about what Adriana had discovered about Tiffani. That woman had a motive. Two motives, since she very likely was Brownie. Plant would have to believe me now. He couldn't keep saying Larry Gilhooly had killed Ginny.

All I got was Plant's voicemail, so I tried his landline. Silas answered. He had no idea where Plant was, and he was cooking Beef Wellington, and if Plant didn't show up in the next forty-five minutes, there would be hell to pay.

Uh-oh. That meant Plant was going to be caught up with either a fancy dinner or a fight or both. Probably both. He would definitely be unavailable. I made some noises about it being nothing and apologized for bothering Silas while he was cooking.

"Okay, Buckingham, we're on our own." The cat jumped down and scampered over to his water dish. Even he didn't want to hang out with me. I wished I had somebody who could discuss the Tiffani revelation. Jonathan might have, but he was gone.

So was Fish. I picked up my copy of *Trout Fishing in America*. I hadn't noticed before, but he'd put another note on the flyleaf.

"Thanks for letting me park in your used graveyard," was written in blue ink at the top of the page. But at the bottom was another quote in black ink:

*"I'm leaving for America, often only a place in the mind...*Richard Brautigan."

Definitely a good-bye. A farewell as strange as Fish was. I did hope he'd find his "America" after Jonathan's interview, and his life would be happier.

And I'd be happier if his friend Joe wasn't still in danger. Joe was always at the back of my mind. Somebody killed Ginny Gilhooly and it wasn't him. I needed to find out who. I got my bag of clues and dumped them on the coffee table: the scrap of wrapping paper, the big folded piece of the same paper that fit it like a jigsaw puzzle, the floaty otter pen, the green fingernail, and the red one.

Did they mean anything? If I were on one of those TV police shows, I could get some fingerprints or DNA from the pen, and maybe the paper, and if they matched, they might reveal the murderer. Especially if the prints belonged to somebody with a motive, like Tiffani.

Buckingham jumped back on the couch, and as usual, seemed fascinated by the green fingernail. He wasn't allowed on the coffee table, but he stood on the couch and loomed over it.

"Okay, Buckingham, what really happened the night Ginny died? How did you get that fingernail on your head? Did Ginny try to pet you, before she was attacked? No. She had that black cat phobia. Maybe she pushed you away?"

The cat almost looked as if he remembered the dark incident.

"Ginny must have been tipsy or drugged or something if she thought she could return the book in the middle of the night. As if we worked 24/7 like robots."

Buckingham meowed. Maybe to say he was definitely not a robot.

"But there was Ginny, on the back doorstep with that book she wanted to return. Then what? Somebody must have been with her, or maybe came up from behind. She must have been clutching the book, and the somebody tried to take it from her."

Buckingham yawned.

"Well, it had to be a struggle, or the gift wrap wouldn't have been torn. And the otter pen wouldn't have fallen out of the bag. Then there's the red fingernail. The attacker must have been grabbing that book hard for the fingernail to break off inside."

Buckingham climbed onto my lap. I hoped it meant he was going along with my scenario.

"So, let's say the killer got hold of the book. Then what? Did he/she thump Ginny over the head with it? Could Angela Duckworth's *Grit* have killed Ginny Gilhooly?"

The cat gave me a disapproving look.

"Okay, it would have had to be a strong person. Like…Larry. Larry is the one that doesn't make sense. If Larry isn't the murderer, how did he get hold of the bag with the partially wrapped book in it? Maybe Plant and Ronzo are right after all."

Buckingham jumped down to the floor and walked away, lifting his tail to show his butt. Okay, he did not go along with the Larry theory.

"You're probably right, Bucky. It's Tiffani. Everything points to her. But she's short and really thin. Doesn't look as if she could lift a sack of potatoes. But maybe she works out. There's a fitness place next to the salon. I suppose she might be strong enough to kill somebody with a book and drag the body away. I know she scares me."

I put the clues back in their bag. They weren't helping one bit.

Besides, I was hungry. I fixed myself a solitary dinner of frozen pasta and bland veggies. Luckily, I had a passable Zinfandel to drink with it.

I was pouring myself a second glass when I realized I'd left my keys in the store. I hated going in there after dark because when the store was lit up in any way, people assumed I was open and would start banging on the door. But it wasn't safe to leave the keys in there. If anybody found them, they could get into the register, and my cottage, too.

I grabbed a flashlight and hoped its dim beam wouldn't attract any book-deprived night owls. When I got back in the store, I found the keys right there on the counter. (What had I been thinking?) As I pocketed them, I heard a raucous bunch of women coming down the sidewalk toward the store. I turned off the flashlight, hoping they hadn't seen the glow. They were singing "Hotel California" at the top of their lungs. I remembered an Eagles tribute band was playing at Fisherman Jack's tavern down the street. These women were obviously getting primed for the music. I peeked across the street from the dark store.

They were not all women. There was one little man bringing up the rear, not singing. He looked like Shannon's Derrick. Oh, dear, the raucous crowd was Shannon and her salon crew and — was that Adriana's mother Luisa? How nice how she was getting a night out.

I shouldn't begrudge them their fun. Shannon deserved to celebrate her homecoming. And at least Tiffani didn't seem to be with them.

Uh-oh. Tiffani wasn't with them. Had she left the party early? Or had she stayed at the house? Were Adriana and Britney alone with her now?

I grabbed the desk phone and called Adriana. No answer. Not good. Adriana pretty much had her phone stapled to her hand. Maybe it was charging. I should call Britney. But I had no idea of her number — it was in my own cell phone back in the cottage.

Should I go to Shannon's house and make sure the girls were safe?

Unfortunately, I didn't know where the house was. But I Googled Shannon's name on the store computer and found an address. It was in one of the newish faux Spanish neighborhoods down by the bay. Not far. Maybe I was being silly, but it felt urgent. If those girls had started blabbering about "Brownie" at dinner, they could be in danger — terrible danger.

# fifty-six

· · ·

## Fish in a Barrel

When I got back to my cottage, I grabbed my phone and purse and started out the door. Buckingham stood directly in front of me, blocking my way. He meowed loudly.

"Okay, Bucky," I said. "You're right. I haven't even called Britney yet." The girls were probably fine. I had let my mind go to a worst-case scenario again. Plant always told me I shouldn't do that.

I sat on the couch, pulled out my phone and saw I had a text — and it was from Britney.

But there was only one word. "Hell."

A chill went through me. I'd never heard Britney or Adriana use strong language. Maybe my worst-case scenario was right, and Tiffani was doing something awful to them. I called Britney back. But the phone rang forever, then went to voicemail. I tried Adriana again and the same thing happened. Why were those little phone addicts not picking up?

This was going from "maybe scary" to terrifying. What if Tiffani had figured out Adriana knew she'd been catfishing Ginny, and wanted to murder her as well? I couldn't bear thinking about it.

"Sorry, Buckingham." I got up and gave him a pat. "I need to check on our friends Adriana and Britney. I have a feeling something awful is going on at that house." I dropped the phone in my purse and ran out to the car. Buckingham let me go without protest this time.

The fog had moved in and the girls' newly-developed neighborhood had no streetlights. The only illumination came from the occasional floodlight mounted on one of the McMansions that lined the winding streets. As I turned onto the cul-de-sac where the girls lived, a shadowy figure in a hoodie darted out of the darkness into the street. I screeched to a stop, only feet from him, and jumped out of the car.

"Are you all right? I didn't see you!"

"Well, duh. You weren't paying attention!" It was Adriana, wearing an oversized jacket I hadn't seen before. Her voice went whispery. "I was waving at you! I've been hiding behind that bush. I was so glad to see you. But then you were just going to drive on by, so I had to stop you. Quick! Let me in."

As she went around to the passenger door, I could see she was limping.

I got back in the car and took a deep breath, then turned to Adriana. "What's wrong with your leg? Are you okay?"

"How could I be okay? They took my phone. Britney's too. And Britney's still in there and she can't even text her mom. I put on Derrick's jacket to kind of disguise myself, and climbed out the bathroom window. I figured if Fish could do it, I could, too. But I landed funny and hurt my leg."

Okay, maybe this was simply about the girls being angry because some grown-ups confiscated their phones. I hoped so. I drove down the street and parked in front of a house about two doors down from Shannon's and looked directly at Adriana.

"Why did you climb out the window? Was it just because somebody took your phone? Why were you hiding behind a bush?"

"I was waiting for my stupid mother to get back. She's so embarrassing. She drank tequila with them — and she never drinks hard liquor. Then she let those ladies talk her into going with them to Fisherman Jack's. I thought all of them were going, but those two stayed behind and started asking questions in a nasty way. They're drunk as skunks."

"Drunk as skunks?" An odd expression for a child. "Who?"

"All of them." Adriana shivered in spite of the jacket. "Do skunks get drunk? Why do people say that? Shannon says it all the time. She said it tonight. 'We're all drunk as skunks and we're going to have a good time. You're grown-up enough to behave yourselves, aren't you, girls?'" Adriana's voice had gone into a nasty sing-song. "Like we're the ones who don't know how to behave."

This wasn't sounding good.

"Adriana, is Britney in danger from these drunks? Is she hurt?"

"Well, she cried when she got slapped in the face, but maybe she's being a drama queen. I got slapped too, but all they did was knock my glasses off." Adriana pushed her glasses farther up the bridge of her nose.

"Britney cried? Maybe that's why she sent me her strange text. It was only one word — 'Hell'."

I kept trying to breathe normally. This was sounding worse and worse.

"Hell?" Adriana pondered this for a moment. "That doesn't sound like something she'd say. Maybe it was auto-correct for 'Help.' She tried to text something before they grabbed her phone, but she didn't have time to finish."

"Who is 'they'? Is it Tiffani?" It was probably time for me to call the police.

Adriana shook her head. "It's Crystal and Ruby-Lee. They're acting like they're cops, trying to make Britney confess what she knows about 'Brownie.' Which is zero. But she was stupid enough to talk about catfishing at dinner."

"Crystal and — Ruby-Lee? But Tiffani — where is she?"

"Tiffani left when Britney started talking about Brownie. Ruby-Lee is the curvy one. She's a physical trainer at the spa next to the nail place. Ginny called her Betty Boobs — because she always wears these low-cut tops. Ginny's emails said she could be dangerous, and she is."

"Dangerous? Like I should call the police dangerous?" I pulled out my phone, trying to decide if I should call Officer Pilchard or hit 911.

"No! Don't. They said they'd hurt our moms if we told." Adriana sank down in her seat. "Oops. Too late. Here comes Betty Boobs now."

Oops indeed. A tall young woman in leggings and a low-cut, glittery red top emerged from the shadows and banged on my window.

I rolled it down. "What can I do for you, Ruby-Lee? Adriana says things are rather unpleasant in the house."

"Rather unpleasant? I'll show you unpleasant!"

Before I realized what was happening, the woman opened the door, grabbed my arm and yanked it hard while yelling at the top of her lungs.

"Oh my god! Oh, my god! You're kidnapping that child!" She had a voice like a drunken foghorn. "Somebody help! Neighbors, you gotta come out here! She's kidnapping this little girl!" She could have felled a horse with that breath.

Another yank on my arm pulled me right out of my seat. A moment later, the hard scrape of asphalt burned my palms as I tried to break my fall. My knees hurt too, and I felt warm blood seeping into my sleeve from something stabbing my arm. I seem to have fallen on something sharp. I lifted myself a bit to push away a piece of broken wine bottle. Good Lord. No wonder I was bleeding. I grabbed the car door handle and tried to pull myself up.

"Look out! Don't let the pedophile get away!" Neighbors rushed out of their homes and surrounded me. "Pervert!" somebody yelled. "Pedophile! Call 911!"

"I already have," Ruby-Lee held up a phone. My phone. She must have grabbed it when she threw me to the ground. But I hadn't seen her make any calls.

"You're all bananas. Camilla's my friend!" Adriana piped up in a squeaky voice. This mob was obviously terrifying her too.

"I can tell the woman's been grooming her," a man said. "That's what they do. I saw it on the news."

"Please. I'm not a kidnapper." I pulled myself almost to a standing position, leaning against my sturdy Honda, but my knee kept giving way. "There are children in danger in that house. Could somebody help me up, if it's not too much trouble? I'd be very grateful." I spoke in as polite a voice as I could muster. But everybody kept looking at me as if I were a ravenous beast about to eat them.

I felt myself sliding down the car back to the pavement, and heard a commotion on the passenger side. People were trying to get Adriana to come out.

"I know this little girl's mother," a woman said. "She's Shannon Fiorentino's maid over there at Number 165. Shannon's been on vacation for months. She went to Africa. I think she was being catfished by some Nigerian romance scammer. Maybe this pervert is in cahoots with the Nigerians."

"I own the Morro Bay Bookshop on Main Steet…" I started to say. But I could see I shouldn't waste my breath. I could have been King Charles and they would have ignored me.

I hoped Adriana would make a run for it. But as the woman coaxed her out of the car, I could see her limp was worse. That jump out the window had done some real damage.

"Did that pervert hurt you, honey?" the woman asked her. "I'll help you walk back to your house."

"Come on, pervert." Ruby-Lee gave me a kick in the ribs that hurt almost as much as my arm. "Get up. I told the police you'd be at number 165. You'll get to lie down when you go to jail."

Dear Lord. The woman was getting away with this. Nobody would even help me get up. The neighbors looked down at me with eyes full of hate. I guess if somebody calls you a pedophile, they own you. People can do what they like to you while they hold you hostage. Like shooting a fish in a barrel.

And I seemed to have volunteered to be the fish.

# fifty-seven

. . .

## One Fish, Two Fish, Three Fish

*A*fter Ruby-Lee marched my aching, bleeding body into Shannon's house, Crystal accosted me with her shrieky voice and pushed me into a leather recliner.

"Whaz wrong with you, lady? Why did you tell these kids about Ginny's boyfriend Brownie? You've shpoil...ruined everything!" Her speech was even more slurred than Ruby-Lee's. She was sipping something greenish that might have been a margarita.

Britney cowered on the blue suede couch, under a matching shawl that made her nearly invisible. The room was decorated in a chilly blue and beige color scheme. It made me shiver.

"Adriana! Where were you?" Britney perked up as the neighbor woman brought her limping friend in the front door.

Adriana rushed to join Britney on the couch. I could see a red patch on Britney's face, and a bruise forming around her eye. She'd been slapped hard. The situation was even worse than I'd feared.

Crystal turned her shrieking anger on the neighbor. "What are you doing here, Nosy Nellie? You've been spying on us all night, haven't you?"

Crystal must have learned her manners from a pack of feral chihuahuas.

The neighbor shot eye-daggers at Crystal, then turned to Ruby-Lee.

"I thought I should stay and watch the girl until the police arrive."

"Who the hell called the cops?" Crystal's face distorted in rage as she screamed that the cops would "shpoil" everything.

But Ruby-Lee ignored her and ushered the neighbor out the still-open door.

"We'll be fine, ma'am. Thanks a lot for your help. Everything is under control." She closed the door and marched up to Crystal, waving one finger like a cartoon schoolmarm. A finger with a nail painted in bright red polish. Revlon's Cherries in the Snow if I wasn't mistaken. Exactly like the nail Plant found in Ginny's copy of *Grit*.

"Crystal, will you be quiet?" More finger wagging. "I had to tell people the bookstore lady was a kidnapper, so the girl wouldn't run away and tell everybody about Brownie. There were people out there, and more standing in their doorways, staring at us. I had to think of something. I didn't actually call 911. I lied."

"What are we going to do with her?" Crystal gave me a once-over. "She looks pretty beat up. Did you do that?"

"Sort of." Ruby-Lee glanced over at me and eyed the growing bloodstain on my sleeve. "I pulled her out of the car, and she fell on the broken bottle all by herself."

Dear Lord. I must look terrible.

"What are we supposed to do with her? I don't have my gun with me. I guess we could bash her over the head, since everybody's going to think we bashed Ginny's head on purpose, because of these blabbermouths." She turned and gave a fierce look at poor Britney.

"Maybe we could find her some Ambien, and she'll fall on her head and die like Ginny did." Ruby-Lee grabbed a half-full wine glass from the coffee table and sat on a blue and beige ottoman in front of the fireplace.

Ambien. The newspaper did say that Ginny had sleeping pills in her system.

"What's Ambien?" Adriana was always the sleuth.

"None of your damn business." Crystal slurped the dregs of her margarita.

Ruby-Lee's voice was calmer. "It's a sleeping pill you should never take." The woman seemed to have a strange motherly streak in spite of her homicidal tendencies. "It makes you walk in your sleep and do stupid things. Even drive."

Adriana jumped up. "Oh, wow. So you think Mrs. Gilhooly took Ambien and drove to the bookstore in her sleep?"

Ruby-Lee might sound calm now, but asking questions of these drunks was a bad idea. I tried to signal to Adriana, but she didn't look my way.

Crystal was quiet too, but quiet like a bomb about to go off. I tried to make myself small and invisible, like Britney.

But Adriana went bravely on. "Nobody bashed Mrs. Gilhooly on the head? The old lady just fell down 'cause she was sleepwalking on drugs?"

"Something like that," Ruby-Lee gave a weird smile.

"It was exactly like that. She did it all by her ownself!" Crystal's voice rose. "She took a buttload of Ambien and was supposed to nod off into Lalaland, but she had to return that damned book. Somehow, she drove to your store and fell on her face onto the concrete step. As soon as I realized she was gone, we drove over to get her to go back home, but by the time we got there, she was dead. That's all that happened."

"Of course, somebody might have bashed her on the head later to make sure she was dead." Ruby-Lee gave a macabre laugh.

Ah. So that's why Ginny's skull had two wounds.

"If it was all an accident, why are you being mean to us?" Adriana was like one of those cats that got killed by curiosity. "And why didn't you just tell the police it was an accident when it happened? Then Joe wouldn't have had to disappear and we wouldn't have had all this stupid drama."

"Well, why did little blondie here have to start talking about Brownie?" Crystal stood and loomed over Britney, who covered her face with her hands and shrank deeper into the couch.

Adriana jumped in to protect her friend.

"She said it to mock me because I told her Camilla and I figured out who Brownie is. Britney thinks my sleuthing is stupid."

"She's right." There was menace in Crystal's voice. "It's stupid. You should mind your own damned business. Tiffani has enough to deal with right now. There's no more catfishing money to pay for her salon remodel and she might have to move back to Bakersfield."

Crystal stomped off to another room and emerged with a pitcher about a quarter full of margaritas.

"So we're right? Camilla, Tiffani is Brownie!" Adriana gave me a big grin. I cringed, hoping the revelation wasn't going to get me bashed over the head. I was feeling too weak to fight or flee. Thank goodness Crystal didn't have her gun.

"No. You're not right." Ruby-Lee downed the contents of her wine glass. "It wasn't just Tiffani. It was all of us. But we had Tiffani write the emails because she's the one who was good in English in high school. And besides, her momma got catfished by some creep on a Christian dating site, so she knew what to say."

Crystal took a swig out of the margarita pitcher and looked at Adriana.

"Don't look so surprised, girly. We had to get money out of her somehow. That old bat wouldn't give Larry a penny, even though he was supposed to be her partner in the business. That old lady pulled the purse strings so tight they screamed."

Wow. All of them. Crystal and all her bridesmaids had been catfishing Ginny Gilhooly together. Amazing. Had they all been there in my courtyard that night, helping to move Ginny's body? Peter Sherwood said he heard giggles in the alley. Maybe he'd been right that it was a "hen night" party for the bride and bridesmaids. Except instead of throwing dollar bills at a male stripper, they moved a body to a homeless camp. How awful.

Speaking of awful, I was getting blood on Shannon's nice leather recliner. Luisa would have a big job getting it clean. My arm hurt like crazy. So did my ribs. I hoped Ruby-Lee's kick hadn't broken anything.

"It was Tiffani's fault the whole thing went to hell." Crystal perched on the arm of the couch and spoke in her normal high-pitched whine. "If she hadn't been such a drunk-tard that she signed her own name to the Brownie email, Ginny would have been willing to give us money forever. And I wouldn't have had to give the old bat all that Ambien."

"What?" Ruby-Lee's voice went up a couple of octaves. "You gave her the overdose of Ambien?" She stared at Crystal. "You told us the old lady took it herself. You were trying to kill her all along?"

Crystal let out a nasty laugh. "Duh. Somebody had to. I mean, it's not like I wanted to do it. That's why I was so mad at Tiffani. How could she be so stupid that she signed her own name!" She took a last gulp of her margarita. "But I forgave her when she drove us in her SUV to look for Ginny. No way could Ruby-Lee and me fit Ginny's fat ass into my little Miata. And Tiff had the great idea to take the body to the homeless camp where Ginny had tons of enemies."

Ruby-Lee gave a smug smile. "And I'm the one who remembered to go back and get that book out of the bushes, so nobody would know Ginny had been there. Otherwise, we might all be in jail right now."

Crystal snorted again. "It's a bookstore, Ruby-Lee. Nobody would have figured out it was Ginny's book. You didn't have to make such a big deal of it. Larry was totally pissed he had to return the damned thing. And you tore the wrapping paper. And left her phone in her damned pocket. Thank God nobody found it."

So that's where my "clues" came from. Ruby-Lee fished the book out of the bushes, tore the wrapping paper and got her fingernail caught in the book. Ginny must have dropped the bag when she fell, and the book and the pen landed in the shrubbery next to the door.

Then the three of them found her and moved the body. I guess it was a small hen party: Crystal, Ruby-Lee, and Tiffani. Women with the jewelry-related names Ginny deplored.

I heard a growing commotion outside. It sounded as if the neighbors hadn't all dispersed after we'd come into the house.

262

The front door burst open, and there was handsome young Ruben Moreno. Holding a gun. A cute pink gun.

"Adriana, are you okay?" he said in a commanding voice. "Where's the pedophile? My aunt says you got kidnapped by a pedophile."

# fifty-eight

. . .

## Kensie's Fishing Expedition

*R*uben rushed into the tense living room and hugged Adriana. "What happened? Is the pedophile still here? My aunt phoned me. She lives down the street. She said you were hurt by some pervert."

"Be careful with that, Ruben sweetie," said a high-pitched voice. "You don't want to shoot the poor girl."

In sauntered Kensie Weiner, wearing an embroidered Mexican blouse, a full skirt, and hoop earrings. She looked as if she intended to audition for some Mexican folk-dance troupe. She wasn't only what my mother called "mutton dressed as lamb," but mutton dressed as Mexican lamb. Did she think that was the kind of bait Ruben Moreno would go for?

She came up behind Ruben, way too close, and grabbed her pink gun out of his hand. With a smirk, she waved it around at all of us.

"So where's the perv? Is it one of these skanks, Camilla?" She aimed the gun in the general direction of Ruby-Lee and took a closer look at me. "Oh, gross! You're bleeding like crazy and ruining that beautiful chair."

Adriana stood up, all smiles, in spite of her sore leg. She seemed to think the cavalry had arrived. Well, maybe they had. I might be hallucinating, but it looked as if we were being rescued by a college kid and Kensie Weiner.

"That one pulled Camilla out of her car and threw her on the street," Adriana pointed at Ruby-Lee. "Camilla fell on a broken bottle from Mrs. Harding's recycling bin. The garbage trucks always drop something, but Mrs. Harding won't pick it up, so my mom has to do it." She limped toward me. "Are you all right, Camilla? I think you need to go to the hospital. You look weird."

"Somebody needs to call my mom." Britney piped up from behind her blue shawl. "And some policemen. We need police to arrest them. These criminals said they were going to kill Camilla and my mom and Luisa, too. They're catfishes. And they stole our phones!" Britney threw off the shawl and stomped over to Crystal. "I want my iPhone back! You stole it! Give me back my phone!"

"They're lying. That's the kidnapper right there!" Ruby-Lee jumped up and pointed at me.

"What, are you high, bitch?" Kensie motioned with the gun for Ruby-Lee to sit back in her chair. "Camilla is a famous New York socialite. Her mother was a Countess. She owns the bookstore up on Main Street."

Of course Kensie would have found out about Mother's dubious title.

We heard a car pull up into the driveway beside the house.

Britney grinned. "It's my mom and Derrick! You'd better give me my phone now, or they'll get you arrested for stealing!" Britney grabbed at Crystal's jacket.

Crystal dug deep into her pocket, pushed two phones into Britney's hands, and ran out the doorway to the kitchen. She probably intended to escape out the back. Fine. As long as she was gone, we'd all be safer.

But oh my, I was exhausted. And dizzy.

Britney gave one of the phones to a grateful Adriana. Then she punched a number on her own.

"She's not picking up! She's in the driveway. Why doesn't she answer?"

Outside, the commotion grew louder. More neighbors seemed to have gathered when they saw Shannon had come home. But all the voices were drowned out by the sudden wail of police sirens.

My head kept spinning around, and I couldn't hold it up. People in uniforms swarmed into the house. Shannon stomped in, barking orders that nobody obeyed. Derrick wanted to see the policemen's badges. And Adriana kept saying I looked weird. Then I kind of lost track and things went dark.

I guess it was sometime later that I woke up in a hospital bed, a tube stuck in one arm, and deep pain in the other. Plantagenet was hovering above me.

"Welcome back, darling. We thought you were gone for a while there. You lost a lot of blood." He smoothed my hair from my forehead. "What an ordeal you've been through."

"The girls?" I remembered Adriana's limp and Britney's black eye.

"They've been patched up and they're fine. They're even going to have their pictures taken for the local paper this afternoon. Everybody's calling them heroes."

"Crystal and Ruby-Lee?" Had all that really happened, or had I dreamed it? "That was Ruby-Lee's fingernail. In the book. I'm pretty sure."

"She may have to wait a while for her next manicure. She and Crystal are behind bars. And will be for some time. There's the kidnapping charge, your assault, defrauding Ginny Gilhooly with that catfishing operation, and of course the small matter of Ginny's murder. The girls had quite a tale to tell the police."

I tried to pull words out of my mental fog.

"Not murder. Crystal said it was an accident. Ginny fell on my concrete steps because she was sleepwalking. Crystal only furnished her with mass quantities of Ambien, or so she says."

Plant gave me a lopsided smile. "I think that's considered murder. Plus, there was a post-mortem blow to the head that cracked her skull."

"That might have been Ruby-Lee. She said she needed to make sure Ginny was dead. Or it could have been Tiffani…"

Misty images kept wafting in and out of my brain. I grabbed Plant's hand and squeezed it.

"I'm afraid I'm losing it. I dreamed that we were rescued by Kensie Weiner dressed in a Mexican costume. And that very good-looking college boy, Ruben Moreno, was there. The one who found Adriana in the spider shack. Dreams can be so weird."

Plant let out a big laugh.

"You weren't dreaming. It was Kensie who called and told me you were here in the hospital. I'm afraid she's been on one of her fishing expeditions. She's been trying to hook poor young Ruben Moreno the way she did with me. She'd been stalking him all weekend. Apparently, she imagined her little Mexican outfit would appeal to his Latinx roots." He laughed again. "But Ruben is a bright boy. When he heard from his aunt that Adriana was in trouble, he returned one of Kensie's texts and asked for her help. I guess she'd told him she carries a gun. So he got her to meet him at Shannon's house. He was pretty brave to go in there to rescue Adriana with it, since he tells me he's never shot a gun in his life. But thank goodness he did. You were in there bleeding to death."

"Did he call 911? Ruby-Lee first said she called 911 with my phone, but later she told Crystal she lied."

"Kensie called 911 as soon as she got the text from Ruben. She was afraid he'd do something stupid before she got there with the gun. She's not entirely useless. If those first responders hadn't got you to the hospital when they did, you might not have made it."

I shuddered. Did that mean I owed my life to Kensie Wiener? A sobering thought.

A nurse came in and shooed Plant out of the room. She gave me a shot of something and I sank back into the antiseptic-scented fog.

# fifty-nine

. . .

## Forty Pounds of Fish

*I* woke to noises from the hallway outside my hospital room.
And two familiar voices.

A moment later, Ronzo walked in, with Bette Midler in tow.

"They wanted to kick me out because of my outfit," Marva said.
She wore a grassy, classic perfume. Balmain's *Vent Vert*, if I wasn't
mistaken. "People can be so intolerant. I told them I'm a personal
friend of RuPaul, so they said I could come in for a minute."

Ronzo laughed, then leaned down and gave me a soft kiss on the
forehead.

"How do you feel, babe? They gave you a blood transfusion, so
you're supposed to have your strength back in a couple of days,
although the doc says it's gonna take a month before you're feeling
back to normal. How's your arm?"

"Not too bad. I think they gave me a pretty strong pain killer."

"So glad to see you're going to be okay," Marva said. "Joe will be so
relieved."

"Joe? Is he okay? Does he know we found out what happened to
Ginny Gilhooly?"

"Yes." Marva laughed. "You've never seen a man so energized. He sang along with the radio all the way back from West Hollywood. I'm so glad we convinced him not to out himself as J.J. Tower. He'd have been beaten to an Internet pulp by now. So many people blame him for the deaths in that fire."

Ronzo took my hand. "Are you strong enough to talk? I gotta hear from you what really happened. Everybody's got a different story."

I launched into my tale of woe. I told him all about how Adriana and I figured out the catfish had to be Tiffani, and we thought Tiffani probably killed Ginny as well.

"Why did you think Tiffani wanted Ginny dead? Because of the wedding?"

"No." I tried to smile. "It was because Ginny evicted Tiffani's mother from her apartment, leading to a fatal heart attack. Smart little Adriana got that information by eavesdropping at the nail salon. So we were sure the culprit was Tiffani. But then I realized the fingernail was the wrong color."

"Somebody's fingernail was the wrong color?" Marva hovered closer, her own nails a fierce orange. "There's a right color nail enamel for committing murder?"

I sort of laughed. "We found a green acrylic fingernail and a red one. But Tiffani always wears purple. So it couldn't have been her nail Plantagenet found in the book."

Marva rolled her eyes at Ronzo and blew me a kiss. She obviously didn't understand a word I'd said.

"I'll see you soon, sweetie," she said. "When you're feeling better."

I reached for Ronzo's hand. "Am I not making any sense?"

"Of course you are. Marva's got things to do, people to meet — you know Marva." He gave me a knowing look. "What I want to know is how you ended up in that McMansion with those two lunatic chicks. Is it where Adriana lives?"

"Adriana and Britney both. Adriana's mom is Britney's mom's maid. It happened because Britney mentioned Brownie, Ginny's catfish, at a dinner party. She was just teasing Adriana. But afterward, when the other diners moved on to Fisherman Jack's, Crystal and

Ruby-Lee stayed behind to see what the girls knew about Brownie. Because Brownie was actually all the bridesmaids. Which even Adriana didn't suspect. And Britney didn't know a thing. But Crystal and Ruby-Lee thought they both did, so they tried to make the girls talk by hitting them and threatening to kill their mothers."

Ronzo looked confused. "So the Brownie emails came from the lunatic chicks? Were they the ones in those *Real Housewives* messages I read?"

I nodded. He looked goofy and sweet, trying to follow the improbable saga without calling me crazy.

He let out a big laugh as the story started to fall into place for him.

"Wow. So you're saying the bride and her posse were catfishing the mother of the groom? Talk about bridezillas! But how did you find out? And, excuse me, but why the heck did you go over to that house instead of calling the cops?"

I tried to give him a quick overview of my saga, but I could see in his eyes that he didn't understand half of what I said. But the dear man kept his cheerful smile in place.

"So the victim took a bunch of Ambien? That's some badass stuff. I knew a guy back in New Jersey who dropped some Ambien one night and drove down the shore and bought, like, forty pounds of fish. The next morning, he had no idea how the fish got in his truck. But he called all his friends and had a killer fish fry. I liked that guy. Always made the best of things."

I should have been grateful Ronzo wasn't acting as if I had lost my mind.

"My mom would eat bread and butter on Ambien. Fat and carbs. She would never do that while she was awake."

Ronzo's expression got serious.

"So, Crystal killed Ginny Gilhooly with Ambien because Tiffani's email mistake outed the catfish scam?"

"Sort of. After she took the overdose, Ginny seems to have driven to my store in her sleep to return the book she bought for the now-despised Brownie. Then she fell on her face on the back steps and died. That's when Peter found the body and went to tell me, then ran off to Marva's house. Meanwhile, Crystal showed up with Ruby-Lee and Tiffani. They wanted to get Ginny back home before Larry arrived. But they found Ginny's corpse instead. Taking Ginny to the homeless camp was Tiffani's idea. Because Ginny had so many enemies there. I think Tiffani's the brains of the outfit."

Ronzo laughed.

"None of these ladies seem like Mensa material, Camilla. So that's how the body disappeared? The three of them came looking for Ginny, found her dead, then took the body?"

"Yes. They were Peter's 'hen party' he'd heard in the alley that night."

Ronzo's phone rang in his pocket. He squeezed my hand and said he had to take it. Maybe he was humoring me, listening to my rambling, and needed an excuse to get away. I guess he'd earned it.

A genuine grin spread over his face. He was really pleased about something.

"Twenty thou over asking?" he said to his phone. "Sweet! Do they know it's as-is? Ratty carpet and all?" There was a brief silence and Ronzo's grin got even wider. "Keep me posted, Oliver."

Since when did Ronzo speak real-estate-ese? He did have a cousin Oliver who was a real estate agent. What was up?

After he ended the call, Ronzo gave me a big kiss and grinned some more.

"We've sold it, Camilla! I've sold my Nana's house. For more than I expected. Now I can settle down here with some cash in my pocket to feed you something besides fish and chips. Maybe buy myself a car so Marva doesn't have to chauffeur me around."

This was amazing. "You're moving to Morro Bay? To be with me?"

His eyes went dreamy and he kissed me again.

"Well, yeah, maybe to be with you. Or maybe because I heard there's a job opening at a bookstore here with Mr. Fishman gone. Or maybe to form a band with one of the greatest guitar players of all time — Joe and I made some big plans on the way back from LA. Or I could get licensed in California and hang out my private eye shingle.

But mostly it's for Bucky, of course, I have to move here to be with my cat."

I laughed. "He's an awfully smart cat."

"Yeah. He listens pretty good. I figure that's in the job description for a bookstore cat. I remember how people always tell you their troubles in there. It's worse than tending bar."

# about the author

**Anne R. Allen** is a popular blogger and the author of the hilarious Camilla Randall Mysteries as well as the comic novels *Food of Love, The Gatsby Game,* and *The Lady of the Lakewood Diner.* Her nonfiction book, *The Author Blog: Easy Blogging for Busy Authors,* is an Amazon #1 bestseller. She's also the co-author, with Catherine Ryan Hyde, of the writer's guide *How to Be a Writer in the E-Age.*

Anne is a graduate of Bryn Mawr College and now lives on the Central Coast of California near San Luis Obispo, the town Oprah called "the happiest town in America." She loves to hear from her readers! Contact her at annerallen.allen@gmail.com

She blogs with *NYT* million-copy seller, Ruth Harris, at "Anne R. Allen's Blog…with Ruth Harris." You can find them at annerallen.com. The blog was named one of the Best 101 Websites for Writers by *Writer's Digest.*

If you've enjoyed this book, we hope you will consider writing a brief review. It will help others find the book. Thanks!

# also by anne r. allen

**THE CAMILLA RANDALL MYSTERIES:**

Chick Lit Noir— Snarky, delicious fun! These books are a laugh-out-loud mashup of romantic comedy, crime fiction, and satire. Dorothy Parker meets Dorothy L. Sayers. Perennially down-and-out socialite Camilla Randall--a.k.a. "The Manners Doctor"--is a magnet for murder, mayhem and Mr. Wrong, but she always solves the mystery in her quirky, but oh-so-polite way. Usually with more than a little help from her gay best friend, Plantagenet Smith.

**#1 GHOSTWRITERS IN THE SKY:** After her celebrity ex-husband's ironic joke about her "kinky sex habits" is misquoted in a tabloid, New York etiquette columnist Camilla Randall's life unravels in bad late night TV jokes. Nearly broke and down to her last Hermes scarf, she accepts an invitation to a Z-list Writers' Conference in the wine-and-cowboy town of Santa Ynez, California, where, unfortunately, a cross-dressing dominatrix named Marva plies her trade by impersonating Camilla. When a ghostwriter's plot to blackmail celebrities with faked evidence leads to murder, Camilla must team up with Marva to stop the killer from striking again.

**#2 SHERWOOD, LTD:** Suddenly-homeless American manners expert Camilla Randall becomes a 21st century Maid Marian—living rough near the real Sherwood Forest with a band of outlaw English erotica publishers—led by a charming, self-styled Robin Hood who unfortunately may intend to kill her.

**#3 THE BEST REVENGE** (the prequel): Read how it all began. In the glitzy 1980s, a teenaged Camilla loses everything: fortune, love, and eventually even her freedom when a TV star's murder is mistakenly laid at her feet. Through it all, she perseveres, and comes to learn that she is made of sterner stuff than anyone might have imagined, herself included.

**#4 NO PLACE LIKE HOME:** Doria Windsor, the uber-rich editor of *Home* decorating magazine loses everything, including her Ponzi-schemer husband, when their luxury wine-country home mysteriously goes up in flames. Homeless, destitute, presumed dead and branded a criminal, 59-yr-old Doria has a crash course in reality…and a second chance at love.

Meanwhile, Camilla Randall is facing homelessness, too, as Doria's husband's schemes unravel and take down innocent bystanders along the way. When the mysterious—and dangerously attractive—Mr. X turns up at Camilla's bookstore looking for clues to the death of a missing homeless man, Camilla joins in the search.

With the help of brave trio of homeless people and a little dog named Toto, Doria, Camilla and Mr. X journey down their own yellow brick road to unmask the real killer and reveal the dark secrets of Doria's "financial wizard" husband.

**#5 SO MUCH FOR BUCKINGHAM:** Camilla makes the mistake of responding to an Amazon review of one of her etiquette guides and sets off a chain of events that leads to arson, attempted rape and murder. Her best friend Plantagenet Smith is accused of the murder and nobody but her shady former boyfriend Peter Sherwood—fresh from a Tasmanian prison—can save him.

Camilla and Plant are caught between rival factions of historical reenactors who are fiercely pro or anti-Richard III. Set against the backdrop of Richard's re-burial in Leicester in 2015, the book is an exploration of the power of false rumors as well as a satire of the Internet communities whose "flame wars" sometimes spill into real life.

**#6 THE QUEEN OF STAVES:** Camilla's boyfriend Ronzo is forced to stage his own death and hide out in a homeless camp after his review angers a homicidal rock band. But he's able to help Camilla keep her struggling Morro Bay bookstore afloat with his unexpected tarot reading skills...until the lover of one of his tarot clients turns up dead on the beach. It's up to Camilla and Ronzo — and the tarot cards — to solve the mystery. Meanwhile, Camilla's ex-husband Jonathan Kahn resurfaces, sparking old feelings, and Ronzo has a new rival: a too-perfect doctor who may or may not be in cahoots with a gang of murderous New-Agers who believe Camilla knows the whereabouts of the legendary lost Braganza emeralds.

**#7 GOOGLING OLD BOYFRIENDS:** Camilla befriends socialite Mickie McCormack, who's going through a painful divorce. Mickie has been Googling her old boyfriends in order to reconnect and "remember who she used to be." Unfortunately, every one of those boyfriends soon ends up dead. Is the serial killer Camilla's old boyfriend Dr. Bob? Or another one of Mickie's old boyfriends? And can Camilla's old boyfriend Captain Rick Zukowski of the L.A.P.D. protect her and her cat Buckingham from being fed to the sharks before she solves the mystery?

**FOOD OF LOVE :** *Romantic-comedy/thriller*

After Princess Regina, a former supermodel, is ridiculed in the tabloids for gaining weight, someone tries to kill her. She suspects her royal husband wants to be rid of her, now she's no longer model-thin. As she flees the mysterious assassin, she discovers the world thinks she is dead, and seeks refuge with the only person she can trust: her long-estranged foster sister, Rev. Cady Stanton, a right-wing talk show host who has romantic and weight issues of her own. Cady delves into Regina's past and discovers Regina's long-lost love, as well as dark secrets that connect them all.

**THE GATSBY GAME:** *Romantic-comedy/mystery*
When Fitzgerald-quoting con man Alistair Milborne is found dead a movie star's motel room—igniting a world-wide scandal—the small-town police can't decide if it's an accident, suicide, or foul play. As evidence of murder emerges, Nicky Conway, the smart-mouth nanny, becomes the prime suspect. She's the only one who knows what happened. But she also knows nobody will ever believe her. The story is based on the real mystery surrounding the death of David Whiting, actress Sarah Miles' business manager, during the filming of the 1973 Burt Reynolds movie *The Man Who Loved Cat Dancing.*

**THE LADY OF THE LAKEWOOD DINER** : *Romantic-comedy/mystery*
Someone has shot aging bad-girl rocker Morgan le Fay and threatens to finish the job. Is it fans of her legendary dead rock-god husband, Merlin? Or is the secret buried in her childhood hometown of Avalon, Maine? Morgan's childhood best friend Dodie, the no-nonsense owner of a dilapidated diner, may be the only one who knows the dark secret that can save Morgan's life. And both women may find that love really is better the second time around. Echoes of the Grail legend bring into focus the nature of nostalgia and the pitfalls of longing for a Golden Age that never was.

These three comic novels are also available in a box set: **BOOMER WOMEN: THREE COMEDIES ABOUT A GENERATION THAT CHANGED THE WORLD**

**WHY GRANDMA BOUGHT THAT CAR:** A collection of short stories and verses—humorous portraits of rebellious women at various stages of their lives. From aging Betty Jo, who feels so invisible she contemplates robbing a bank, to neglected 10-year-old Maude, who turns to a fantasy Elvis for the love she's denied by her patrician family, to a bloodthirsty Valley Girl version of Madam Defarge, these women—young and old—are all rebelling against the stereotypes and traditional roles that hold them back. Which is, of course, why Grandma bought that car...

### Nonfiction by Anne R. Allen

### HOW TO BE A WRITER IN THE E-AGE: A SELF-HELP GUIDE

Co-written with Amazon superstar Catherine Ryan Hyde, this guide offers warm, friendly advice on how to start and sustain a writing career. You'll see a lot of books out there about how to write, and a whole lot more that promise ebook millions. But this book is different. It helps you establish a professional writing career in this time of rapid change—and answers the questions so many writers are asking: Does an author still need an agent? Can new writers still get published by Big Five publishers? What about digital-only imprints, mid-sized publishers, small presses—or should everybody self-publish? Do you need to spend endless hours on social media? How do you cope with rejection, depression, bad reviews and other downsides of the writing profession? Anne and Catherine answer all these questions and more in this fun, information-packed book.

### THE AUTHOR BLOG: EASY BLOGGING FOR BUSY AUTHORS

Anne's easy-does-it guide to simple, low-tech blogging for authors who want to build a platform, but not let it take over their lives. She'll tell you why an author blog doesn't have to follow all the rules that monetized business blogs do. You'll learn the secrets that made Anne a multi-award-winning blogger and one of the top author-bloggers in the business—and why having a successful author blog is easier than you think.

Printed by Amazon Italia Logistica S.r.l.
Torrazza Piemonte (TO), Italy

61198442R00161